For many years, Kim sent he
never made it off the slush
back to Nottingham Trent U
Creative Writing.

Before graduating, she received five offers of representation from London literary agents which was, as Kim says, 'a fairytale… at the end of a very long road!'

Kim is a full-time writer and lives in Nottingham with her husband, Mac.

ALSO BY K.L. SLATER

Safe With Me
Blink
Liar
The Mistake
The Visitor
The Secret
Closer
Finding Grace
The Silent Ones
Single
Little Whispers
The Girl She Wanted
The Marriage
The Evidence
The Widow
Missing
The Narrator
The Bedroom Window
Husband and Wife
The Married Man
Message Deleted
My Husband Next Door

THE GIRLFRIEND
K.L. SLATER

bookouture

BOOKOUTURE

First published in 2022 by Bookouture, an imprint of Storyfire Ltd.
This paperback edition published in 2026

1

Copyright © K.L. Slater 2022

The moral right of the author has been asserted.

All characters and events in this publication, other than those clearly in the public domain, are fictitious and any resemblance to real persons, living or dead, is purely coincidental.

All rights reserved.
No part of this publication may be reproduced, stored in a retrieval system, or transmitted, in any form or by any means, without the prior permission in writing of the publisher, nor be otherwise circulated in any form of binding or cover other than that in which it is published and without a similar condition including this condition being imposed on the subsequent purchaser.

A CIP catalogue record for this book
is available from the British Library.

PB ISBN 978-1-83618-835-3
EB ISBN 978-1-80314-791-8

Printed and bound in Great Britain by
Clays Ltd, Elcograf S.p.A.

Papers used by Bookouture are from well-managed forests and other responsible sources.

The authorised representative in the EEA is Hachette Ireland
8 Castlecourt Centre
Dublin 15 D15 XTP3
Ireland
(email: info@hbgi.ie)

Bookouture
An imprint of Storyfire Ltd.
Carmelite House
50 Victoria Embankment
London EC4Y 0DZ

An Hachette UK Company

www.hachette.co.uk
www.bookouture.com

CHAPTER 1

COLE

SATURDAY, 10:25

Cole Fincham paces around the perimeter of the party marquee, and only when he's sure he's out of sight of the house and his wife, Jennifer, does he take out his phone and read the generic text regarding his business bank account.

> *You have exceeded the agreed limit on account ending 193. To minimise fees and allow items to be paid, please pay in cleared funds by 2 p.m. today, 30 OCT.*

His heart starts up again. That new, hard thud accompanied by a sense of slight dizziness is back. Cole has experienced it for the past few days, since he'd heard the bottom might drop out of the building contract that was going to help rebuild his business. He pushes his phone back into his pocket and takes a couple of deep breaths. He's a bit stressed out, that's all it is. Cole knows he needs a plan, and he'll get on to it first thing Monday morning. He'll take the bull by the horns and face his business bank manager who's been ringing on a daily basis and leaving him increasingly frosty messages.

But the bank isn't his only problem. There's something else that's going to destroy his family unless he can think of an answer.

He's reminded of one of his father's favourite sayings: 'There's a solution for every problem. You just have to be creative enough to find it.' And luckily, Cole *is* creative. Endlessly so. Despite what seems to be insurmountable problems today, he feels sure he will look back in a few weeks and laugh.

After all, this is Cole's thing. Ducking and diving is what he's good at. When others crumble, he squares up to the problem and this time it will be no different. However, this weekend is out of bounds. It's their much-anticipated annual family Halloween bash. Cole and Jennifer, together with their two kids, Miller and Sylvie, host a big party every October, circumstances allowing. In addition, this year, it's a chance to show off the newly renovated house. Cole has invited a couple of very important business associates and their wives. Giving them a night they won't forget could literally make or break the deal he is so desperate to tie up, particularly if the Beesley contract ends up going south.

Cole has been told by a reliable source that his company is in with a chance of winning the tender for a luxurious apartment complex to be marketed as a Live-Shop-Eat destination built on the river next to the leafy suburb of West Bridgford, lying immediately south of the city of Nottingham and in a desirable enclave near Trent Bridge. If he is successful, the deal will put an end to his financial worries. If he pulls it off, that jumped-up business banking manager will be begging for his business and apologising for his brusque communications.

'Cole?' Jennifer's voice calls out from close by. His heart rate ramps up another notch. 'Where are you hiding?'

Jennifer emerges from the tent, her wavy brown hair tied back with a patterned scarf showing off her pretty round face. Cole used to affectionately call her moon-face in their early years and she'd always laugh, saying she found it quite cute. Jennifer looks good for her mid-thirties even though she frets about her weight – unnecessarily, in his opinion.

'Hey, gorgeous!' Cole wipes the sheen of sweat from his forehead and pastes a smile on his face as he emerges from around the side of the marquee. 'Just checking out the lanterns. They're going to look amazing when they're all lit.'

Jennifer frowns, scanning his face for indications of any problems. He thinks he might sound a bit nervous and she is good at spotting such signs. This only increases his stress levels. 'They've called me down to see the inside of the marquee. Have you seen it yet?'

He shakes his head. 'I waited for you, so we could see it together.'

The team leader of the Marvellous Marquees staff, a tall, whip-thin woman with a sallow complexion, appears at the entrance. 'Come through, guys! It's looking totally amazing. I hope you're pleased.'

Cole and Jennifer follow her inside, through Pennywise the clown's yawning black mouth with its sharp little teeth jutting just above their heads. Cole had walked into the kitchen earlier to find Jennifer explaining to five-year-old Sylvie that the scary clown was just like a picture. It wasn't real. If only Cole could say the same for his mounting problems.

'This has got to be one of the coolest designs we've done to date,' Cole hears the woman say. 'Ready?'

The interior is pitch dark when suddenly... *Whoosh*! The space is illuminated around them. Eerie purple and red swirls of light climb the walls and a creeping carpet of green fog crawls malevolently across the glittering dance floor.

'Wow!' he says, trying to inject some enthusiasm into his voice. 'This is amazing.' In fact, the unnerving effect just makes him feel even worse.

'It's incredible!' Jennifer's eyes pop at the Perspex round tables that will each seat up to ten guests. An enormous hollowed-out pumpkin sits in the centre of each one, filled with black and red roses.

Thousands of tiny twinkling LED white lights cover the black walls, which lifts the gloom and perfectly showcases the projected show: moving classic horror animations around the walls including Dracula, Cruella, Frankenstein's monster, vampires, bats and, of course, a coven of cackling witches that fly in endless circles up above their heads on sparking broomsticks.

Cole looks at his wife's stunned face and leans close to her as she hisses in his ear, 'How much has all this cost?'

'Irrelevant. Nothing's too much to celebrate my gorgeous wife's birthday.' She gives him a look as if to say, *yeah right!* But she's smiling and that's always a good sign.

Cole's phone pings in his pocket with another text. He waits until Jen walks away before taking it out and glancing at the notification.

God, not this. Not now. His heart begins thudding in a flurry of irregular beats again.

'The kids won't believe this,' Jennifer says, looking around. 'You should go up to the house and get Miller to come down here, Cole. I've been trying to get him out of his room all day. Tell him the photos of tonight will get him loads of street cred when we post them online. The other kids will be begging to be mates with him.'

'Wait here,' Cole offers. 'I'll give him a shout.'

He strides out of the marquee, relieved to be away from Jennifer's intense stare. After a few steps he stops and stands, looking up to the sky with his eyes closed, silently repeating the texted threat. Cole's lungs are demanding far more air than he's managing to currently get in and he tries yet again to gulp more.

'Is everything alright, sir? You look... unwell,' a young man asks hesitantly. Cole recognises him as one of the Marvellous Marquee team.

'Yes, yes. I'm fine,' Cole says irritably. These people, they get everywhere.

He feels trapped and slightly panicky. Sweat pools, sticky and cold, at the base of his spine.

Infuriatingly, he realises the young man is still staring at him, so Cole starts walking across the lawn. The house looks enormous from down here. A swathe of glass and natural Nordic spruce timber that Cole had specially imported, at great cost, from Scandinavia. One of the best features of the house is its ability to open wide at the back, the glass walls disappearing and pulling the garden into the inside space.

He still finds it hard to imagine he helped design and implement the extensive renovations. Pity his old man isn't here to see what he's achieved after so many years of telling Cole he'd never amount to much.

He reaches the patio and trips. The whooshing sound increases in his ears, making him feel wobbly and faint. He hears a noise, a sharp crack below him. Did he drop something? He stares down at the ceramic patio tiles he'd had to wait months for and they seem to undulate below his feet. He feels... weird.

'Miller.' Cole still feels a bit breathless. 'Miller!' he tries again, this time bellowing as loud as he can, up at his son's bedroom. His surly thirteen-year-old son appears and peers down from the open window, his eyes dark with resentment.

'Get yourself down to the marquee,' Cole barks. He's sick to death of pandering to him. It's time he fell into line. 'Your mum needs you.'

Cole does not wait to hear Miller's inevitable objections and usual display of insolence. Jennifer doesn't know but they had an altercation earlier. A bad one. Cole doesn't want to put up with any more teenage attitude; he's had enough for one day. No, Cole can only think of getting out of the house and, suddenly, nothing else matters. He walks through the house and out of the front door, holding on to the walls in an effort to keep his balance.

With difficulty, he climbs into his brand-new, white Range Rover Vogue and speeds blindly off the drive, the tyres screeching as he pushes the accelerator to the floor.

His phone starts to ring and when he glances at the name on the screen, he knows he's reached the end of the line.

Everything he cares about is poised to disintegrate.

CHAPTER 2

MILLER

10:35

When he hears the front door slam and the growl of his dad's engine, Miller runs downstairs, jumping down two steps at a time. He glimpses his little sister, Sylvie, sitting reading on their gran's knee in the living room before he rushes past on his way to the patio.

He steps outside and pauses in front of the kitchen doors. This is the exact spot his dad stumbled. From what Miller could see from upstairs, his face had looked a funny colour and his eyes were wide and weirdly staring.

His dad had tripped and lurched forward, trying to steady himself, and that's when Miller had seen his phone skidding across the patio slabs. He turns in a full circle now, scanning the area but he can't spot it. He walks over to the small, neat row of topiary hedging adjacent to where his dad had been standing. He crouches down and feels underneath each one and he finds it on his third attempt. Miller stands up and pushes the phone into his pocket.

'Mum!' he yells, starting to walk down the garden. 'Mum!'

Jennifer emerges from the marquee and sees Miller shouting and waving his arms. She walks up the lawn to meet him halfway.

'What is it?' Jennifer calls. 'Is everything OK?'

'Dad shouted up to me. He was stumbling all over the place,' Miller says tearfully. 'I think he might have been drinking again and he's taken the car.'

'He'll be fine, don't worry,' his mum says, but Miller can see her top teeth are digging into her lower lip. His dad had his annual health check at the doctor's recently, which showed his cholesterol and blood pressure were on the high side. The doctor had prescribed some tablets and Miller had heard his mum telling him he needed to cut down on his drinking and eat more fruit and veg, too. 'Did Dad say where he was going?'

Miller shakes his head and looks at his mum's face. Her features have been blurred by the thick fancy dress make-up she's been trying out. Her mouth is a wide bloody slash and her eyes have been made up to look red-raw and very sore.

Jennifer sighs and slides her arm around his shoulders. 'He'll be back soon and he hasn't been drinking, I'm sure. There's no way he'll want to miss the party. Come down here and see our amazing Halloween marquee. Your schoolmates are going to be queuing up to come next year.'

Miller scowls but says nothing. He hasn't got any mates so he doubts that very much; there's just one boy coming tonight and he's the class geek whose father is in business with his own dad. Miller doesn't care. His little sister is excited for the party but he'd rather be alone anyway. That way you can do exactly as you please.

Someone calls his mum away and Miller slips his hand into his pocket and slides his finger lightly over the smooth glass screen of his father's secret silver iPhone. A thrill shivers through him because he knows the six-digit passcode that opens it.

A few weeks ago when his parents had friends over for dinner, Miller had been at the top of the stairs about to come down for a glass of water, when his dad had slipped out of the dining room and answered a call in the hallway.

At the time, Miller could hear everyone laughing in the other room at a story his mum was telling them. His dad had pulled out the phone and spoken in a kind of angry hissing voice and said, 'Are you crazy, ringing me at this time? You know full well I can't talk tonight.'

Miller had stepped back into the shadows in his bare feet and peered down from between the balustrades, so he could observe his father without detection.

His dad had paced back and forth, listening to what the other person said on the other end and then he'd clapped a hand to his forehead and sat down on the bottom step. He'd said some things that had made Miller hold his breath that long, he'd felt lightheaded. Then Cole had said, 'OK, OK, there's no need for that. I'll come but it won't be until late now. I'll have to get a cab over because I've been drinking.'

Then the dining room door had opened, and the noise of laughter had spilled out into the hallway. Miller had watched as his dad had stood up and, in one smooth movement, slipped the silver phone in his pocket, and pulled out his normal black phone.

'There you are!' His mum had laughed. 'What are you doing out here?'

'Just someone ringing in sick for tomorrow.' He'd waved the phone in the air.

'Work, work, work,' Miller's mum had sung out as she'd gone back to their guests. 'It'll be the death of him, mark my words!'

His dad had waited until she'd gone back in the other room and had then slipped the silver iPhone out of the other pocket again. He'd tapped the screen and Miller had clearly seen the sequence of numbers in the dim light.

Zero-seven-zero-three-one-seven. That figured: the date of Sylvie's birthday. She'd always been his dad's favourite and, even though he would never admit it, Miller knew it to be the truth. Sylvie didn't give their parents any trouble. Sylvie loved everyone, even Miller.

Now, Miller takes his hand out of his pocket. His chest feels tight and heavy. Maybe he should destroy the iPhone so his mum never has to find out the truth.

But first, Miller thinks, he will take the phone up to his bedroom to examine it.

He will take his time and go through everything that's on it. That's the sensible thing to do.

CHAPTER 3

COLE

He parks the Range Rover and rushes inside. She is waiting for him.

'I don't know what you think you're going to do about all this,' she hissed. 'I can ruin you!'

The look on her face... Cole has never seen her expression so twisted and steeped in fury. Cole shrugs and gives her a little nonchalant smile that masks his panic. 'That's up to you. If you don't want to listen, that's fine. But it's happening anyway, regardless of what you think. I've made up my mind.'

He turns away from her and, as he does so, he hears a shuffling movement and a clatter. When he spins back, it's already too late. A flash of metal, a blur of a raised arm.

He baulks, crying out as a searing pain splits open the back of the head. He stumbles forward and manages to steady himself on a chair. For a moment or two everything goes black and then his vision returns, and he tentatively takes a few steps towards the door.

'Next time, I'll do a proper job and you won't be getting up,' she hisses behind bared teeth as he staggers past her. 'You'd better remember that and keep your mouth shut.'

He pushes forward and the momentum takes him to the door. She shoves him from behind and he falls into the hallway. Managing somehow to get up again, he makes his way out to the car.

His skull is throbbing with pain and it's so hard to think straight but the one thing he knows is that he needs to get away from her.

The driver's seat feels comfortable and supportive, the soft leather hugging his body. Cole closes his eyes and waits for his head to clear. One minute, two minutes… five… he isn't sure how long he's been sitting here. But his eyes open and the dull thud at the base of his skull feels bearable.

The party… he has to get back.

Cole turns on the ignition, presses his foot down on the accelerator and breathes a sigh of relief as the car begins to move.

His head is clearing and, somehow, he will sort it out.

He can do this.

CHAPTER 4

JENNIFER

10:52

I get back from picking up our fancy-dress outfits and park outside the house, my frown intensifying as I see Cole's car is still not back on the drive yet. I glance up at the sky. It looks like the rain is going to hold off after all. The caterers should be just about finished setting up and I've already signed off the marquee's interior. I just need Cole to turn on his phone and get back here.

My husband didn't get home until after nine this morning after a late business dinner in Edinburgh last night. He's spent the last hour pacing around the garden like a bear with a sore head, periodically checking the weather app on his phone. Then out of the blue, Miller has announced that Cole's taken himself off without telling anyone where he was going, or when he'll be back.

Although it isn't completely out of character for him to behave like this, and I'd usually be raging at his impulsive behaviour, Miller's words echo in my head: 'I think he might have been drinking again and he's taken the car.' Surely Cole wouldn't be so stupid… not after his drink-driving ban a couple of years ago.

I stare out of the kitchen window, a slippery, cold squirming in the pit of my stomach. I try to tell myself it's just Miller getting it wrong. He's prone to exaggeration like any teenager.

Everything in his life tends to be either brilliant or disastrous… usually disastrous.

I've got a good view from here in the kitchen of the tiny LED lights arranged in an archway around the marquee entrance, and of the dozen enormous silver lanterns, each containing an outsize church candle, equally spaced around the perimeter. I try to steer my thoughts back to the party and the things that are yet to be done in preparation.

The luxury black marquee option cost an extra twenty per cent on what was an already outrageous quote but, as the manager of Marvellous Marquees had cleverly remarked at the time of booking: 'Do you really want your Halloween party looking like a wedding reception, madam?' I feel so lucky that, thanks to Cole's business acumen, we are in the fortunate position we're able to splash out on such frivolous things, and can throw a party at all in the midst of a very bad economic recession.

Just over a year ago our fortunes had seemed to change. Cole said the business was doing so well we could afford to take more money out. We had new cars and he pulled some guys off other jobs to carry out extensive renovations on this house, including an enormous kitchen extension. Tonight's event is the culmination of all that coming together.

The party is due to start at seven p.m. prompt and guests will begin arriving anything up to thirty minutes before. Cole has scheduled the day down to the millisecond. In just a few hours, the hair and make-up girl gets here to transform the whole family into ghastly ghouls – even Miller, if I can prise him out of his bedroom – and now Cole has gone AWOL. I fan out my fingers and admire the glittery black talons I had done at the salon yesterday, each nail delicately hand-painted with a shimmering silver spider web.

Sylvie runs into the kitchen and fans her hands out too, touching her fingertips to my nails. 'Mine too, Mummy, look!'

I took her with me and the salon technician gave her purple glitter with a tiny orange pumpkin on each nail.

'They look perfect!' I kiss her on the top of the head. 'Where's your brother?'

'He's gone back up to his bedroom.' Sylvie folds her arms in a huff. 'He says he doesn't want to go to the party.'

I get that a house full of drunken adults dressed up isn't Miller's thing, but we throw a party nearly every year, so he really ought to be used to it by now. I'm often reminded of the age gap of our kids at times like this. Miller constantly stuck in his teenage angst, as opposed to Sylvie, who looks at the world through a permanent sparkly lens. We only ever thought we'd have the one child but then… well, things changed pretty much overnight.

Just over six years ago, Cole had an affair with a young admin assistant who worked in his office. I found out when Ellen, my sister, spotted them acting all lovey-dovey together at a bar in the next town when he was supposed to be working late. With Ellen and Mum raging in the background about his deceit, I kicked Cole out of the house without a second thought when he admitted it. I felt devastated when he left without complaint and moved into the twenty-three-year-old's bedsit.

Echoes of Mum's illness when we were kids, together with the feelings of fear and rejection I experienced back then, returned with a vengeance. Six months later, the affair fizzled out. When Cole got down on his knees on the doorstep and literally begged me to take him back, I didn't need to think twice. I wanted our family life back and I believed him when he swore it would never happen again.

Deciding to have another baby was part of our pact to recommit to each other and to our family and having Sylvie had worked. Our bond felt stronger than ever.

I grin now at Sylvie's annoyance with her brother. 'Well, if Miller doesn't come down, we'll go upstairs and tickle him with our witchy nails until he changes his mind!'

She giggles with delight and runs upstairs to tease him about what I've just said. At thirteen years old, Miller's sphere of interest is currently limited to gaming, football, and food. Lots of food. I have to try and limit his time spent gaming and I simply can't fill him, appetite-wise, at the moment. But he seems to be spending more and more time in his bedroom after all that trouble at school.

'He must be going through a growth spurt, Jennifer,' my mum, Kris, said last week. 'Just don't let him get fat like our Damian.'

Damian is my sister Ellen's son, and Miller and Sylvie's cousin.

'It's not Damian's fault he's piling on weight, Mum. Ellen needs to overhaul his diet.'

I often joke that my sister and I weren't raised in the same house. She never seems to care about teaching eleven-year-old Damian to eat properly or attempt to get him interested in sports. Damian's dad didn't stick around once Ellen told him she was pregnant. He'd relocated to Dublin before she'd even given birth and is now married with two kids, and he sees Damian only sporadically. Every time I go round there, Damian is in his bedroom, too.

Ellen really struggles with her own weight, and I literally had to beg her to come to the party tonight because she hates dressing up. 'Think about Damian, Ellen,' I'd reasoned with her. 'He'll love being a vampire for the night and it'll get him out. Miller will look after him; they'll have a great time.'

My husband doesn't know I've bought Ellen and Damian's outfits for the party. Ellen was 'let go' from her job as a temporary nursing auxiliary at a local hospital at the end of summer. I'm not supposed to know about this, but Mum confided it was due to Ellen being constantly late and ringing in sick.

'Come and be a glittery witch like me, Auntie Ellen!' Sylvie had begged. Ellen had only grudgingly agreed only when I'd offered to pay for their outfits.

My birthday is mid-October and, most years, Cole insists on marking it with a Halloween party later in the month. We've done so for nearly all the years of our fifteen-year marriage apart from the last couple while he's been remodelling the house. So this year, now the renovations are finished on the large 1930s Goodchild-built house, Cole wanted to go for it big-style. It has become quite the annual event for our friends and family and, this time, Cole has invited some of his most important business associates, too.

I look around me at the space-age glossy white kitchen cabinets and arctic-white floor tiles that feel warm as toast on my bare feet thanks to the underfloor heating running throughout the house. Outside, the hired catering team have already done a test run, firing up the stainless-steel outdoor kitchen – including a brand-new wood-fired pizza oven. I think about baking with my nan as a child, sliding trays of fairy cakes into her tiny, basic Belling oven and feel the pang of nostalgia. She died when I was just eleven but I'd swap all this fancy equipment to see Nan's humble cooker there instead.

During our marriage, we've struggled financially for many more years than we've been well-off, so when I look around me at all this space-age splendour, it still doesn't feel like mine. When you are born with working-class blood running through your veins, I'm not sure you ever fully believe the financial struggle is truly over. It always feels like disaster is waiting around the corner to jump out no matter how well you're doing in life.

My phone dings with a text alert and I snatch it up from the marble worktop Cole had shipped over from Italy. Hopefully the message will be from my husband, telling me he's on his way back home.

Cole is very particular about the annual party set-up and it's not like him to relinquish control. His phone is either turned off or he's in a no-signal area. Either way, it's not unusual. His work is so unpredictable and relentless, sometimes his plans can change in an instant and I'm used to him just taking off and then texting me where he is later.

But the message isn't from Cole; it's from my sister. If Ellen's making an excuse why she can't come after all tonight then I'll be annoyed. Sylvie will be so disappointed.

Jen, could you lend me £100 asap? I can pay it back next week. I'll explain everything when I see you later.

I stare at the message, irritation prickling across my chest. Another request for a 'loan'. It started happening back in January when we'd first moved into the new house. Her requests for cash are always accompanied by a promise to repay but of course that never happens. Somehow, I never feel I can mention that fact to her. Probably something to do with how she raves on about the 'amazing' house whilst always comparing it to the lack of facilities in her own rented semi.

There's no love lost between Ellen and my husband. He'd be furious if he knew about her relentless cadging, so I haven't mentioned it. Particularly as he's so laid-back about money, never questioning how much I spend, and he insists on transferring an amount each month into my personal bank account. What annoys me more than anything about Ellen's lending requests is that they are almost always issued without a single please or a thank you.

I sigh and open my banking app, ignoring someone knocking on the kitchen glass door. I'm going to have to tackle this issue with her, but now is not the time. I want to relax and enjoy the party later, and I want all our friends and family to have a great night. Fresh tensions between my sister and I will only set everything on edge and could threaten to ruin the evening. It's just not worth it for a hundred quid.

I log into the app and transfer the money over out of my personal account, pressing send just as there's another knock at the kitchen door. It's a young woman from the marquee company.

'Sorry to disturb you, Jennifer, but there are two police officers at the front door,' she says nervously. 'They say they need to speak with you urgently.'

CHAPTER 5

SARA

11:00

Sara's heart is heavy as she strokes baby Rory's soft, downy head. Her milk is no longer satisfying him. Consequently, he is feeding every couple of hours, day and night, and it's exhausting her.

She glances at the clock: not even noon, and she'll be alone until tomorrow evening at the very earliest. He has promised her he'll try his best to get back here by late afternoon, but she knows by now how these things go. He always underestimates how early he can get away.

Sara checks her phone again but there is still no message. She lowers her eyes and watches her son feeding. He has his father's hair, nose and mouth but her eyes. It was wonderful last night, the three of them snuggled together on the couch in their little family unit.

Mercifully, as she watches, Rory's vampire-like sucking slows and his swollen eyelids finally close.

She carries him through to the bedroom and lays him down in the cot at her side of the bed. She opens the window and breathes in the fresh, damp air.

She watches the glimmer of the water as the river catches the light. The Trent runs in front of the Grade II listed converted vicarage where she rents the top-floor apartment that runs the whole length of the house. There are two smaller, but still substantial, apartments downstairs. Both are also owned by the landlord, Mr Friedmann. He lives in one and rents out the other to a professional couple who Sara hardly ever sees.

She closes the window, pulls the blind and turns around, her silk robe falling open. She stands still, studying her naked body in the mirrored wardrobe.

Sara has enjoyed keeping fit for the whole of her life. She loved taking part in all kinds of sports in school – living in her native Stockholm until she was eight – and she'd continued when her mother died and her surgeon father moved them both to England so he could take up a senior position at the Queen's Medical Centre in Nottingham – the largest hospital in the UK, back then.

Sara's body has always been naturally firm, hard and functional. She's never had curves but thanks to her devotion to the gym she's remained as strong, lithe, and flexible as she was in her late teens. Her fiancé tells her constantly how much he loves her body but since giving birth to Rory, she's noticed he doesn't rave quite so much about it.

Her previously neat, pert breasts look larger and too heavy. Her nipples are cracked and sore from over-feeding the baby and, even though she's lost all the pregnancy weight and enrolled in a sit-up and squat fitness app, her stomach still looks distended by the birth only six months ago. She stands erect, pushes back her shoulders to activate her once-iron stomach muscles but nothing happens. Her brain sends the command and the muscles promptly ignore it.

She turned twenty-eight almost two months ago but today she feels forty. Is this really the utopia that was supposed to be motherhood? The magical state she's waited for the whole of her adult life? The glossy magazine pictures, the online articles all eschewing the limitless wonders of being a parent. It is supposed to be the best feeling in the world, and yet…

Sara pulls her robe together and ties it in a double bow. Two patches of dried milk decorate the front and, at the hem, a bloom of Rory's vomit, which she tried unsuccessfully to sponge off earlier while juggling the screaming baby.

She looks around critically at the minimalist living space. She'd loved this apartment when they'd viewed it a year ago.

'It's so big and stylish,' she'd told him. 'I can work wonders with it. A modern industrial style will look amazing.'

As a child, her parents had gone out socially a lot and had rarely taken her with them. But this once, they had brought her along to a housewarming party in Stockholm. The hosting couple had converted an old paper mill into a chic, three-storey house with a stark industrial interior. Sara had been entranced by the unusual furnishings compared to the traditional patterned rugs and dark, dreary furniture at home.

The couple's three children had run around mixing with the guests and Sara had never heard them even once being told to be quiet or ushered up to their bedrooms. When the parents had spoken to the kids, it had been in a loving, interested way.

Those people had become enshrined in Sara's young mind as the perfect family compared to her own home where there was little emotional warmth and children were most definitely regarded as inconveniences to be seen and not heard.

She'd been trying to recreate the paper mill family feeling here and has failed miserably. Her fiancé has been forced to travel for work for longer periods after the birth. Sara has felt for some time as if she and baby Rory are rattling around in the cool, unyielding space. Even with the heating on and stylish lamps dotted around the dark corners, her bones feel constantly chilly in this, her first full winter here.

She can feel the old desperation growing. The loneliness is creeping in again and taking a stranglehold like knotweed. It's the same feeling she experienced when her widowed surgeon father worked such endlessly long hours. That sense of being alone in the world when everyone else at school went home to warm, loving families at the weekends and she'd be collected by yet another agency nanny she hadn't seen before… it was a sadness that had followed her into adulthood.

Now her father has gone, she's a wealthy woman thanks to his savvy investments and property portfolio that Sara has sold off… but financial security is not the thing she craves the most.

What she really aches for is the time they will be a proper family like he is always promising when they talk at length about their future together. That's what she wants for her son above anything else.

She's always known he was married with children. He'd said, that first night, that he was divorced with a couple of kids but that Jennifer, his ex-wife, had taken the children abroad and refused to let him see them.

But Sara has seen his 'ex'-wife and children in the fabulous house she'd believed he was renovating for the two of them and for Rory. But that was OK because Sara knew how men worked. She'd learned from a good teacher. Her mother would smile and nod when her father spun his lies about attending yet another medical conference. When he'd left, her smile would fade and the vodka would come out of the drinks cupboard. Then she'd tell seven-year-old Sara all about what he was really up to. 'Sleeping with some slut he's met at the hospital,' she'd rant and rave. 'But it's me he loves. It's me he really wants to be with.' She'd tap the side of her nose with a long red nail. 'As a woman, you need to play dumb and stay smart. Remember that, my darling.'

Sara doesn't care he's lying. He's besotted with her and his new adorable son. She's been playing dumb and staying smart and it's working. She knows where Jennifer shops, where her kids go to school. And she's engineered an ingenious insurance policy to keep herself and her son front-centre in his life. Now that financial contracts have been signed and sealed, he literally cannot function without her. He can't simply shrug her off like a garment he's grown tired of. Whether or not he quite realises that yet remains to be seen.

During the long hours she's spent alone, Sara has explored all her options. Every single angle has been interrogated. At one stage she even started to think that maybe she'd be better off cutting her losses and simply facing the pain of being without him. Everyone said time was a great healer and maybe that was true. Even if, deep down inside, she couldn't believe she would ever fully get over him. Not now she had his baby. From the moment her son was born, her world tipped on its axis and she'd started to formulate another plan. A better one that would make their bond stronger rather than push him away.

So far she's been able to battle the bad thoughts, but she can feel their strength growing. Thinking back to before, she has secretly begun to feel afraid of what she might be capable of.

They had met at a business networking event just fifteen months ago. He'd pursued her relentlessly, suggested they go back to her place. She'd known he was likely to be married although he hadn't been wearing a ring. The best ones always are. She hadn't asked any questions, hadn't wanted to know the answers.

When she'd discovered she was pregnant so soon after they'd met, she'd been nervous of how he might react. He had certainly been overwhelmed when she'd told him. He had cried with joy. She glanced down at her left hand now as she recalled how, a week after she'd told him she was pregnant, he had asked her to marry him. This dazzling two carat diamond teardrop set in a platinum band was the proof of his commitment, surely?

Sara loved Cole with all her heart and she trusted him completely. She did. Things weren't the way she wanted them but she had faith it would come right. So she had committed to get through this difficult time until she could have it all. And it would happen, Sara would make sure of that.

After the baby's birth, and on her health visitor's insistence, Sara had made an appointment to see the doctor, who'd adjusted her medication and referred her to see a counsellor. She hadn't been yet. She'd felt so tired, so low and out of it. She needed him working less and in her life more. She needed them to be together… for her baby to thrive in the warmth of his own family. When she imagined the situation, she felt the promise of her own healing within.

'Just a few more months and it will all be sorted,' he kept promising.

Before he'd gone away this time, he had placed the tiniest, lightest butterfly kisses on her damp cheeks. 'When I'm not with you, I think about you all the time,' he'd said. 'Never forget I'm with you every moment of every day, Sara. Both in heart and in spirit. You only need to close your eyes and know I'm there with you.'

She loved the poetic way he spoke to her, the way he gazed so intently into her eyes. She felt cherished and safe. Yet once he'd left the apartment, once he went back to travelling up and down the country with his work, the feeling didn't last long.

The only thing that stopped her falling further down was the thought that very soon, she would have all of him.

She would not settle for anything less and she wouldn't allow anything to get in the way of that. No matter what she had to do or what she had to force herself to believe in order to achieve it.

CHAPTER 6

JENNIFER

11:15

I rush out of the kitchen to the front door. Two uniformed officers stand on the step beyond the open door, talking in low voices.

'Hello, how can I help you?' I manage to say, blood whooshing in my ears.

'Are you Mrs Jennifer Fincham?' the tall one asks.

'Yes,' I say. 'What is it? What's wrong?'

He makes their introductions but all I catch is 'Nottinghamshire Police'. My heart hammers on my chest. All I can think about is how unusual it is that Cole isn't home yet. Miller thought he might have been drinking but I've been watching him all morning and I hadn't seen him touch a drop. It's a long time since he's drunk alcohol in the morning but for the last year or so, it's become Cole's go-to way of relaxing after a busy period at work. It used to be much worse than the odd beer. He'd even joke about pouring vodka over his cereal but after a near-accident on the motorway and a subsequent driving ban, he seemed to come to his senses. Could it be he's had more alcohol than I think, and been driving under the influence?

'Mrs Fincham?' the shorter officer says. 'May we step inside for a moment?'

I move back and usher them inside. 'It's my husband, Cole, isn't it? Has something happened?'

They move just inside the hallway and then stop. 'Is it possible we can sit down? Somewhere private.'

Silently, I lead them into a small room off the hallway. We sit around a small table.

'I'm so sorry to have to tell you that your husband, Cole, has been involved in a serious road traffic accident, Mrs—'

'What? Is he… is he OK?'

'His vehicle hit the barrier and then rolled off the A453,' the officer says gravely. 'I'm so sorry, but his injuries were substantial and he passed away at the scene.'

The walls bend in and out around me. 'Oh dear God, no…' I lean my elbows on the table and cover my face with my hands. Every part of me is shivering. I don't know what to do, I—

The shorter officer cranes his neck to look at the door and then I hear my mum's voice.

'Jennifer? Is everything… oh!' Mum rushes in. 'What's wrong, love? What have you told her?'

I stand up and collapse into her arms. 'He's dead, Mum! Cole is dead!' I feel a shudder travel all the way through her as I press my face into the warmth of her shoulder.

'What happened?' she gasps.

The police officer repeats what he told me and then Mum is talking to them both, asking them questions. Words like *death* and *injuries* are muttered in hushed voices.

'A family liaison officer is on her way to assist and support you in this—'

'What caused the accident?' Mum says as I lift my head. 'I mean, had he been drinking, or—'

Before the officers can respond, the door bursts open and Sylvie skips in, her face split by a wide smile.

'Miller says he's not coming down for the party and you can't make him... oh!' Sylvie freezes in the doorway when she sees the policeman. I step away from Mum and wipe my eyes quickly. I have to battle the rising bile in my throat for Sylvie's sake. 'Mummy, why are you crying?' she says in a small voice and nestles into the side of Mum's leg when she holds out an arm.

I turn to see the young woman from the marquee company approaching. 'Is everything alright, Jennifer?' she says with concern.

'Can you take Sylvie, please?' I say, my voice shaking now. 'Just while I sort out—'

'No, I want to stay with Granny!' Sylvie objects.

'I need Granny to stay here with me to listen to what the police officers are saying,' I try to explain. I can't take in all the detail of what they're saying but I know Mum will.

'Of course,' the woman says brightly, holding out her hand to reassure my daughter. 'Come on, Sylvie, I'll show you some of the tricks we use in the marquee to scare people.'

Sylvie looks at me, then at the two policemen and the young woman. She wants to stay but the pull of being shown the tricks is too strong and she allows herself to be led outside. I turn back to the officers.

I take a deep breath. 'What about the other driver? Was it their fault?'

'We can confirm there was no other vehicle involved in the accident,' the tall officer says carefully. 'For reasons that are yet to be ascertained, Mr Fincham's vehicle left the road and rolled over on to its roof. He is the only casualty.'

So, nobody else was involved, his car veers off the road. He must have been drinking after all, then. My heartbeat jumps up to my throat and I feel really, really sick. Had I missed the signs when we were in the marquee together... was Miller right? I hadn't smelt drink. He hadn't slurred his words...

'You said he died at the scene. Do you mean he was...' My voice breaks and Mum reaches for my hand and squeezes it. 'Was he already gone before the ambulance even got there?'

The tall officer hesitates before saying, 'I'm sorry, it's too early to confirm the exact details, Mrs Fincham. But rest assured an ambulance did get to the scene very quickly and the attending officers confirmed that the paramedics attempted to administer CPR to your husband.'

The family liaison officer's name is Mandy. She's young, probably in her mid-twenties. I look at her bright, willing face and wonder if she's in a relationship, or has a child. She's kind and clearly wants to help but she seems a little nervous, like she's worried she might say the wrong thing. I feel skittish around her. I wish she wasn't here.

Currently, together with Mum, she's trying her best to calm me down. We're in the living room. Mum rang my sister when the police officers left and Ellen came straight over with Damian and took the children upstairs with her, away from where the horror is unfolding.

'I want to see Cole,' I say again, trying to stand up on legs that just don't have the strength to support me any more. 'I have a right to see my husband. I want to see that it's him, that they haven't got it wrong. I'll... I'll drive myself.'

'You will be able to go and identify Cole, Jennifer, but you have to give them time to get him ready for you,' Mandy says.

A stainless-steel gurney, a white sheet with blood splatters... Cole's broken body and smashed-up handsome face...

I let out a wail. 'It's not right! He's all alone in there. He's... all...' Big sobs that rack my body. Mum grips my shoulders, holding me tight like she used to do when I was a child and I'd wake with night terrors and try to get out of the windows, the doors, the house. Always trying to escape from a horror only I could see.

'Listen to Mandy, love. We have to do things the right way, even though it's painful.' Mum's voice is a little firmer now. 'There are two children upstairs, Jenny. Two children who need their mum, who can't fail to know something is very, very wrong. We have to get them through this, that's the priority. Cole would want you to make sure they're OK. Wouldn't he, now?'

I nod, mopping at my snotty nose with a tissue. My eyes feel so sore and swollen I can barely see through them.

'I'll check all the details, find out when you'll be able to see him,' Mandy says in hushed, calm tones. 'The main thing is you try to get some rest and I'll come over first thing to tell you what I've found out. OK, Jennifer?'

'She'll be fine,' Mum says, standing up. 'You get yourself off now, Mandy. I'll look after her. Thanks for everything.'

They walk to the door, speaking in very low voices.

When Mum returns, she sits with me, her arm around my shoulders. My tears have dried and I feel numb, unable to move. Mum talks to me, her voice soft and reassuring but I can't process what she's saying.

After a while she stands up, leaves the room. Time passes. I don't know how long it is before I hear the doorbell and Mum is back again with Dr Mantel from the local surgery. Mum used to work there part-time a few years ago and has obviously pulled some strings and managed the impossible. A house call.

'I'm OK,' I mumble. 'Mum shouldn't have bothered you.' Then I start to babble, asking the doctor disjointed questions about driving under the influence and the signs of stress. When he glances at Mum, I realise I'm not making much sense and I clamp my mouth shut.

Dr Mantel spends a few minutes checking my vitals. 'She's bearing up, Kris,' he tells Mum. 'Her blood pressure is slightly high but that's to be expected considering the shock.' He hands Mum a prescription and she shows him out.

Thirty minutes later, Mum returns from the chemist.

'Take this, love.' She hands me a pill and a glass of water. 'You're in shock and it'll help you relax. I'll look after the kids while you rest.'

I take the tablet and allow her to lead me upstairs. I lie on my bed and she closes the curtains before kissing my forehead and closing the door softly as she leaves.

I stare up at the ceiling, feeling empty and hollow.

I just want Cole back. That's all I want. We're so happy. He loves me and the kids. Everything he does is for us and we're all so close.

I just can't imagine my life without him.

CHAPTER 7

The sedative Mum gave me about one o'clock this afternoon has knocked me out for hours, but of course the devastation of Cole's death is still waiting to finish what it started.

When I wake up about seven p.m., I have a banging headache. The enormity of what's happened hits me and I swing my legs off the bed and sit up too quickly, feeling dizzy. I stand up slowly and walk into the bathroom. My legs are wobbly but I manage to use the loo and then move to the sink where I splash cold water on to my face to try and dispel the fogginess in my head. I hear the door open and Mum appears behind me.

Wordlessly she wraps her arms around me from behind. 'Come downstairs, Jenny,' she whispers. 'You have to eat something and the kids are asking to see you. We haven't told them anything yet but… I think it's time they know the truth.'

I can't stomach the thought of food, but I do need to see my children. They have to hear it from me.

Downstairs, Ellen is waiting with Damian. At first, she can't seem to meet my eyes but I understand. You don't know how you're going to react in a situation like this until it happens.

'Thanks for coming over, Ellen,' I croak and that breaks the spell. She rushes over and hugs me, rests her forehead on my shoulder. 'I'm so, so sorry, Jennifer,' she says, a sob breaking up the flow of her words. 'Anything I can do, you just have to say and…'

Her words fade out as my little girl appears. Sylvie's eyes dart all around the room, as if the police officers might still be here. Miller is behind her. He says, 'Where's Dad?' His face is long and pale, his expression blank.

'Come and sit here, both of you.' I pat either side of the sofa. 'I have something to tell you.'

Sylvie walks over, sits down and immediately nuzzles up against me. I slide my arm around her and wait for Miller. He walks a few steps inside the living room and then stops. 'What's up?' he says, looking from me, to his gran, to Ellen. 'Why have all the marquee people gone home? Where's Dad?'

'Where's my daddy?' Sylvie asks in a small, fearful voice.

In their own way, they know. They already know something is very, very wrong but they can't possibly imagine how bad it is or understand how their lives will change forever once they hear the truth.

'Miller? Sit here.' I pat the seat next to me again. 'Come on.' Reluctantly, he sidles over and sits down, leaving a few inches of space between us.

Time seems to freeze in this, the moment before I break open the awful truth. A thick silence hangs in the air, waiting for me to destroy their world. I take a breath, look at Mum and she gives me a tiny nod.

It's time.

'I've got some very, very sad news to tell you both. Daddy… your dad…' I glance at Miller. 'You know he went out in his car earlier? Well… he had a very bad accident.'

'What? Is Dad OK?' Miller asks, his voice high and tight.

'He's not OK. It was a very serious accident.' I reach out to both and lay a hand on theirs. 'I'm so sorry, Miller, Sylvie, but your dad… he died. The car left the road and rolled—'

'No! You're lying!' Miller stands up, his face dark with rolling emotion. 'He's not dead! Dad can't be dead, he—'

Mum rushes forward as his legs buckle.

'I... I want my daddy!' Sylvie cries out, her sweet features knotted into a mask of pain and suffering. 'I want Daddy!'

'Oh sweetie, come here.' Ellen runs across to Sylvie and holds her close.

I sit there staring ahead, my head swimming with the harrowing sounds of my children's grief. The sounds no mother ever wants to hear. We're hardwired to protect them from the horror life can rain down on us with little or no warning. This feels so wrong. My heart is breaking.

'He's gone,' I whisper, trying to focus on the family photograph on the windowsill. It was taken last Christmas at Lapland UK: the family treat Cole surprised us with because the business was doing so well. We'd travelled down to Ascot and stayed over the night before so we could get an early start. Miller had initially complained he was too grown up, that it was just for little kids like Sylvie, but in the end he'd loved it, had hardly been able to sleep. And Cole, he had been the biggest kid of them all, splashing out cash like a millionaire, whirling the kids around every last ride and attraction there was left to see before he'd finally agreed to leave when it was closing. I squeeze my eyes closed against the sharp pain of the memory.

'Jennifer?' Ellen says sharply. 'Come on, now. Focus. Miller's asking how the accident happened.'

'Did another car hit Dad?' Miller demands, his anger and denial almost tangible. 'Did the police arrest them?'

I sit up, the pain and grief on my children's faces snapping me back to my senses. Sylvie is turned into Ellen, quietly sobbing.

'We don't know exactly what happened,' I say, my voice gravelly and rough. 'The car left the road and rolled over but there was no other vehicle involved. The police say they're appealing for witnesses but they said… he didn't suffer. Dad wouldn't have known what happened, Miller.'

'No one can know that,' Miller said darkly. 'He might have known he was going to die. He might have been in terrible pain and—'

'Miller. Think of your sister,' Mum said quickly, noting Sylvie's horrified expression.

'I'm just saying,' Miller persisted. 'He might've known.'

'They said he didn't suffer,' I whisper. 'One thing I know is certain is that he loved you both so very, very much.'

I hold out my arms and Sylvie rushes from Ellen into my embrace, but Miller just stands there seemingly devoid of emotion and eerily staring into space.

'Was anyone in the car with Dad?' he says faintly.

We all look at him. 'What?'

He repeats it with some impatience. 'Was Dad on his own in the car, or had he got a passenger in there, too?'

It feels like a strange thing to ask and something I haven't even considered. Cole had left the house alone. Miller had seen that for himself. He'd even called down the garden to tell me.

'He was on his own,' Mum says firmly. 'The ambulance came and the paramedics tried their best to save him, but… your dad was very badly hurt, love, and, in the end, they couldn't do anything for him.'

My children are inconsolable. Sylvie with her open, honest display of emotion and Miller with his closed-down reaction. Both of them hurting, both desperately sad and grappling hopelessly with their grief.

And here I sit, their mother… the one person who is supposed to know exactly what to do to comfort my children. And yet I feel like I can't reach them. I'm no help at all because I'm stuck in my own swamp of devastating denial.

I can't believe my husband, the love of my life, is gone. I just can't.

*

I'm in bed and the room is dim and cool. I don't know what time it is but it's deadly silent and very dark outside. My phone is somewhere but not charging on the bedside table as it would usually be.

Sleep is a distant memory. I've been in a liminal state with hell all around me but, somehow, I've found a pocket of silence in the middle of it all where I can hide. I lie on my side, eyes open and barely blinking, staring at Cole's side of the bed. The quilt is undisturbed, the pillow straight, underlining his forever-absence.

Everything is a blur and I'm not really thinking in the ordinary sense of the word. Probably thanks to the sedative. But then, out of nowhere, random moments present themselves with startling clarity. Like the minutes after the police officers left and before Mandy, the liaison officer, arrived. I'd started babbling. Fretting about ridiculous stuff.

'I don't know what we're going to tell everyone… I mean… the party,' I'd kept stammering to Mum. 'The marquee, the holograms inside and—'

'Leave all that to me,' Mum had said as she'd held me in a tight embrace. 'You just worry about yourself and the kids. Nothing else is important, Jennifer. Do you hear me? Nothing.'

That's when my whole body had started aching, my skull reverberating with the words of the police officers.

I'm so sorry, but his injuries were substantial and he passed away at the scene.

Up until about a year and a half ago, Cole used to go to the gym three times a week without fail and, work schedule allowing, he'd also try to pull in a couple of early runs. He was a picky eater back then and consciously avoided junk food. He would have turned forty early next year but rather than his healthy approach gathering momentum, it went haywire instead. The most worrying change had been in his drinking habits. From drinking moderately, he'd suddenly started coming home smelling of booze… and after he'd been driving. If he'd stayed home, he'd have his first beer just after the kids got home from school and he'd graduate on to wines and spirits as the night went on. I'd just been grateful the kids were in bed by then and not around to see their father stumbling around.

I'd tried to talk to him about it, asking him what was bothering him because clearly something was. But he'd fobbed me off. 'I'm just tired, I'm just so busy at work, I'm just winding down.' *I'm just this, I'm just that…* I couldn't break through his smokescreen so in the end I'd given up asking.

Then Cole underwent a routine annual medical screening and it was discovered his blood pressure was dangerously high and his cholesterol was concerning, too. I'd tried to get him eating more fruit and veg, yoghurt for breakfast instead of the greasy fry-ups he now favoured. I'd begged him to stop the extensive work travel and spend more time with me and the kids. Most of all, I'd started hiding away the booze and that had made him really angry.

It was unnerving because I knew how bad he could get. One day, a year or so before that, I'd come home unexpectedly from a day trip to Hathersage in Derbyshire where I'd accompanied Sylvie and her playgroup as a volunteer helper. I'd found Cole fast asleep on the sofa with a half-empty bottle of vodka propped up beside him. Over in the chair, Miller had sat, oblivious, watching football highlights.

I'm ashamed to say I lost it with Cole in front of the kids, yelling at him that he needed to get serious help with his drink problem. Without a word, Cole had grabbed his jacket and stormed out of the house. He'd jumped into his car and screeched off the drive. That was the day he'd hit the central reservation on the M1, miraculously escaping the vehicle without injuring himself or hurting anyone else. In short, he was prosecuted for dangerous driving and lost his licence for a year. It had been the humiliating revealing of the ugly underbelly of our apparently successful life.

After that he'd seemed to pull himself together. He confided he'd been stressed about some business problems but that they were now resolved and things were back to normal.

Cole was a great dad, an attentive and loving husband. He travelled the country during the week to maximise the pool of work his building company submits tenders for. Suddenly, there was a lot more money.

'I hate staying away from home,' he always told me before he went. 'One day I'm going to stop all this and we'll never be apart for a single day.'

Everything he did, he did for us, his family who adore him. And now, he's gone.

His life extinguished within minutes while we were all getting ready to party.

CHAPTER 8

SARA

22:00

She'd been woken ten minutes ago by the ding of a text notification. Her heart had leapt at the thought her love was in touch at last.

HI SARA.

She'd rubbed her grainy eyes and frowned as she read the curt message. No kisses, none of his usual affection and he nearly always called her 'darling' rather than by her actual name. Also, she realised, he never typed all in block capitals.
She'd sent a message back by return.

Where have you been? Can you talk?

Nothing for two minutes then another text.

SEND ME A NAKED PIC

What? Her heart pounds in the face of this unrecognisable communication. This doesn't sound like him at all.
She looks over longingly at Rory sleeping peacefully. One of

the rare times she could have caught up on her sleep but now the message has disturbed her. She sits bolt upright on the edge of the bed and reels off another message.

You're not making any sense. Call me.

She tosses the phone down on the bed and pads naked to the en suite. When she's flushed, and as she re-enters the bedroom, the phone starts ringing. She rushes over and snatches it up.

'Darling? Is that you?' she says breathlessly. 'Is everything OK?'

Silence.

'Hello?' She takes the phone away from her ear and looks at the screen. The call is still live, each second ticking through on the counter. 'Baby, is that you?'

She presses it closer to her ear and thinks she can discern faint breathing.

'Who is this?' Her voice hardens. 'I'm going to put the phone down unless—'

The call ends before Sara gets a chance to finish. Before she can think better of it, she presses the call back button. It rings once before being diverted to answerphone. She calls again and the same thing happens. The third time she calls, it does not ring at all and goes directly through to the answerphone.

'Nobody calls this phone but you. No one else knows the number,' he'd told her one night when they were out for dinner. She'd smiled, knowing the real reason, of course. She was his dirty little secret and the phone was a way to keep her well away from his wife and family.

But she'd pushed the unhelpful thoughts aside. Life was good. She was crazily in love and he'd promised her they'd be together by Christmas. That was good enough for her. She'd believed him. She had to hold on to the hope, however flimsy.

Sara glares at the phone, which remains infuriatingly silent. She lies on the bed staring at the ceiling, listening to the soft rasp of baby Rory's breathing.

It has been twelve hours since she's heard from him. None of the promised calls or text messages have materialised – until these last two strange ones. Something is wrong, it has to be. He's probably lost his phone and some saddo has texted the only number in it. But then, how have they opened his phone without the passcode?

She picks up her own phone and finds his other number in her contacts. This is the phone everyone else calls him on. The phone Sara has been instructed to call only in an absolute emergency. Well, now she is worried.

Her call goes through to his answerphone. His voice sounds jaunty and professional on this recording.

Just then her phone dings again with a text notification. Rory stirs in his basket but does not wake.

Sara opens up the message. It reads:

I AM DEAD.

She holds the phone in a shaking hand and stares at the text message with the three simple words that rock her world sent in block capitals.

I AM DEAD.

The text has been sent from *her* phone. The phone he never uses for business but just for her.

Then, *I AM DEAD BITCH.*

CHAPTER 9

JENNIFER

SUNDAY

I thank God for my sister, Ellen, and for my mum. They've cocooned me in a safe space: my own bedroom. The curtains are closed and the room is reassuringly dim.

They are looking after me, Miller and Sylvie. They dealt with the fallout from the party, just took it all in their stride.

'There's no way we could let the party run,' Mum told me when she brought me a cup of tea in this morning. 'Everyone is in utter shock and sending you their love and condolences.'

This morning, some of Cole's employees had come and taken food for themselves and had taken the rest to a few local foodbanks and homeless shelters in the city.

Mum says, 'The liaison officer has been on the phone. Someone has to identify Cole's body, possibly tomorrow. I'm very willing to do that for you, Jennifer. I honestly think it's for the best, so you can focus on yourself and the children.'

'I'll do it,' I say, taking a sip of scalding tea. 'It has to be me.'

'Right. I'll tell Mandy. She wants to come over later this morning to see how you are.'

I shake my head. 'No. I know she means well but her being here just stresses me out more. Can you call her and say I don't need her to come today?'

Mum nods. 'I know it seems impossible, but try and get some rest, love. You're going to need all your strength.' She leaves the room, closing the door behind her.

It's giving me more time to think through everything that happened before the accident. I don't know whether that's a good thing or just makes everything worse.

'Was he drunk? He couldn't walk straight when I saw him on the patio,' Miller had remarked and we had to tell him to be careful what he said in front of his little sister.

Cole had not been over the limit, the police had since confirmed.

'Balance issues and slurring words can be signs of severe stress,' Dr Mantel had explained when I'd told him Miller had seen his father almost fall over. 'Has there been a lot going on in his life recently?'

'Nothing any more than usual. He has a high-pressure job but business is good and Cole has always coped brilliantly with it.'

The doctor had seemed unconvinced. 'People can get used to an inordinate amount of stress and often don't notice the warning signs until it's too late.'

I've thought about what the doctor said and I now concede it's possible Cole was more stressed than I thought. I've never had any involvement in his business or in finances of any kind. I might order online, pay the old household bill or tradesman on the credit card but that was the extent of it. Since we've enjoyed Cole's business success, I don't have to think too much about if there's money in the bank to cover purchases.

That's always the way Cole has preferred it. I look after the house and the kids and he earns the money. Some women would think me foolish but at the beginning of our marriage I used to drive Cole crazy accounting for every single penny. I knew it stemmed from the fear of ending up with nothing again, out on the streets and sleeping in a hostel when Mum had ended up in hospital.

When we got better off, we'd toasted a great new deal Cole had secured and he'd said, 'Let me take the weight of the financial responsibility, Jen. You find it hard and I don't, so why sweat about it?'

I'd jumped at the chance. Why wouldn't I? Not everyone is ambitious, striving to build a successful career. I've always felt my role at home is important. I trusted Cole implicitly and it was a way of escaping the fear and dread of revisiting the past. It's served us well for all of our marriage.

So I don't feel guilty because it's what Cole wanted. When we got back together after his affair, we agreed to talk about everything. If he had problems, he'd have discussed that with me. I know he would have.

I'm shaken from the distraction of my thoughts by raised voices from downstairs.

'I've told you… she's just lost her husband. You'll have to come back another time.'

'Trust me, she'll want to see me,' a woman retorts. I don't recognise the voice. 'Please, just tell her I'm here and that it's urgent!'

Against the backdrop of Mum's voice rising in volume, I haul myself up out of bed. I pull on a loose pair of yoga pants and a T-shirt and set off downstairs, raking my fingers through my hair as I descend. I notice all the Halloween decorations in the hallway and around the front door have been removed.

'Who is it?' I call out.

Mum sees me and pushes the door half-closed against the visitor. Her face is flushed with indignation.

'Her name is Sara Nordstrom,' she whispers. 'She's insisting she sees you but you don't have to, Jennifer. You're grieving.'

'Please,' the woman's voice calls out from the doorstep. 'I just need a few minutes.'

I don't know anyone of that name but I can see Mum is getting flustered. 'It's OK, I'll see her.'

'I can stay with you, if you—'

'It's OK, Mum. I'll sort it.'

Mum frowns and pushes the door to a bit more before whispering, 'She says you don't know her but that she has some very important information to tell you.'

'About what?' A spark of hope ignites in my chest. Maybe this is someone who witnessed the accident, who can give the police information on what actually happened on the A453 yesterday. But… how would she know our address?

'She says it's about Cole.' She hesitates. 'She has a baby with her. A little boy.'

Something in the way Mum looks at me makes my blood run cold. I step forward and Mum retreats towards the living room. She hovers just outside the room as I open the front door.

Sara Nordstrom is not what I was expecting. She's young, probably only in her late twenties and very attractive in a sort of icy Nordic way. Her skin is lightly tanned and she's not wearing much make-up but still looks very put together. She has striking blue eyes and short buttery-blonde hair that's been brushed back from her face and tucked behind her ears. The tiniest diamond glitters at the side of her nose.

She carries a baby boy – who looks about six months old – in a papoose. I avoid meeting her eyes. Her presence makes me feel uncomfortable and I wonder again why she's here.

I catch movement over the road and see the owner of the house opposite – who I've not had a chance to speak to yet – craning his neck to get a better look.

'Thank you for seeing me, Jennifer,' she says as if she knows me. 'I just need a few minutes of your time, I know—'

'You'd better come inside for a moment,' I mumble, ushering her in.

Like me, she is also wearing yoga pants – possibly even the same brand – but she is achingly slim and toned with no sign of the extra padding that spoils the outline of my own.

I close the door and we stand there in the hallway. Mum pops her head out of the living room. 'Everything OK, love?'

'It's fine, Mum.' She nods and closes the door softly. I fold my arms and look at the woman. 'So, what can I do for you?'

'Thank you for seeing me, Jennifer. I'm Sara Nordstrom and this is my son.' She sounds confident but she keeps looking away from me and jiggling her son even though he isn't making a sound.

'How do you know my name?' I hear my words but I feel separated from them. As though the real me is standing way back from her and I'm just going through the motions, being as polite as I can manage in view of what's happened.

'I… I knew your husband, Cole. We've never met, I know, but… I only just found out about you.'

I feel dizzy and sick. I glance at the baby and point to the comfy seating in our oversized hall. 'Let's sit down a moment,' I say weakly. 'As you can imagine, this is not a great time for me.'

'I know. I'm so, so sorry for your loss.' A look crosses her face and for a moment I think she's about to crumble with something that looks remarkably like my own grief. 'I… it's a terrible shock.'

Why would it be a shock for her? A crawling sensation starts on my skin and I cross my arms and rub my elbows.

She sits down. 'Rory is getting heavy. He's growing so fast and…' Her voice fades out as I silently repeat the name in my head. *Rory*. Cole had always liked that name for a boy. He'd suggested it for Miller but I hadn't been keen.

'Jennifer?' Her face comes back into focus.

'I can only give you a couple of minutes. As you can imagine, I'm trying to come to terms with my husband's death,' I say shortly, sitting down and perching on the end of the cushion. 'Why have you come here? I don't recognise you and I don't know your name.'

The baby grizzles and Sara pops a dummy in his mouth.

'It's Cole I know very well. Knew,' she says sadly before looking at me, her eyes serious. 'I'm sorry. I know this will be hard to hear. But I am your husband's girlfriend. And this is his son.'

'Excuse me?'

Time freezes. My instinct is to laugh at the audacity of her, the rubbish she's spouting. But my mouth has turned instantly dry and my throat feels as if it's closing up. I'm instantly sensing something horribly authentic about her claims on a level I can't explain.

Although I'm trying hard not to, my eyes gravitate like magnets to the child. His dark hair, smooth olive skin… he is the image of Miller as a baby except Miller has soft brown eyes and the baby's are the icy blue replicas of his mother's. My insides have turned to liquid.

'Believe me, Jennifer, I'm in shock, too. I swear I didn't know Cole had a family… that you were here, in this house. He told me he was divorced and travelling the country on work business on the days he was away from home.'

I make a sound of mockery. 'And you believed him?'

He told you he was working away and you *believed him.*

I fix her with a laser-like gaze.

'When we met, he said he *had* been married and that he had a couple of kids but that you'd taken the children abroad and refused to let him see them.' Sara meets my glare. 'That's what he told me.'

'You must think I'm an idiot.' I stand up and point to the door. Inside I am soft and bleeding but a steelier part of me speaks. 'You need to go. You need to leave this house right now.'

If someone had asked me before today to predict how I'd react to a situation such as this – a woman invading my world and tearing it apart with a few well-chosen words – I'd have sworn I'd physically throw her out of the house. But I have no strength left in me. Her poisonous rhetoric has robbed me of any energy I have left. I want to call her a liar, say I can see straight through her outrageous claims but inside I am quiet. As though some deeper part of me can sense the truth.

'This is a massive shock for me too, but I have to be straight with you now,' she says, raising her voice slightly. 'I know it must be incredibly hard for you to hear all this, it's hard for me to face it too, but I swear, I'm telling you the truth.' She's still sitting on one of the big squashy Loaf sofas that we pile on as a family when we're ready to go out. Our family photographs sit in frames on the hall table next to her. In fact, the last time Cole came home, he sat right there to take off his boots. Right where she is now, holding the baby boy.

I realise she hasn't moved an inch despite my order for her to leave.

'Have you finished?' I say quietly. 'Have you said what you wanted to say? Because if so, congratulations. You've done what you came here to do.' I stand up and fold my arms. 'And now you can get the hell out of my house.'

'You can't just push us aside,' she says simply. To say she apparently loved my husband, she's hiding her grief remarkably well. 'I know you're hurting, but so am I and… I'm not going to disappear and neither is my son. Cole's son.' She hesitates before adding, 'And I'm afraid there is more I need to say. A lot more.'

'Well, I don't want to hear it!' I ball my fists, trying and failing to keep calm. 'Who even *are* you? How do I know you're not some random woman off the street… a ghoul wanting to cause trouble? I can't deal with this now. I can't—'

'He wanted to be with us and we were going to move in here together when the renovations were finished. He just couldn't bring himself to tell you.'

'The renovations were finished months ago, as you can see.' I look at her sharply. Pictures of the two of them in the master bedroom forming in my head. 'Have you been here before?'

She shakes her head. 'He told me he wanted it to be finished before I saw it, but I found the address in some of his paperwork. I—'

'Enough! If you don't leave now I'm going to call the police.'

She shakes her head and lifts her chin slightly. 'I won't be going anywhere until I'm good and ready because all this belongs to *me*.' She sweeps an arm around. 'This is *my* house. The Range Rover Cole was driving yesterday was *my* car. Pretty much your whole lifestyle is currently funded by me. So what I want to know is—' she bounces a fidgeting Rory on her knee as I try my best not to collapse in a heap in front of her '—would you like to start this conversation again, or do you and your family want to get the hell out of *my* home?'

CHAPTER 10

I bury my face in my hands. The stuff she's saying is nonsense. The profits of the business have paid for the renovation of this house and for the new cars we bought when Cole got his driving licence back. I can't understand why she'd say all this.

I look at her and whisper, 'Why are you saying these things and trying to hurt me? What kind of monster are you?'

'I don't want to go down the road of blame and revenge, OK?' Sara sighs. 'I'm not a monster, whatever you might think. I know what it feels like to hurt, believe me.'

'It doesn't sound like that to me,' I say. 'Any agreements you've made with Cole – if that's even true – are between you two. It doesn't concern me or my children.'

She gives a wry smile and shakes her head at my apparent naivety.

'I'm afraid that's just not true, Jennifer. I can ask my solicitor to give you a full overview of the agreement,' she says. 'In the meantime, can we just try to get on and get through this awful mess? For the sake of ourselves but mainly, for the sake of our kids?'

My eyes fall to Rory. Again, I'm struck by how he looks so much like Miller did as a baby… and it's an unavoidable fact he looks like Cole, too. If it's true and this tiny boy is the product of Cole's affair with Sara, it means he is also the half-brother of my two children. I pinch the top of my nose. I don't know what to do, it's all so… *awful*. It's impossible to call.

Sara sits silent and calm, waiting for my reaction.

'You're not the first, you know,' I say. 'Cole has had an affair before.' A deflating sensation pulls me down further. I want to hurt her back but my own words only serve to confound the disappointment I have in myself that I'm openly admitting the fact I've taken him back after he's been unfaithful before. She doesn't flinch but continues to watch me coolly, dashing my hopes that her face will fall when she realises she's nothing special. Now it's my turn to wait.

'For this to work, we have to forget what's happened before,' she says simply as if it's an easy option. Her eyes are bright and clear, not red-rimmed and sore like my own. 'We both loved Cole, but he's gone now. He's never coming back.' She presses her lips together. 'But we two women… we're still here! So are our kids. We all have to get through this somehow.'

Frankly, I don't care how she gets through it. If what she's telling me is true, I only care about the impact on my children. That means I need to think carefully before closing her down.

I must have been around thirteen years old when I heard Mum talking to her friend Brenda over a glass of wine in the kitchen one night. Ellen was up in her bedroom at the time, and I'd come downstairs to get a drink when I'd heard voices. I'd stopped outside the door to listen.

'If he refuses to leave then you should take the children and just go,' I heard Brenda say.

But Mum sounded defiant. 'Why should I lose this house and subject us to all that upheaval? I won't do it. I know you don't understand, Bren, but I'm doing what's best for me and my kids. Even if everyone else, including you, thinks it's the wrong decision.'

I've always remembered that conversation and when I was older, even now as a mother myself, I kind of admire Mum for choosing the unpopular path because it would be easier for her girls. She wasn't to know about Dad's financial problems back then and that we'd end up losing the house anyway.

Sara leans forward as if she can tell I'm distracted.

'People follow what's gone before them like sheep, as if there's a precise formula for how life should be lived. We grow up learning strict rules for how to react in any given situation. If your husband has an affair, you kick him out. The mistress is always the evil one, right? But I've learned life is rarely that simple. Cole lied to us both. We don't have to choose to continue with that pain and inflict more on ourselves just because we're supposed to hate each other.'

I think about the sharp cut of loneliness that had sliced through me when I'd lived alone with Miller when Cole left me before Sylvie was born.

'You're strong, Jenny,' Mum had said. 'You can get through this.'

Ellen had hugged me close… and Ellen *never* hugged me close. 'I'm so proud of you, sis, showing that rat you won't be messed around.'

But Mum and Ellen weren't there in the long, dark evenings after I'd taken Miller up to bed. When all I could think about was Cole being with that other woman and loving her instead of me. And now… now, I'm facing not only his death, but the harsh realisation he's done it again. Not only has he been unfaithful after he swore on Miller's life he'd never betray us again but this time, he's been living an entire other life away from me and his children. There are degrees of betrayal and levels of hurt. Cole had sunk to a depth I know I'll probably never be able to fully recover from and trust again.

'Do you want to talk about it?' Sara says, wrapping a protective hand around the baby's tiny hunched back. 'Shall we just try and sort out this mess without hurting ourselves or our children even more?'

I look at Sara now, at the shadows under her eyes. I look at baby Rory, so innocent in all of this, the half-brother of my own two children. I think about what Cole has done to us all and what my children might think of me in years to come if I shut their stepbrother out of their life.

'We can talk,' I say, meeting Sara's eyes. 'But first, I need a little time to absorb what you've told me.'

CHAPTER 11

Sara Nordstrom leaves the house and we agree I'll call her about coming back over to talk about the situation. Mum is reading Sylvie a story in the other room, so I don't disturb them. I get myself a glass of water, take a deep breath and call the only person who will be able to debunk Sara's outlandish claims. Corinne Waterman, Cole's accountant. She doesn't pick up so I leave a voicemail and then sit there staring at my phone, waiting.

Corinne's name was on a short list of people I left with Mum to inform them of Cole's death yesterday. Mum told me she managed to speak to them all, so I know Corinne is aware of the situation. But ten minutes later, Corinne hasn't returned my call so I call her again. There's still no answer and I leave another message.

'Please call me the instant you pick up this message, Corinne. I need to speak to you urgently regarding Cole's finances.'

I tap my fingernails on the table. Stand up, stretch and sit down again. Still no return call.

Another five minutes then on my third attempt, Corinne finally picks up.

'Jennifer, I'm so sorry, I left my phone in the other room.' Her voice drops respectfully. 'Please accept my sincere condolences on Cole's passing. It's a terrible shock for us all but... for you and the children... I just can't imagine.'

'Thank you,' I say. 'Someone's been here... a woman. She said a lot of things about financial matters that just don't make any sense, like Cole and I don't own this house. I know you'll be able to put my mind at rest—'

'I'm relieved you called me. I've been desperate to get in touch since I heard the news but I had to give you a day or two of space.'

'Is it true, what this woman is saying?'

She hesitates. 'Can I come over to the house right now?'

'Tell me, Corinne. Please.'

'I understand you're concerned and need answers and I'll keep it as short as I possibly can. But there are matters I simply must discuss in person with you as soon as possible, Jennifer. It's for yours and your children's sakes. Please.'

I falter. 'Are you saying it's true… that she owns this house? Corinne, did you have anything to do with this?'

'No, of course not! But… it's complicated. I'm leaving now, OK?'

When the call ends, I sit staring into space. I didn't get the reaction I wanted from Corinne. Far from telling me Sara is completely off the mark, there is clearly bad news that she wants to say in person.

Twenty minutes later she's at the front door. Mum approaches before I can get there.

'I'll get this, Mum,' I say. 'It's Corinne, Cole's accountant.'

'Jennifer, what's happening?' Her brow is furrowed with concern. 'You shouldn't be making any big decisions yet. You're still in shock.'

I haven't yet told her the rubbish Sara Nordstrom has spouted, nor why I've agreed to speak with Corinne. My eyes land on Cole's shoes under the hall table. He was always leaving shoes down here, one of my pet hates. Everywhere I look, everywhere I walk… everything reminds me of him. All the times he'd slip off his coat, throw his keys into the dish and tell me he was glad to be home… now I know the truth about where he'd really been most of those occasions and how he might have left us financially, it makes me sick to my stomach.

I open the front door and Corinne stands there looking efficient and concerned in her slim-cut grey trousers, sensible heels and short red jacket. I've never seen her do casual, even on her frequent golfing weekends when she's been known to drop paperwork off at the house for Cole. Her salt and pepper hair is pulled back into a severe ponytail and her grey eyes look hooded with concern.

'Again, I'm so sorry to hear about Cole,' she says. 'I know what you're going through. I lost my sister a few years ago and I doubt I'll ever get over it.' She follows me through to the kitchen and I close the door behind us. 'If I could have avoided coming here at this very sad time, I would have done so but… well, as you made contact, I considered it unavoidable.' We sit at the table and she slips on her reading glasses before taking a sheaf of papers out of her briefcase, some bearing Cole's business logo and his signature.

When she seems satisfied she has everything to hand, she places her forearms on the table and laces her fingers together. 'Tell me what happened, Jennifer. What, exactly, did this woman say?'

The way she seems to anticipate a problem makes me nervous, but I explain how Sara Nordstrom turned up at the door unannounced and what she said. 'It can't be true, can it? That this woman owns my house and other assets?' I look pleadingly at Corinne but when I see the serious look on her unsmiling face, I know it's going to be bad.

'I'm so sorry, Jennifer.' She gives a little shake of her head as if she can't quite believe it herself. 'From what you've told me, what she says is true.'

'But… it can't be! I mean, I wasn't involved in Cole's financials at all,' I say weakly, my head pounding with the aftershock of Sara's outrageous claims. 'Whatever arrangement he made was his doing, not mine. I left him to deal with all that.'

'But as far as the law is concerned, you are a director of this company whether you actively took part in running it or not.'

'It's the way we've always done it. Cole deals with the business, I deal with everything else.'

She gives me a look over her spectacles like a stern schoolteacher who is trying and failing to drive a point home to a student who isn't paying attention.

'I'm afraid you've got to realise that things have now irrevocably changed, Jennifer. It would be considered professionally negligent of me if I failed to give you a clear understanding of the current position.' She picks up a piece of paper bearing lists of figures and pushes it towards me. 'A year ago, Cole was on the verge of bankruptcy. The business, like many others, had suffered terribly in the recession, and, for want of a better phrase, he was up to his eyeballs in debt. Without new contracts, he was going under fast with his business bank about to call in several loans.'

I stare at the figures in front of me, which frankly don't make much sense. Cole never mentioned to me how desperate things were. He occasionally grumbled about the effect of the recession, but he brushed off my questions, insisting the problems were already sorted. But *bankruptcy*? 'I literally had no idea,' I murmur through the numbness of my shock. His drinking problem… had Cole been trying to drown away his problems?

'Then last year he told me he'd found a new investor and his fortunes were transformed. Someone, not a director of the business but who bankrolled the renovation of this house, funded the repayment of several bank loans that were already in default and provided a large sum of money to enable Cole to take a director's loan from the business. Up until yesterday, he'd effectively been using this loan to fund his current lifestyle.'

The marquee party, the designer clothes, the holiday to Disney World Florida he'd just been about to book…

Corinne continues. 'The new investor insisted everything was done completely above board and through the correct legal channels and so water-tight funding and loan agreements were drawn up and signed. I assume you are at least aware of this detail?'

I look at her, clueless. 'No. I literally had no idea.'

In response, Corinne pushes several sheets of paperwork towards me. All of them bear my signature, together with Cole's own. 'These are the agreements I'm referring to, Jennifer,' she says gently.

My head is swimming. I can't look at this stuff. 'You told me you had nothing to do with it and yet you've been Cole's accountant for years. You know all about it!'

'This agreement was none of my doing. Cole came to me with the paperwork that Miss Nordstrom's solicitor and accountant had prepared and I advised him not to enter into what essentially amounted to a financial headlock.' She indicated the paperwork in front of me. 'But you clearly knew of the arrangement because you have signed it.'

I push the paperwork back to her. 'Cole often asked me to sign paperwork to do with the admin of the business,' I splutter. 'I never checked anything… not for years! I just signed. I – I trusted him.' I stop talking then, mortified and ashamed at what I'm being forced to admit to myself, as much as to Corinne.

I'm not a stupid person. But it's true I'd blindly trusted my husband in every area of our lives. I was so certain of his loyalty to us, it never as much as crossed my mind he might be unfaithful again… or financially deceitful. I'd trusted him with every last penny we had to our name.

I look out of the glass at the garden. The oversized black party marquee crouches at the bottom end of the lawn like a harbinger of doom. I wince at flashbacks of Cole walking around the perimeter, looking at the lanterns, Miller calling me in a panicky voice from the patio.

Somebody needs to call the company to pick it up. I can't look at it any more.

I cross my arms and stare down at the baffling paperwork. I haven't taken care of myself. I've failed to maintain an overview of even the most basic of details. I've never checked so much as a word or figure on anything I've signed. I never questioned Cole about his travel or accommodation arrangements when he'd say he was working away yet again. My throat burns. I've been an idiot. A gullible, naive idiot.

'This paperwork confirms that you both signed away any jointly owned assets to be used as collateral against Miss Nordstrom's loan in the case of default,' Corinne confirms.

It's too much for me to get my head around. My brain can barely cope with even the simplest explanations. 'What does this mean, in lay terms? What happens to us now? I mean, OK, I've made a mistake in signing this stuff but… how do we get out of it?'

Corinne lowers her eyes and presses her lips together. 'Jennifer, I can't stress how serious this is. The deeds of this house bear Sara Nordstrom's name. The money in your joint bank accounts effectively belongs to her and several other assets are owned by her.'

'Like the new cars,' I say faintly, remembering her words.

'As part of the loan agreement, you both signed to agree that in the event of Cole's death, all of the assets covered by it will revert to her immediately for the purposes of settling the debt.'

'He's been having an affair with her!' I blurt out, the emotion rising in me like a tidal wave. 'She has a baby with him, do you know about that? She says he was going to move them both in here. That's a lie! I know it's a lie.' Tears spill unchecked down my swollen cheeks.

Corinne shakes her head sadly. 'I'm so sorry, Jennifer. I honestly didn't know the extent of Cole's relationship with Miss Nordstrom; I've never met her. But I confess that due to the highly irregular nature of their financial arrangement, I guessed there was a little bit more behind it.'

'So, what do I do now?' I wail, wiping my face with the back of a hand. 'There must be some way to put this right, some legal loophole that protects us. I can't have anything to do with that woman. I don't want her, or her baby, anywhere near me or my kids so I need you to deal directly with her.'

Corinne twists one side of her mouth up. 'Sadly, she's well within her rights, if she chooses, to evict you and your family from this house immediately. She could, if she were so inclined, issue an instruction through the courts to freeze all your joint bank accounts and assets unless and until the loan is paid in full.' She hesitates. 'I must ask you something, even though I think I know the answer: are you personally able to satisfy the debt?'

I let out a bitter laugh. 'Everything was tied up jointly with Cole. He transferred some spending money each month for me, but he made all the financial decisions and dealt with the admin.'

'How did you leave it with Miss Nordstrom after her visit?'

I shrug. 'I told her I was willing to talk things through in the morning just to get rid of her. I've now decided I'm not going to do that. Any agreements he made will be negated… surely you agree?'

'Jennifer, my advice is very simple. Don't do anything rash.' Corinne shuffles the paperwork in front of her into a neat pile before finally meeting my eyes again. 'These agreements appear watertight. Unless you're happy to move out of the house lock, stock and barrel, you should talk to Sara Nordstrom and try to come to an amicable agreement. Try to keep on the good side of her at least for the interim to buy us some time.'

'What? Are you seriously saying—'

She holds up a hand. 'I, in turn, will revisit the agreements in view of Cole's death and explore if any weak angle exists that we can potentially exploit.' She inclines her head to one side as I open my mouth to protest. 'I can only imagine the horror of finding yourself in this situation when you are trying to come to terms with your husband's untimely and tragic death and, of course, I'm here to support you, Jennifer. But unless you want to find yourself and your children on the streets, as far as I can see, you really have very little choice but to hear what she has to say.'

CHAPTER 12

When Corinne leaves, Mum sees her out, and I sit at the kitchen table with my head in my hands.

'Jennifer?' Mum cautiously approaches me when she comes back in and touches my arm. 'It can't be that bad. What did she say? And what did that Sara woman say?'

For a few moments I just let my hands take the weight of my head. Then I look up into Mum's drawn, concerned face.

'Honestly, Mum, I don't know where to start. It's… beyond my worst nightmare.'

'Come on.' Mum defaults to her tea and sympathy mode. 'Sylvie's watching a cartoon, so I'll make us a nice hot drink and then you can tell me everything. A problem shared is a problem halved.'

I laugh sadly but she continues.

'We can certainly have a good crack at it, can't we? It's the ideal time to get this off your chest.'

When she brings the tea over and a box of fresh tissues, I tell her. I tell her everything.

'That little baby is *Cole's son*?' Her eyes widen. 'Did she know he had a wife and family when she took up with him?'

'Apparently not,' I say sardonically. 'But she could be telling me anything. I can't ask him now, can I?' My eyes begin to prickle.

'So, she claims to have thought she was the only woman in his life? Where did she think he was living, if not with her?'

'She claims they've been living together as a couple for the last year and—'

'Rubbish! Cole has been living here; you can't live in two places without someone noticing!'

I look at her. 'How much is Cole out of the house, supposedly working, Mum? He's away practically all week, sometimes.' She falls quiet. She knows as well as I do it's perfectly possible for him to have maintained another relationship under the guise of work. Particularly as I've been so gullible. Made it all so easy for him. 'He's had plenty of time on his hands because, unbeknown to me, he hasn't really been working at all. According to Corinne, the business *has* no work. A year ago, we were nearly bankrupt. Can you believe that? I never had an inkling.'

Mum frowns and I can almost see the cogs turning as she tries desperately to get her head around it all. 'But look at this house and your lifestyle… if Cole had no money and no work, how could you afford to live like this?'

Which brings me to the next crippling blow. 'Because of *her*. Apparently, everything we have belongs to Sara Nordstrom.' I wave my hand around the kitchen. 'She owns this house, the new cars… everything we have is hers, or has been paid for by money she lent to Cole. This woman who I didn't even know existed until today.'

Now Mum is the one with her head in her hands. 'It can't be true… it can't!'

'I thought the same, but Corinne has just confirmed it. Seems Sara's father died and left her well-off. For some unfathomable reason, she decided to lend a good chunk of it to Cole. But this wasn't a friends' arrangement, it was a proper loan; she had it all set up legally.'

'But… could there be some mistake? Maybe Sara is exaggerating about some part of it at least… I mean, the house?'

I shake my head. 'Corinne confirmed everything and she didn't pull any punches. So I know Sara has been telling the truth, about the financial situation at least.'

'She might be lying about the baby being Cole's son, though,' Mum retorts and then, clearly remembering his previous affair, says, 'Even though it's not beyond the realms of possibility, I suppose.'

I throw my hands in the air. 'Have you seen the baby? He's the spitting image of Miller at that age and he strongly resembles Cole. His hair, that little dimple on his chin…'

Mum looks at the floor. She has obviously seen the resemblance, too.

'Anyway, a simple DNA test will establish that truth. In the meantime, Corinne says Sara is well within her rights to evict us from this house and put us on the street. And just to add insult to injury, all the money in our bank accounts belongs to her. Every penny of it.'

'*What?* How is that possible?'

I shake my head, my eyes swimming. 'It's just too awful for words. She's tied us up in knots and the worst part is… I signed all the paperwork like a complete idiot. I had no idea what it was; I trusted Cole implicitly. Lots of business documents have needed signing over the years and I did it all without question. I've effectively signed away the roof over my children's heads.'

'You and the kids can come and stay with me if necessary. There's no question you're going to be homeless so don't go upsetting yourself about that.'

'You live in a one-bedroom flat, Mum.' Three years ago Mum moved out of her council house and into an over-sixties managed complex in Netherfield, a town about a twelve-minute drive from here.

'It will do for a night or two until you get yourself sorted, won't it?'

Just when I think Mum understands the gravity of what's happening, she shows she hasn't really grasped what I'm saying at all. Nothing is going to be sorted *in a night or two*. We are penniless, about to become homeless and up to our eyeballs in debt that will never be repaid unless I invoke voluntary insolvency procedures. Which means I'll never get a mortgage, probably won't even pass the rental checks on a new place. But that's just one part of it. Even if I can somehow shed the debt, I have no job, no way of providing a reasonable income overnight to get us a decent place. Visions of us moving into a hostel blindside me and I let out a faint wail.

'You've got to fight, Jennifer.' Mum takes in my hopelessness. 'You can't just give in. Has she actually said she wants you out of the house?'

'Not exactly, but—'

Mum sighs with relief. 'There you go then! It isn't as bad as you first thought, is it?'

I don't know whether to laugh or cry. A woman, who's been having an affair with my husband for I don't know how long, has been living with him for the last twelve months, gives birth to his son and finally, a year ago, puts in place a watertight legal strait jacket, which means she doesn't just own Cole, but me and the children as well. I'm not sure how much worse it can get.

I push back my chair and stand up. 'I'm going to have a lie-down upstairs,' I say.

'Just a minute, Jennifer. Hear me out. What are you going to do? If you're not careful you could put yourself in an even worse position. I know that's difficult to imagine but losing the roof over your head will soon put things in perspective.' Mum waits until I'm looking at her. 'What was Corinne's advice?'

'She said unless I want to find myself homeless, I need to try and come to a compromise with Sara.' Just the thought of being beholden to that cheating woman sickens me to the bottom of my stomach. Panic takes hold of me. 'I can't see her again, Mum, I can't! I don't know her, and the kids have no idea they have a half-brother. It's sick. I can't let her worm her way into our life. I can't do that to them.'

Mum's voice is calm. 'You know, one way of looking at it is that Cole betrayed you both. If this is all true, he played you both, didn't he? Maybe she feels as bad as you do.'

'There's one major difference, though,' I say bitterly. 'She's in a position of strength. She holds all the cards financially and, because of that, she has choices. She doesn't have to talk to me, or come to a compromise. She could just throw us out with the sounds of it. So, I'm asking myself why? What's in it for her?'

'I suppose you're only going to find that out if you talk to her, Jennifer. How did you leave it... when she left here earlier, I mean?'

'She's coming back in the morning, supposedly to talk. I can't stand the thought of it.' I put my hand in the pocket of my yoga pants and draw out a small pink and white card and slide it across the table. 'She left me her contact details. Maybe I should just cancel until I can think straight.'

Mum picks up the card and studies it. She turns it over but there's no detail on the back. Just her name and mobile phone number. That's all I have to go on. It's all I know about her. I stare out at the garden for a moment or two. Sylvie's doll's pram is abandoned on the grass. Her bicycle with its stabilisers lies on its side on the patio where Miller saw his father stumble and fall.

'Here's my opinion for what it's worth,' Mum says. 'I think you should get Sara back over here to talk, see what she has to say. I'll take the kids over to Ellen's so you can speak to her in private.'

'And say what? "I'll do anything you want, just don't throw us out on the street"? I don't think so.'

'That attitude is helping no one, Jennifer, least of all you,' Mum says sternly. 'All I'm saying is you two need to talk as a matter of urgency. There is the welfare of three children at stake here and that needs to be forefront in both your minds. At least find out exactly what she's thinking. Hopefully, it won't be as bad as you think.' Mum hesitates before saying, 'She might be a decent person underneath it all, love, you never know.'

Maybe Mum is right and, by some miracle, another conversation with Sara Nordstrom won't be as bad as it sounds. Sadly, I have a horrible feeling it will probably turn out to be a hundred times worse.

Mum kisses me on the cheek. Turning back in the doorway, she pins her eyes to mine.

'Above all, remember this. *You* are Cole's legal wife, and she is just his girlfriend. That has to count for something in the eyes of the law, surely?'

CHAPTER 13

COLE

FIFTEEN MONTHS EARLIER

Cole looked around the hotel function room with a heavy heart. He was proud of Fincham Developments, the construction business he'd set up from scratch. But he wasn't cut out for this: standing around talking to people with inflated egos. Trouble was, most of them also had deep pockets and, in this game, a business was only as strong as the contracts it had in the bag at any given time.

Cole considered himself lucky. If there was one thing he'd always naturally excelled at, it was putting on a show. Giving people what they wanted. He could blag himself out of almost any situation. He could talk to anyone and build a rapport – from one of his site labourers, to the CEO of a multi-million-pound building investment company, and he could do it all in a respectful yet relaxed, open manner.

Cole was very, very good at hiding what he really thought. It was probably, he thought, the singular perk of having a critical father who openly pegged him as a failure from a very young age. Cole learned to shrug his shoulders each time and walk away with a smile on his face when inside, he crumbled a little more.

He walked to the free bar to get himself a lemonade in a gin glass. All around him people stood cradling glasses filled with wine, whisky and even champagne. His attention was caught by a tall, heavy-set man holding court in the corner. The people around him soaked up every word he uttered and laughed in unison, in all the right places.

Cameron Beesley. Owner of one of the most successful property companies in the Midlands. Cole had had his eye on him since he'd walked through the door but he soon resigned himself to the fact there was no real chance of getting anywhere close enough to speak to him.

As Cole took his drink from the bartender, someone walking past nudged his arm and the drink slopped messily from the glass. Cole tutted and pulled out a handkerchief to mop his olive-green cord jacket.

'I'm so sorry! I'm so clumsy. Please... forgive me.'

A woman, much younger than him, stood mortified. She'd been at a couple of these events and had caught his eye before. But he'd never spoken to her. 'Can I help you clear that up? I'm so, so sorry.'

'No harm done,' Cole said, stuffing the handkerchief back in his trouser pocket. He lifted his glass. 'Just between you and me, this is only lemonade. It won't stain.'

She laughed and Cole couldn't help noticing her graceful long neck, her piercing blue eyes and smooth, radiant skin. Close up she was even more of a stunner, no doubt about it. He attended quite a few of these networking events and you saw lots of the same faces. But he'd definitely remembered *her* face.

'I'm Cole Fincham,' he said, offering his hand. 'I think I've seen you here before.'

'Sara Nordstrom. I've been helping organise the last few networking events.'

They chatted for a few minutes. Cole told her briefly about his business and Sara said she'd been doing some PR work for an agency which had led her to events management.

'You come to these things a lot then?' she said, taking a sip of her fizz.

He nodded. 'A necessary evil, I'm afraid. It's where I hear about a lot of the tenders coming up and, despite the idle chatter, it's a great way to pick up new contacts and, potentially, new business.'

'Is that what we're doing, right now?' she asked cheekily, leaning into him a little. 'Indulging in idle chatter?'

'No, I didn't mean…'

She laughed. 'I'm only teasing. Got your eye on anyone in particular?'

Cole shrugged and glanced over to the group in the corner.

'Ahh, Mr Beesley.' She grinned. 'He's always on everyone's wish list.'

'You know him?'

She nodded. 'I got to meet him through the agency I work for. One of my first jobs was to meet with him and get him on board with the proposed PR campaign for the new Live-Shop-Eat project that he has in the early stages of development.'

Cole almost choked on his lemonade. 'That's the very project I'm hanging my nose over,' he said, astonished. 'But there's not a cat in hell's chance of getting anywhere near him with his entourage.'

Sara nodded and looked up at Cole with her crystal-clear eyes. 'He's always very popular. Me? I prefer chatting to more interesting and better-looking people.'

Cole felt his cheeks heat up a little. It was years since he'd felt like this in the company of a woman… like he was a schoolboy again. Embarrassed and desperate to impress. Jennifer's disapproving face flitted into his mind. He was almost relieved when she said, 'There's someone I need a quick word with. I'll just be a couple of minutes… don't go away!'

Sara turned and walked a few steps away to place her glass on a vacant table. Cole's eyes travelled down the back of her as if they had a mind of their own. She had the perfect figure in her smart, navy fitted dress. Narrow shoulders, nipped-in waist and smooth brown legs, her calves defined in her towering heels. Jennifer's voice came into his head. 'You couldn't pay me to wear heels that high any more.' He smiled, remembering how Jennifer herself had loved wearing heels in her twenties, too.

Cole watched until Sara had disappeared into the throng of people. It was funny, really, how this lovely young woman had got him into a bit of a tizzy. Here he was, approaching forty and a family man... she must be at least twelve or thirteen years younger. He wasn't used to flirting any more and neither should he be. He'd made a terrible mistake in the past but he'd pledged to stay faithful and he intended to continue to keep that promise. He had big business problems on the horizon and was here to try and resolve them with a juicy big contract.

No, he certainly didn't need any complications in the shape of a young woman well over ten years younger than him, but... God, he'd forgotten how it felt to have such a strong, instant attraction to someone. It had been so long! And incredibly, he could tell that Sara felt it too. It was a chemical reaction that couldn't be faked. Then it occurred to him that maybe Sara had a boyfriend and that's why she'd removed herself from what was potentially a dangerous situation. It was the sensible thing to do.

Cole decided he'd finish his drink and get out of here in the next five minutes. Miss Nordstrom had put him on the backfoot, and he felt uncomfortable. At times like this, there was sometimes nothing left to do but remove yourself from the situation... from the *temptation* that lingered there.

Cole drained his lemonade before patting down his pockets. Satisfied he had his keys and his phone on his person, he began to make his away across the room to the exit, raising his hand and nodding a farewell when he spotted the face of someone he recognised. He was about halfway across when he heard someone call out his name. His eyes fixed on Sara over in the corner, waving her hand and beckoning him.

Beside her, Cameron Beesley had turned away from his adoring audience to smile broadly at Cole and jerk his head by way of an informal summons.

That's when Cole realised he was being invited to join them.

Later, Cole, Sara and Cameron Beesley sat at a round table in a private members club in the trendy Lace Market area of the city. They had been among the last stragglers to leave the networking meeting and when Cole had tried to shake Cameron's hand to thank him for the invitation to visit his offices the next day, Cameron, a large gregarious man with a ruddy complexion, had wafted the gesture away.

'No goodbyes yet, my good man! We've only just started. This afternoon is just the warm-up. I insist you and this lovely creature join me and my party for dinner and drinks at my private club.'

Cole had escaped to the bathroom and texted Jennifer.

Got a possible lead for a hot new contract. Could be late back.

When he saw the two delivery ticks, Cole turned off his phone and returned to join the others, his head buzzing with the elation of winning an appointment the next day with Cameron to discuss his latest Live-Shop-Eat construction project, but also with the effect of the alcohol. Cole had lost count of how many times his wine glass had been topped up during the afternoon.

Cameron had insisted on Cole joining him in drinking bottle after bottle of the eye-wateringly expensive Pouilly-Fumé he'd ordered for the group. Every fibre of him knew he should call it a day.

'I'd love to join you, Cameron, I really would,' Cole began. 'But I have to get back to—'

'Nonsense! I won't hear a word of it. You're my guest and, as such, you need to come… you don't want me thinking you're being rude, now, do you? No excuses. Tell him, sweetheart.' Cameron leered at Sara, pressing his red, shiny face close to hers.

'Cameron's right!' she agreed happily whilst discreetly leaning back from him a little. When Cameron turned away to settle the drinks bill with a waiter, Cole noticed the smile slip from Sara's face as she rolled her eyes at him. He nodded, understanding immediately.

She was like him, just doing and saying the right thing to make the right impression.

After a long dinner and more drinks at the private club, Cole found himself in a cab with Sara. She giggled as his head repeatedly lolled on to her shoulder, despite his efforts to keep it upright.

When he next opened his eyes, the vehicle was stationary and Sara was gently shaking his shoulder. 'Wakey, wakey… time to get out.' She grinned as Cole stared blearily at her, trying, and failing, to make sense of where he was.

'Where… I need to…'

She helped him out of the car and when the fresh air hit him, he felt his knees begin to wobble.

He looked up at the smart glass and steel apartment block in front of him.

'Where is this?' he whispered, his head spinning.

'I've brought you home with me like a little stray dog,' she said softly, her breath warm on his cheek. 'Just until you get sobered up.'

'I can't, I mean… I have work to do, and I need to prepare for…' He couldn't remember the detail but he knew it was something important.

Her face fell, her full lips opening slightly. She leaned close enough to Cole that he could smell her vanilla scent. He felt himself react on a visceral level. Even though his mind was foggy and trying to resist, he could feel the thrill… the danger, throbbing powerfully through his body. He watched as the red brake lights of the cab came on at the end of the street before it turned and drove out of sight.

Now, the street was quiet. 'What time is it?' he said, failing to make sense of his watch.

'Just come up for a coffee,' Sara said, linking her arm through his. 'When you've sobered up a bit, I can call a cab to take you home… OK?'

Cole nodded. That seemed reasonable. He allowed her to lead him to the brightly lit foyer of the upmarket building where a doorman stood ready to admit them.

He'd have the coffee, thank Sara for the introduction to Cameron and then get a cab back home.

He could hardly go home to Jennifer yet anyway. Not in this state.

CHAPTER 14

NOTTINGHAMSHIRE POLICE

MONDAY

DI Helena Price is just about to divert her desk phone before lunch when the call comes through. She pushes away her notes from this morning's meeting with Superintendent Della Grey and picks up the phone.

'Morning, ma'am,' the voice on the line says. 'My name is Sandy Singh from the Collision Investigation Unit. Do you have a few minutes to chat?'

The unit, known within the force as the CIU, consists of specially trained collision investigators who assist the Roads Policing Unit or the RPU. The phone call probably signals a fatal road traffic accident in the area.

'Go ahead,' Price says, taking a sip from her water cooler bottle.

'Two days ago, there was a fatal RTA on the A453, the dual carriageway between the M1 motorway and Nottingham. The Range Rover overturned, leaving the road and the driver died at the scene. We're sending over a full report this morning, but my boss asked me to give you the heads-up it's coming.'

Helena knew the busy, fast road well. She often used it during her workday and also to access the motorway from her home in Ruddington to visit her widowed dad, who still lived independently in Kirkby-in-Ashfield, a town just off Junction 27 of the M1.

'The Range Rover was the only vehicle involved in the incident?'

'That's right. As per usual, the vehicle was recovered and is currently being examined for any mechanical defects or other evidence that may help to confirm what happened. So investigations there are not quite finished but our concern is with the driver's post-mortem results, a Mr Cole Fincham. We've just had those through and it's not quite adding up. I'm about to email everything through to you, DI Price, so if you'd like to take a look and get back to me with any questions, I'd be more than happy to assist in any way I can.'

When the call ends, Helena looks over to a nearby desk where DS Kane Brewster is tapping his keyboard with one index finger while simultaneously loading a Snickers bar into his mouth with the other hand.

'Brewster,' she calls. 'Got a minute? There's some info coming through from the CIU regarding a fatal road collision on the A453 two days ago.'

Brewster stands up immediately and walks over to her desk, wiping his sticky fingers on a handkerchief.

Helena opens her emails and clicks on the newest one. Several attached documents begin to load.

Brewster moves closer and peers over her shoulder at the screen. 'Anything interesting?'

'Pull up a chair.' She clicks on the first document, which fills the large monitor within seconds. She scans the form, murmuring, 'Scene of the accident looks standard by the sounds of it. Debris collected, tyre skid marks measured at the point the vehicle left the road. No surprises there.'

Helena clicks her mouse a couple of times and another report loads. 'Ahh, here we go. There's a hitch with the post-mortem findings. Looks like there was something that sparked the pathologist's concern... a head injury.'

Brewster wheels an office chair over and sits down next to Helena as she scans the document.

'A head injury is hardly unexpected in the process of rolling two metric tonnes of Range Rover Vogue off the A453,' Brewster remarks, peering closer. 'Says he suffered internal injuries, too. Very nasty.'

'He had a fractured skull but indications were the head injury in question had taken place *prior* to the road accident. They've done the other standard tests including toxicology, but those results will take a while to come back.'

Brewster frowns. 'Seems there was no apparent reason for the vehicle to leave the road – no obstacles, or other vehicles, and the driver's drug and alcohol levels were normal – this head injury could have caused a haemorrhage or similar and forced him to lose control of the car. Essentially, it could have been the thing that killed him.'

'Precisely,' Helena murmurs, clicking through the other attachments before turning to Brewster. 'We'll need to have a chat with the pathologist to get all the specifics. What have we got on today?'

Brewster pulls the corners of his mouth down and shakes his head. 'Nothing major that can't be moved around, boss.' He counts on his fingers. 'There's a follow-up on the corner shop attacks at Sneinton, the community policing presentation later this morning, and then a team meeting on current cases after lunch before we visit the couple whose son was killed in the music festival explosion.'

'OK, see if you can get us a slot with the pathologist in the next couple of days, Brewster. Just a quick chat will do, so we know exactly what we're dealing with here.' She glances over at his desk. 'When you've finished your Snickers, of course. No rush.'

Brewster grins and pulls his chair away. 'I'll get on to that right away, boss.'

Before she clicks out of the email, Helena reads the last attachment: general information on the deceased. The driver was a Cole Fincham, thirty-nine years old and the managing director of his own building company, Fincham Developments. He leaves a wife, Jennifer, and two children aged thirteen and five. Helena reads the address again. Dovedale Road at West Bridgford. She has a friend who lives a few doors down from this address and the number of the Finchams' property suddenly leaps out at her. This was the house that had been sold and then shrouded in scaffolding for the best part of a year with builders going to and fro most days. The one that had seemed to take forever to finish because all work stopped for a while. Helena has a feeling the Finchams had only moved in there in early spring, so they hadn't been living there for a year yet. How tragic.

'Sorted.' Brewster's voice breaks her out of her thoughts. 'The pathologist will see us on Wednesday just before he breaks for lunch at twelve o'clock. Beats me how these people can eat after what they've been doing all morning.' He frowns. 'All those Y-incisions and electric saws are bound to—'

'Yes, alright, Brewster. At this rate you'll put yourself off your own lunch.' Helena glances at the enormous cool bag wedged under his desk. He brings it every day, packed full of sandwiches, cakes, drinks and usually the odd chocolate bar. 'Or knowing you, maybe not.'

CHAPTER 15

JENNIFER

I've spent the whole morning turning my discussions with Sara Nordstrom and Corinne over in my head. Replaying every detail I'm able to recall, trying to find an anomaly or inconsistency in Sara's claims.

Last night, heeding Corinne's advice, I called the number on the card Sara had left with me.

She picked up after a few rings. I heard the baby grizzling in the background.

'Jennifer Fincham here,' I said stiffly. 'If you can get over to the house again tomorrow, I thought we might discuss things a little more calmly.'

'I see.' Sara's tone was equally cool. 'Well, I can come over early afternoon tomorrow if that's—'

'That's fine,' I agreed, keen to bring our brief exchange to a close.

I want this awful conversation over and done with as soon as possible so I can move on. I refused another sedative last night and so didn't sleep a wink. All I did was think everything through and the only thread of hope I have is if I can get her to agree to allowing us to stay another year in the house – although I can't even begin to imagine how much rent she'd want – then it would give me time to get back on my feet. More importantly, maybe… just maybe by way of a miracle, it might give Corinne the time she needs to find a legal way out of this mess for us.

I sit on the bed and look back at Cole's pillow. It's plumped and perfect, as if he might be back any moment to lay his head down. It's been a few nights since he slept here at the house because of his 'work'. Very hard work it must have been, too, coping with a new baby and his young girlfriend in his other house instead of the out-of-town budget hotels he used to tell me he was staying in around the country as he fought for business in the dog-eat-dog world of construction.

'Where are you tonight?' I'd sometimes ask vaguely, as I pottered around in the kitchen or leafed through a magazine.

'Just some cheap and cheerful Premier Inn in a town I've forgotten the name of.' He'd kiss my forehead and tangle his fingers in my hair at the back of my head, sending a frisson of pleasure cascading down my spine. 'One thing I know for certain is I'll be counting the minutes until I'm back in my own bed with my gorgeous wife.'

My eyes slide across to the dressing table mirror where I can see myself reflected. A naive, gullible woman who swallowed every lie without challenge and who soaked up every meaningless, flattering comment. The compliant wife who could be relied upon to sign every item of business paperwork and ask no awkward questions.

Some people might even say I deserve everything that's now happening to me. But they'd be wrong.

It's an official staff training day at the kids' schools today but Mum has already spoken to the respective headteachers to tell them about Cole's death and informing them that Miller and Sylvie will be absent for at least this week. They both kindly offered the services of the school counsellor when the children feel ready.

Mum takes the kids over to Ellen's, giving me time to have my dreaded conversation with Sara.

I take a quick shower, wash my hair and towel dry it. Then I comb it back from my face in a slick, damp ponytail. I use a wash-off face cleanser and scrub so, although I don't apply any make-up, I have a bit of colour in my cheeks at least. I dress in clean, comfy clothes and go downstairs.

When I walk into the kitchen, I don't focus on the high-end designer stuff. Instead, I see Sylvie's Barbie dolls scattered across the table. Miller's Marvel comics that litter the emerald-green velvet sofa next to the glass doors. Cole's GoPro camera and phone chargers that remain plugged in at the wall, the long wires snaking across the worktop. 'Can't you take these somewhere else?' I used to complain endlessly. 'It spoils the clean lines of the marble.' Laughably, that was the sort of problem I had then.

It still looks like home here. A family home in which we'd planned to raise our kids in safety and with love. He'd said he wanted that as much as me and naively, I'd believed him.

I grab a pen and notepad out of the drawer and sit down at the table. On a fresh page, I jot down some questions:

Why did you make such a punishing financial arrangement with Cole? Where is all your money from? Do you intend to evict me and my children from our home? If so, is there a temporary arrangement we can agree to, in order to avoid this?

I feel lower than ever writing down my biggest fears, but I need a framework for our conversation when she gets here. It's important I remain focused when she's glancing around my home and looking at me with those cool, blue eyes like she's the puppet master of my life.

The doorbell rings. She's early.

I jump up but then I force myself to walk, not run, to the front door. Mum's words play again in my head, giving me strength.

You are Cole's legal wife, and she is just his girlfriend. Except she owns my house.

Sara stands on the doorstep with baby Rory, who's fast asleep in a leopard-print BabyBjörn papoose. My shoulder and neck muscles tighten further when I note again, in the angle of his face and the slope of his nose, I can see Cole.

'Hello again, Jennifer,' she says.

I open the door wider and step back. 'Come through.'

She comes inside and I close the door. She doesn't wait for me to invite her to follow me into the house. She slips off her ankle boots and walks through the hallway where she'd sat last time. I follow her through. As she walks past open doors to other rooms, her head turns this way and that as she takes in the size of the accommodation.

'It's a stunning house,' she murmurs. In the living room, she sits down without an invitation and unbuckles the baby, his downy head bobbing back and forth as she moves. She doesn't look like a grieving girlfriend to me.

'Cole and I designed every detail from scratch,' I say archly. 'We wanted it to be a family home that was completely to our own tastes. We loved it here.'

Sensing hostility, she steals a glance at me but does not comment and I feel satisfied that the barb has been received as intended. Then I remember Corinne's advice.

You should talk to Sara Nordstrom and try to come to an amicable agreement.

I should be careful. Riling Sara is not going to help me to secure my children's future and *that* is my number one priority above any point-scoring.

'Can I get you a drink?'

'Thank you,' she says. 'A glass of water is fine.'

In the kitchen, I take a glass from the cupboard and run ice-cold filtered water from the Quooker tap. Pity I haven't got any powdered arsenic to add to it, but sadly it's not something I keep in the cupboard. She seems so cool and, to say she's claiming to have been in a serious relationship with Cole, shows no sign of trauma due to his tragic death.

When I return, she's in the process of starting to feed Rory. I've no problem with breastfeeding mums. I fed both my own children myself after all. But something about her exposing her smooth, still-perky breast so unselfconsciously… it makes me want to throw my head back and howl.

Rory latches on and she grimaces. Thirty seconds later I can see the pain etched on her face. I can still vividly remember the pain of the mastitis I suffered with Sylvie.

'Have you tried using silicone shields?'

She shakes her head. 'He won't feed when I use them. I'm so sore, I don't know how long I can continue but…' She glances at me. 'I'll feel like a failure if I don't do at least eight months, ideally longer.'

'I read some research that said the first three months are the most important. Once you've done that, your baby has a real head start in getting all the best natural nutrients and benefits.'

'Really?' She gives me a surprised look. 'I didn't know that. Thank you.'

I shrug, wishing I'd stayed quiet.

I've left my list of questions in the kitchen, but I think I can remember them. 'I've got lots of things I need to ask as you can imagine, but there's one thing that's more important than anything else,' I say.

'Please, go ahead.' She traces her fingers gently over her baby's feathery hair.

Here goes. I take a breath. 'Are you going to evict me and my children from our home?'

She looks pained. 'I really don't want it to get to that, Jennifer. Remember, finding out about you and the children was a big shock for me, too. I want to try and strike a compromise that means you and your children can continue to live here. If you're open to that.'

A rush of relief relaxes my shoulders but my gratitude is short-lived. One word bounces around my head, drowning out everything else. That word is: *why*? Why would she try to come to a compromise? Why would she not just kick me out so she can live in this nice big house alone with baby Rory?

Words are cheap, and this is a woman who most definitely cannot be trusted. But *if* I can just get some breathing space… if I can just get a year where we're settled to recover from Cole's death, it gives me a fighting chance to work towards having a normal life again one day. I could return to working as a teaching assistant. I left my job when Miller was born and never picked up my career again. Back then I had plans to train as a teacher. But Cole wasn't keen on me returning to work and I was besotted with Miller.

'I'd like to work towards a compromise. I just need some time to recover from all this and plan for our future.' It almost kills me to acquiesce, but what other choice do I have? This is our home and I never want to leave it but… it's a start, at least, if we can stay here. Corinne might come up trumps and uncover some legal loophole that renders the financial loans null and void on Cole's death. At the same time, it's important I find out what Sara's long-term plans are.

'That's good to hear.' She looks relieved, which I find a bit strange seeing as she's the one with all the power.

'Obviously, you're not going to let us continue to live here indefinitely. You'll want to sell this place in due course to recoup your money, I presume.'

'I will want to sell the house at some point, but not yet. Not for a good while actually, and that's where the compromise comes in. I have a proposal of sorts… a rather unusual one. All I ask is you hear me out before shooting it down.'

It must be pretty radical if she's expecting me to close it down. She sits Rory up and mops herself briefly. Her skin is smooth and taut. Cole must have loved looking at her body. I think about my own skin, lightly patterned in places with silvery stretch marks. I'm relieved when Sara covers her modesty with a muslin cloth while she winds Rory.

'I'm listening,' I say.

She stops rubbing the baby's back and looks at me. 'How would you feel about me and Rory moving in here?'

'Moving in?' I frown.

'Rory and I could come and live here with you and your children. We'd agree on a trial period first and—'

'Are you having a laugh?' I feel a bolt of anger shoot into my chest. She'd almost had me fooled! Yet again I've been too open and gullible. Taking her at face value when I already know what she's capable of.

'No, Jennifer, this is not a joke. I can assure you I'm perfectly serious.' She reaches for her glass and takes a sip of water. 'Are you familiar with the term "nesting"?'

'For a married couple, yes.' She's referring to an increasingly popular living arrangement where, to minimise upheaval, the children of estranged parents remain living in the family home and the parents come and go around them, providing care on a rota. But there's no way I'm staying somewhere else for even a night and leaving my children in the care of a stranger. Especially someone who's been having a secret affair with their dad for goodness knows how long.

'I know a couple who are practising nesting,' she says, ignoring my shocked face. 'The parents alternate between staying at the family home and a small flat. The kids stay put and barely notice the new arrangements. It's a healthy alternative to the children being put through the pain of big change and the damage such upheaval can cause. I'm not suggesting we get a flat and alternate care but we've got three kids here that need us to sort out this mess. I'd pay the bills for the first few months and we'd try and build something out of this unusual situation we find ourselves in. We'd be doing it for the sake of our children. That's all I want out of this.'

'It works well, I'm sure, for some families. When a couple have been together. But this situation is completely—'

'It can work just as well with two mothers.' She's been rubbing the baby's back for what seems like an age, her eyes bright and focused on me. 'Admittedly the couple I know haven't got the complications we two have between us, but—'

'Complications? You mean the fact you've been having an affair with my husband? And the fact you've gone one step further and had a child with him, too?' I shake my head in frustration. 'I can't understand why you'd even want to consider living with your married boyfriend's family… it's madness!'

Corinne's words echo in my head.

She's well within her rights, if she chooses, to evict you and your family from this house immediately.

'I told you, I didn't know Cole was still married,' she says carefully.

I give a bitter laugh. 'Clearly you can now see there's no merit in that story!'

'He told me you'd split up because you were constantly at each other's throats, and he'd asked for a divorce for years.'

'That's rubbish!' I cry out and the baby startles and whimpers. I drop my voice. 'That is utter rubbish. We *never* discussed splitting up and we had a policy of never arguing in front of the kids.'

She's still rubbing the baby's back quite firmly. Rory's head is lolling this way and that, and he looks pale. But she doesn't seem to have noticed.

'I think you're making him a bit queasy,' I remark, and she turns him the other way to feed.

'I didn't come here to upset you, Jennifer; I came with a genuine desire to try and work something out between us.' She looks at me.

'That's what doesn't make any sense. Why are you so hellbent on working something out? Why do you want to pay our bills and effectively take money away from your own child?'

'I don't look at it like that and in any case, I have plenty of money. Thanks to my father's property portfolio and investments, I probably have more money than I need. Some things – like family – are more important than money will ever be. That's what I want for my son: a loving home with his blood relatives. I know what I'm proposing is very unconventional but why can't it work if we're both willing to give it a chance?'

'For one thing, my children don't know you and they don't know Rory is their half-brother,' I respond shortly. 'Bringing strangers into our home is bound to make them feel very uncomfortable when they're already grieving for their father.'

'Agreed. Rory isn't used to having people around, either. That's why I'm not suggesting for a moment we embark on a full nesting arrangement but start with just the basic principles. Simply sharing the same space that is the house.' She looks around the large living room. 'We can have our private areas and we can even use the communal areas like this one on a rota if you'd prefer, at least in the beginning.'

What she's proposing is preposterous to me. I can hardly bear to look at her, never mind contemplate living with her. But I'm between a rock and a hard place.

It's crazy. It's impossible. But it could also be a lifeline.

'Why would you want to do this when you could have everything all to yourself?' I know I'm pushing it, but something isn't adding up. It's time I started to ask questions of people and not just blindly accept what I'm told. 'You have the option to kick us out and live here with Rory or sell up and disappear off into the sunset with your money. Rory is too young to be affected by Cole's death so he's not going to suffer in the same way my two kids are.'

'Hard for you to believe, I know, but I'm not a cruel, unreasonable person, Jennifer. I don't want to see you and your children displaced in the middle of a tragedy. You didn't know about me and that was a shock, but I didn't know about you, either. I thought my future was with Cole and that there was only me and Rory in his life. And there's something else, too.' She pauses for a moment before saying quietly, 'I have no one else, OK? A few acquaintances, sure. But now Cole has gone, I am alone with my son, who also has no one in the world but me and now he has… he has—'

'… a half-brother and sister,' I finish for her.

'Yes. And more than anything, I want Rory to know family life. I never had the benefit of that myself.' She sighs. 'Cole is gone now. It's a very sad but irreversible fact. But you and I, Jennifer, we are still young and very much alive. Wouldn't it be wonderful if we could make something positive out of all the lies and heartbreak for our children's sakes?'

I study my bitten, flaking nails and then push my hands under my thighs. She is painting a cosy picture for the future, but there is a treacherous mountain of lies and betrayal to unpick before we can get there.

'Can we put what has happened behind us and see if we can get on for the sake of our children?' Sara says, pinning her eyes to mine. 'Do you want to at least try?'

CHAPTER 16

MILLER

At his aunt Ellen's house, Miller sits and watches as his cousin, Damian, painstakingly assembles the base for the Lego Hedwig he has built. The intricately designed owl sits on the floor beside him, its beady black eyes seeming to bore into Miller's very soul.

'It's taken me two weeks to build the actual bird. The wings were tricky,' Damian drones on. 'The kit is for age twelve plus and some people in my class needed help with it, but I found it easy-peasy.'

'That's nothing,' Miller scoffs. 'There are eight-year-old kids on YouTube building the Hogwarts Castle kit and that's age sixteen plus.'

'I can't wait to show my dad when the owl is fully mounted and on display. Mum says it's going to take pride of place in the living room,' Damian remarks, ignoring Miller's comment.

'How's your dad going to see it?' Miller says, smelling blood. 'My mum says he wants nothing to do with you, now he has a new family in Ireland.'

Damian looks up and regards Miller through narrowed eyes. 'That's not true. I saw him at Easter when he came over with work.'

Miller gives a harsh laugh. 'Easter is ages ago now. It'll be Christmas soon and you've only seen him once this year.' His heart cramps when he thinks about his own dad and how he'd loved Christmas. He'd insisted Miller built a snowman with him every year, even though that sort of thing was meant for little kids. Miller had secretly loved doing it, but now he'd never ever do it again. Not with his dad.

Damian shrugs and selects the next piece to slot on to the base. 'He might be coming over this Christmas, anyway.'

Miller clenches his teeth. The pain in his stomach is gnawing away at him. He is hurting so bad, and he really, really wants Damian to hurt, too.

'Bet he doesn't. Bet he's just saying that but really, he wants to stay in Ireland with his other kids who aren't fat and crap at sports.'

Something flashes in Damian's eyes. 'At least I know I'll see my dad again. Your dad is dead now and you'll never—'

Miller springs off the bed and pushes Damian hard. He lets out a yelp and topples over as Miller turns, kicking the snowy owl across the room. The model hits the wall and disintegrates, Lego pieces flying out at all angles. As Damian yells for his mother, Miller stamps down hard on the partially assembled base.

Footsteps thunder up the stairs and the door flies open. Aunt Ellen and the boys' gran stand there, their mouths hanging open. Behind them, Sylvie pushes her head between their legs and gasps dramatically at the chaotic scene before her.

The momentary silence is shattered when Damian begins to howl.

'He's broken Hedwig and he said my dad hates me... he said I'm fat and rubbish at sports...'

Aunt Ellen rushes forward and crouches beside her son, pulling him close to her. 'What the hell happened here?' she demands, glaring up at Miller. 'What have you done?'

'He said my dad is dead and I'm never going to see him again.' Miller folds his arms and stares at the drizzle that runs in never-ending rivulets down the windowpane. He bites down on his tongue to combat his stinging eyes.

Damian begins to yell back in response. 'He said it first, he said—'

'Let's just all calm down, shall we?' Miller's gran steps forward and slides her arm around his shoulders. 'There's lots of hurting and upset in our family now and it's really important we pull together and support each other, not be unkind.'

The pain and fury inside Miller does not subside. His entire body buzzes, like a swarm of bees is continually chasing up and down, from his toes to his head and back again. It never ceases for a moment. He can't think straight because of it. He can't do anything to take his mind off it. He just wants to curl up and shut out the world.

'I can't put up with behaviour like this, Mum. We know how quickly he got out of control last time,' Aunt Ellen says to his gran, as if Miller isn't standing there. 'I know he's in turmoil, but if he's going to upset our Damian then Jennifer will have to find someone else to look after him.'

'The boy is heartbroken, Ellen,' his gran says. 'He doesn't mean what he said and, besides, it sounds like Damian held his own well enough.'

'It took me ages to build that bird.' Damian sniffs, rubbing at his eyes with meaty, loose fists. 'I really wanted to show it to my dad when he comes over at Christmas.'

Miller catches the meaningful look between his aunt and gran.

'He won't come, Damian,' Miller says, looking out at the rain. 'They tell you what you want to hear but it's all lies. That's all families ever do to you. Lie.'

Aunt Ellen bundles Damian downstairs to recover and Miller locks himself in the bathroom. After a short time, his gran stops trying to persuade him to come out and she goes downstairs, too.

When he hears them talking down there, Miller sits on the floor with his back against the bath panel and stretches his long legs out on the cool tiles.

He takes out his dad's secret phone and scrolls through the WhatsApp messages again. He can tell there are lots of messages missing because there are sometimes long strings of messages from her, but his dad must have deleted lots of his own.

He still loves his dad with all his heart but this phone proves that Miller hadn't really known him at all. His trusty, dependable dad who was the best fun had also been very deceitful for a very long time. Miller knows that to be the truth now. His mum would never believe he'd cheat on her. *Never.*

Even thinking such a thing about his beloved dad physically hurts like someone has stabbed him in the heart. When he'd first opened the phone in his bedroom at home, he'd almost decided to wipe it clean without looking any further. But his curiosity had got the better of him and he'd opened the deleted photograph folder. That had been very interesting.

The woman – Sara – had sent his dad rude pictures. Lots of them. In many, she hadn't worn any clothes at all. When he'd first seen the pics where she'd cupped her breasts and pouted into the camera, he'd nearly fainted. Miller hated her, but the pictures excited him, and that in turn made him feel ashamed and disloyal to his mother.

All the photos are accompanied by short messages she's written. *Miss you, Can't wait till tonight* or *This is all yours, love Sara.* It's both gross and fascinating, and he simply cannot stop himself looking.

There are other pictures too in the later messages. So many images of a baby boy.

Rory, she calls him. *Rory's missing his daddy* or *Your boy looks just like you, honey.*

When he looks closely at the baby, Miller feels like someone has reached in and torn out his heart.

His dad had had another son. A baby boy who looks helpless and perfect and has never brought any trouble to the house like Miller did in the summer term when the headteacher had contacted home.

Jealousy, and other uncomfortable feelings he can't name, squirm in his belly, making him feel sick. He wants to delete all the photographs so badly and yet something inside won't let him.

Now Miller looks again at the baby's ruddy plump cheeks and his trusting, big blue eyes staring up at the camera and a curious feeling prickles in his chest as he comes to a realisation.

This baby boy is not just his dad's son. He also belongs to Miller in a way, too.

CHAPTER 17

JENNIFER

WEDNESDAY

I spend the next couple of days in a daze while arrangements are constructed around me. Mandy, the family liaison officer, calls round and asks to speak to me. Mum makes a pot of tea and sits with us.

Mandy clears her throat. 'I wanted you to know that you're now able to visit the Chapel of Rest to see your husband,' she says solemnly. 'I can accompany you, if you'd prefer or—' she looks at Mum '—other close members of the family.'

I look down at my hands. 'I don't think I can do it,' I say quietly.

'Sorry. I… I thought you'd said you wanted to see him.' She sounds confused and looks to Mum to confirm, but Mum stays quiet.

'After everything, I… I just don't know if I can do it.'

'I understand,' Mandy says. 'Of course, it's your decision alone.'

'Myself or Ellen, that's Jennifer's sister, can identify the body,' Mum says. 'There's no need for Jennifer to put herself through that.'

'No. Of course,' Mandy says. 'I'm so sorry to have to go through all this when everything is still so raw, but I want to keep you fully informed of developments.' She hesitates. 'Unfortunately, because Cole's death was sudden and unexpected, the coroner will need to carry out an inquest following the post-mortem. This means your husband's body will not be released until the inquest has taken place and you won't be able to register his death.'

'Or arrange his funeral?' Mum gasps.

'I'm afraid not,' Mandy says.

I can't stand the thought of a funeral, anyway. Not yet. I have this terrible tug-of-war taking place in my head. Do I try and remember the man I loved and thought I knew, or allow my feelings to harden and protect me against the cheat and liar I've since discovered he was? How do I deal with the loss when I have so many conflicting feelings fighting for attention?

When Mandy has gone, Mum comes in and closes the door.

'I know you're struggling, Jenny,' she says softly, placing her hand on my arm. 'It's your decision alone whether you want to see Cole's body. We can take the burden of it if you'd prefer.'

I'm taken aback by the tears streaming down my face. 'I just don't know how to feel, Mum. If I don't go, I'll feel like I'm letting the kids down but if I do it, I feel like I'm trivialising the terrible things he's done. The way he betrayed us with *her*.'

Mum takes my hand in both of hers. 'Just give yourself permission to feel it all, Jenny. The sadness, the anger, the heartbreak… let it come. All your feelings are valid. You don't have to choose between them.'

Even as Mum drives me to the hospital, I'm questioning whether I'm doing the right thing. But Mum's pep talk helped. I can still see Cole despite my feelings. I can do it because it's something I need to do for myself and for my children. So I can tell them that I saw their father one last time and that he looked at peace.

We don't talk much during the fifteen-minute journey to the hospital. Mum doesn't ask any searching questions or comment on Sara, Rory or ask about the financial disaster I discussed with Corinne and I'm grateful for that.

At the hospital, I stand back and let Mum do all the organising. A few minutes after we arrive, we're directed outside across a parking area to the hospital chapel. When we get inside, Mum squeezes my hand and walks over to the desk to speak with the man sitting there.

When she comes back, Mum says, 'He's ready for us, love. We can go through to see Cole now.'

The room is small and painted cream. There's a silk flower arrangement on the low table and the carpet is that wiry grey sort suitable for heavy footfall.

'I can give you some time alone with him,' Mum says gently. 'If you'd like that?'

I nod, my eyes fixed on the long low table in the middle of the room that bears my husband's lifeless body. There is a lot of folded white fabric and not much of him visible.

Mum leaves and the door closes with a soft click. Just a few days ago, Cole was still alive. Vibrant and excited about the party.

'It's going to be an amazing night,' he'd told me. 'The best celebration for my birthday girl.'

We'd kissed. His lips soft and warm against mine. His strong arms encircling me as he pressed his body closer.

'I love you so much, Jen. I know I've been a bit grouchy lately because of work but... I'm so happy with you and the kids, you know.'

'Course I know that, you big softy.' I'd grinned, kissing him on the nose and pulling away to make coffee.

I take a few steps and look down at him. He's smaller now. His strength has evaporated and his skin looks shrunken and stretched like paper. I can only see one side of his face because they've arranged softly pleated fabric around the rest of him. One hand lies on top of the shroud and I place my fingertips on it. His flesh feels cold and unyielding.

'The day you left for your last work trip, you said you loved me, Cole. You told me you were happy with me and the kids,' I whisper. 'I know now that was a lie because all that time you'd been with Sara. Telling her you want to be with her, that you were planning to move her and your new son into *our* house.'

I'm slightly breathless but it still doesn't feel like I've said enough.

The words come out in a rush. 'You betrayed me, and you betrayed our children. How could you do that to us? How could you leave us with nothing? Part of me hates you for that. Do you hear me? I hate you for what you've done.'

I lift my fingers away from his hand, my voice cracked and raw. I realise then his skin is a strange colour. They've put something on it that's shiny… they've applied a little make-up.

In a rush, I remember Cole's smooth, tanned skin in life. He never looked pasty because he spent a lot of time outside and he always smelt good. He did a good job of pretending he loved us. His tender touch that always seemed so loving as we talked into the night when the kids were in bed, making plans for our future. The wonderful family holiday to Disney World he'd been about to book and that we were going to surprise the kids with at breakfast next week, on the morning they went back to school after half-term.

How could I have been so wrong about the state of my marriage? How could I have failed to spot the clues that my husband had another family, another life? Our rock had been betraying and lying to us all on a daily basis for well over a year.

More than anything I want to discount everything Sara Nordstrom said about their relationship but she has a son and I can see he's Cole's child even without a DNA test.

Cole's frozen face blurs beneath me as my eyes fill with tears and a whip of anger flares up into my chest.

'I can never forgive you for what you've done to us, for how you've left your children with nothing!' I spit out the words, the effort nearly choking me. I can't stop the sobs and I just let them come, racking my whole body. After a minute, the fury drains from me as fast as it came, and I feel empty and spent.

I stand a little taller and take a breath before speaking.

'I loved you, Cole. I really loved you. My heart is breaking that you're gone.' I press a hand to my chest. It feels so tight and I can't seem to get enough air in. 'If you can hear me then please… I beg you… help us. Your children are struggling with their grief. Losing you is bad enough without losing their home, too. Send Miller and Sylvie strength.' I cry quietly, bringing my hands together in prayer and closing my eyes. 'Please, God, send me the strength to somehow get us through this mess. Forgive me now for what I might have to do to protect my children and keep our family safe.'

That last bit is really important because I'll do anything it takes to protect my children and keep our family together. The secret I'm holding proves that.

CHAPTER 18

SARA

Sara moves around the flat with more vigour than she's had since she first moved here when she'd been pregnant with Rory.

She systematically fills three large, open packing boxes with the belongings to be transported to the new house by the removals company on Friday morning. She's also got a couple of large black bin bags filling steadily with items she no longer wants or needs.

Rory is at a local private nursery she's used before. He's booked in for the day to give her the time and space to get things done. To move on. That's what it feels like… moving on to a new life with her son.

Sara hums to herself as she works. She's enjoying thinking over the hurdles she's traversed in order to be moving into the new house.

Sara knew Jennifer would go for it, she just knew, despite the other woman dithering and taking time to think about it. It's clear she is riddled with doubts and Sara always expected that. But the odds are stacked so overwhelmingly against Jennifer that some part of her clearly realised she'd be an absolute fool to turn down Sara's offer.

The house is fantastic. Far better than she'd anticipated. Sara had seen plans, of course, and some photographs of how Cole had envisaged the interior. She knew it was going to be big and grand but wow, actually spending some time in the space was another thing altogether.

Jennifer was subdued, very obviously grieving for her unfaithful husband, which Sara found interesting. She's missing Cole too, of course she is. Baby Rory will never know his father and will only have photographs to remember him by.

Sara had told Jennifer some things that weren't true: that Sara had been unaware he was juggling two relationships, that she was unaware they lived in the new house. What choice did she have? There was no way Jennifer would agree to her and Rory moving in if she knew the truth about the real reason she'd targeted Cole at the networking meeting.

Cole had told Sara so many lies, too, but what was the use in trying to understand why? She would never know. It was far better to accept it and move on. She hadn't invested the whole of herself and her life in a man as Jennifer had done. At least there was that.

Coming over to England as a child had been a difficult time. It had been just Sara and her father, no other family. The loss of her beloved mother had still felt so raw. 'Life goes on,' her father had told her. 'We start again here, in our new home. It's what your mother would have wanted.'

The hospital had put Fredrik in touch with a nannying agency and Sara's first nanny was recruited.

The independent school she attended was a nightmare. Nobody wanted to be near the quiet, new girl who barely spoke a word and, when she did, was so heavily accented they claimed not to be able to understand a word. It made Sara even more withdrawn but slowly, she realised her English was in fact good and it was just their way of excluding and undermining her.

At dinner, the only part of the day she spent any time with her father, he would talk about his new colleagues, about how welcoming they'd been and how the hospital was a pleasant place to work.

She'd had everything she wanted, materially, growing up. But Fredrik Nordstrom had lived only for work. When he felt happy, he worked. When he was sad, he worked. A talented and respected surgeon, he had been in great demand in and out of the operating theatre. This meant that young Sara had to be left with nannies when he travelled around. Nannies who often did not warm to Sara's insolence and what were considered unreasonable demands and so tended not to stay in the post very long.

Sara felt sure, looking back, she must have been a nightmare, but she'd just wanted to be loved.

Sara could not recall him asking even once if she liked her new school, had made any friends, or got on well with the new nanny. Fredrik tended to prefer the approach of, 'You seem to be getting on well, too. We're really very fortunate to have settled so quickly.'

But Sara did not feel settled then and she did not feel settled now.

When her mother had still been alive, contentment had been found in the cold winters with roaring fires, blankets and dogs, snuggled together on the bed. She cherished the image of her beautiful, gentle mother carrying in two mugs of hot chocolate and sitting down to chat for a while.

In England, that life was no more.

To survive, Sara convinced herself she needed no one. She would rely, she decided, only upon herself and, for inspiration, she turned to the Nordic winters she missed so much.

She assumed none of the warmth and bustle of Stockholm's wonderful Christmas markets with their merriment and spiced glögg. Instead, Sara moulded her public persona on the frozen lakes her mother would take her to wild-skate on and the short, dark days of winter.

Her solitary nature and inclination to fantasise was noticed by the nanny and that was the start of a string of child psychologists, each one with a different opinion and treatment plan.

As she grew older and became more beautiful, Sara focused on making the most of her looks. She was no longer ignored by men and she thrived on the attention. The physical closeness the one-night stands provided helped somewhat but Sara found she could not sustain the intimacy. The protective cold front was so ingrained now, it had become who she really was.

Sara had been surprised how homely the Fincham house had felt to her, an outsider. It had that comfortable, relaxed vibe about it that reminded her of the paper mill couple she visited as a child. Sara wants that same warm environment for Rory. The strength of the love she feels for her son had taken her completely by surprise. She wants, more than anything else, for him to grow up around love and laughter. She yearns for family Christmases and long summer days playing with other kids on the beach for her son.

Everything she never had as a child. Everything she does not know how to create alone.

Jennifer loves her children too, Sara understands that. In agreeing their informal nesting arrangement, she was keen the children should not discover Sara and Rory's real identity. She'd asked Sara not to mention Rory was their half-brother and she had agreed while wondering at the naivety of Jennifer in not realising that Miller already knows far more than she does.

It's been hard work, getting so many arrangements sorted out the past few days but now the time has almost arrived for her plans to finally come to fruition.

Moving on was something she'd had to do for the whole of her life. But this time… this time she is hoping she will finally be able to put down some roots.

CHAPTER 19

NOTTINGHAMSHIRE POLICE

'Ahh, Helena, always a pleasure to see you.' Rolly McAfee, the pathologist, is a wiry little man who, according to Brewster, is known unofficially among some officers as Roland Rat. This is on account of the continual rodent-like quick movements of the pathologist and the off-putting tic he has of twitching his nose when discussing medical details.

McAfee puts down his sandwich, the strong smell of tuna mixing with formaldehyde as the detectives move closer.

'Sorry to interrupt your lunch, Rolly,' Helena says, glancing at Brewster, who has turned a whiter shade of pale as he always tends to in the depths of the morgue. Their sporadic visits here are among the only times Helena has witnessed her colleague going more than an hour without a snack.

'DS Brewster.' McAfee nods curtly, acknowledging him rather less enthusiastically. Like many pathologists who have been forced to acclimatise to their working environment, he has no patience with 'yellow-bellied detectives' as Helena has often heard him referring to them.

She knows the exact moment that, as a younger DS, she'd gained a new-found respect with McAfee. She'd been attending a particularly challenging post-mortem of a tragic young man who'd stepped in front of a train. She'd been so invested in McAfee's summary of the case, she had completely ignored a senior detective vomiting in the stainless-steel sink and had continued to ask the pathologist searching questions about the injuries sustained.

McAfee brushes past Brewster now and washes his hands before theatrically pulling the sheet from Cole Fincham's body.

'So, here we have a thirty-nine-year-old male with good muscular and respiratory health. He got bashed about a bit when the vehicle rolled, as you might expect.' Helena notes the contusions, bruising and general injuries on Fincham's limbs and torso.

'We understand he suffered some serious internal injuries,' Helena adds.

'Correct. But none of that killed him.' He beckons the two detectives to the end of the trolley where the three of them stand together behind what is left of Cole Fincham's head, a mass of exposed bone and tissue. 'Bit messy this end, I'm afraid,' McAfee says in his signature conversational manner and Helena thinks she detects a slight wobble in Brewster's usually sturdy six-foot frame.

'The officer from the CIU said you'd found an existing head injury,' Helena remarks.

'Indeed. Whilst examining his skull I found a linear fracture of the base of the skull here.' Using a metal wand, McAfee twitches his nose and indicates the spot at the top of Fincham's head and the bottom of his skull. 'There were also numerous haemorrhages and a subdural haematoma, all causing bleeding in the space that surrounds the brain. But it's this linear fracture that happened ante-mortem.'

'You're saying a blunt force trauma occurred *before* the accident,' Brewster says faintly.

The pathologist nods. 'We're talking about a blunt force trauma so severe, it was akin to him being whacked on the back of the head with a baseball bat.'

'It beggars belief he was in a position to drive at all if that's what happened to him before he even got into the car.' Helena frowns.

'Victims of brain injury don't always behave as we might expect.' McAfee scuttles forward slightly, and peers down at Fincham's injuries. 'At the moment of an impact such as this one, the brain may crash back and forth inside the skull. We call this the primary injury. Immediately afterwards, it's usual for the person to experience some confusion or memory loss. They can suffer blurred vision and dizziness or even lose consciousness.'

'But you're saying that probably didn't happen in Fincham's case?' Brewster says.

'That's right. A much smaller percentage of people may appear perfectly fine following the primary injury before their condition rapidly declines. As the brain undergoes a delayed trauma, it swells and pushes against the skull. This is known as the secondary injury and this stage can be fatal. It's my opinion that our Mr Fincham here received his primary injury not long before he got into his car and the secondary injury occurred whilst he was driving.'

'And that's probably the reason he lost control of the vehicle, bearing in mind there were no other distractions,' Helena murmurs. 'Which means that the secondary injury killed him, not the actual accident.'

'That's precisely what I'm saying, DI Price,' McAfee says. 'As usual, you're spot on.'

Back in the car, Brewster winds down his window.

'Do you really have to do that?' Helena shivers, pulling her jacket closer and folding her arms. 'There's a force ten gale blowing out there.'

'Sorry, boss, but I've got to clear my head of that stench or I'll be stopping at the side of the road and throwing up.'

Amused, Helena looks at his peaky face. 'It really got to you in there... yet again.' She looks out of the window and points. 'Aren't you stopping at the golden arches today?'

She can't remember the last time they drove by this particular McDonald's branch – the closest one to the station – without Brewster diverting to the drive-through.

He winds up his window and shakes his head. 'Can't stomach it today. The smell alone is enough to make me want to—'

Helena holds up a hand. 'Drive on, Brewster. We'll just have to hope you toughen up in time, eh?'

'Yeah, well, Roland Rat doesn't help. He gives me the heebie-jeebies.' Brewster scowls. 'I heard something creepy about him in the canteen that I can't get out of my head.'

Helena turns in her seat, interested. 'Go on, then.'

Brewster wrinkles his nose. 'I heard he's a taxidermist in his spare time. You know, he stuffs dead animals.'

'Believe it or not, I do know the meaning of the word taxidermist.'

'Yes, but fancy doing it *for fun*. Stuffing dead animals in your spare time when you've spent all day taking dead humans to bits and then putting them back together. Somebody ought to give that guy a psychometric test.'

Helena grins. 'Well, taxidermy wasn't against the law the last time I looked. Horses for courses and all that. Anyway, regardless of his unsavoury hobby, McAfee knows his stuff. It didn't take him long to pick up on the blunt force trauma injury at the base of Cole Fincham's skull.'

Brewster stops at a red light and glances at Helena. 'Can you honestly believe that someone coshed him at the back of the head that hard, and then he just got in the car and drove away?'

'I trust McAfee's opinion and I think that's probably exactly what happened,' Helena remarks. 'And extrapolating on from that… if McAfee is right, it means that we've got a brand-new murder case on our hands.'

CHAPTER 20

JENNIFER

'Are you out of your crazy little mind?' Ellen slams a flat hand down on the worktop and glares at me. 'No wonder that boy of yours is so screwed up!'

'Hey!' I point a finger at her. 'Leave Miller out of this. His dad just died, remember? Have some respect.'

Ellen steps closer, her eyes blazing. 'How about you have some respect for *yourself*? There's a radical thought. I thought you'd have learned that lesson last time he left you, but—'

'Girls, girls! I'm begging you to calm down. *Please*.' Mum pinches the top of her nose and screws up her face. 'This is like having you both back at home when you were hormonal teenagers.'

'Before you got taken into hospital for alcohol poisoning, you mean?' Ellen turns on her. 'Before we were left to fend for ourselves and Jennifer ended up living rough?'

I feel like turning on my heel and just leaving them to their bickering.

'Mummy, I can't sleep.' Sylvie's hushed little voice cuts through the stormy air like butter, dissolving the tension. My daughter, with her corkscrew curls and Peppa Pig pyjamas, looks at us all in turn like we're naughty schoolchildren. She looks at me, her gran and her aunt, then her bottom lip wobbles. 'I wish Daddy was here.'

Mum rushes forward and scoops Sylvie up in her arms. 'Lucky that Gran knows just the cure when you can't sleep. Warm milk and an oaty biscuit.' A ghost of a smile crosses Sylvie's rosebud lips as Mum carries her over to the other side of the kitchen.

A hand claps down on my shoulder. I turn and Ellen rests her cheek against the top of my arm. 'I'm sorry, OK? I want to tear this woman, this Sara whoever-she-is, from limb to limb. You're trusting a woman who betrayed you in the worst possible way and I don't want you to hurt any more than you do now, Jen. That's all.'

'I know.' I place my own hand over hers and squeeze, thankful for her concern despite her acerbic tongue. 'But it's a hard one, Ellen, because if I turn down her offer, I literally have nothing. And, more importantly, the kids will have nothing. On top of losing their dad.'

'You have us, Jen! Me, Mum and Damian. We're family and families pull together at the worst times.'

I smile. In the face of my sister's kindness, I can hardly point out that Mum lives in her age-restricted apartment complex and Ellen in a tiny, rented house and always needs me to sub her to just get through the month. With some financial support from Sara – and I've decided I'm not going to feel guilty because God knows she owes me – I can start, very slowly, to rebuild a life for myself and my children. Nothing is guaranteed, but it's a chance I won't have if I turn Sara's offer down. I have to fight for what we built together and Cole just handed to her on a plate.

As Ellen says, Sara did betray me, but so did Cole and I can't forget that. It's easy to pile all the blame on the other woman, paint her as some kind of femme fatale who bewitched my innocent husband, but it wasn't like that. Cole knew what he was doing. Sara maintains she believed Cole to be divorced and estranged from his children. That might be the truth; perhaps

I'll never know. One certainty is that Cole himself knew. And he chose to betray all of us again and again and again.

I'm trying to put a brave face on it in front of my family, but I'm scared. I'm scared of making the wrong decision, of trusting someone else – someone who has already shown they are incredibly deceitful.

I'm scared of making a terrible situation even worse.

It's getting late. Mum is staying with us tonight and Ellen has gone home to Damian, who is still apparently upset over the spat with Miller in his bedroom.

Mum had told me what happened. 'Miller is hurting, love. Try not to be too hard on him. He's still very young to be coping with tragedy on this scale.'

I'd tried to speak to him about the incident, but as soon as I mentioned it, he said he felt sick and had to rush upstairs to the bathroom.

Earlier this year, Miller went through a bad time at school. He was being bullied by a group of older boys and we only found out when another parent asked us if we knew what was happening every day after school. They'd wait for him outside the gates and terrorise him all the way home and he'd never said a word.

We contacted the headteacher and the boys were promptly excluded. Weeks later, the phone rang one afternoon and it was the school again. Miller had been caught by a teacher taking lunch money from a younger boy. When they'd searched his bag, they'd found a lot of cash and it transpired Miller had been running a bit of an extortion racket with the younger kids.

Up until this time, Miller had been a considerate boy who had a good group of friends. He played in the school football team and enjoyed a full social calendar with his mates at weekends including cinema visits and bowling, among other activities. Then he'd seemed to change overnight. So we were shocked. Ashamed.

Cole had laid into Miller. For one awful moment I'd thought Cole was going to strike him, but thankfully he'd managed to cool himself down.

Slowly and with the help of the school counsellor and other support staff, we'd managed to get Miller on the right path again. We'd discovered he had no real friends left and had enormous trust issues in making new connections to his other classmates.

It's far from being a restful night. I'm carried back and forth on a tide of emotions. Grief, hurt but also hope.

Tomorrow morning, Sara will move in here and, although I haven't a clue how I'm going to deal with that, it's a step closer to carving out some time to set this awful financial mess straight.

CHAPTER 21

SARA

FIFTEEN MONTHS EARLIER

Once Cole got inside her penthouse apartment after leaving Cameron Beesley's private members' club, Sara noticed he seemed to sober up. The disorientation was gone as he walked into the large lounge that overlooked the river and the glittering lights of Trent Bridge.

'This is impressive,' he murmured. 'What did you say you did for a living again?'

'Right now, I'm in PR.' Sara walked up behind him and slid her hands around his broad chest. 'Before that I dabbled a bit in events management. I like to do a bit of this, a bit of that.' In one deft movement, she'd stepped to the side of him, brushing her body against his. 'Thing is, Cole, I tend to get bored quickly. Unless something is special enough to hold my attention, that is.'

He swallowed hard and she watched with amusement as his Adam's apple bobbed up and down. 'Is that right?' His voice sounded deep and croaky. Sexy.

Sara moved directly in front of him. She'd kicked off her high heels at the door and so now, she stood much shorter than Cole. Five-foot-four to his six-feet. She liked her men tall, always had, and she hoped he liked his women short and petite. By the hungry look in his eyes, she thought there was a very good chance he might. She'd been briefed well.

Cole looked down at her and she turned her face up to his. Sara watched his eyes flutter over her fine features, her piercing blue eyes, her naturally plump lips. She knew all her best features and she knew exactly how to accentuate them.

Cole had hazel eyes with tiny amber flecks and long dark lashes. Sara liked the way he wore his hair slightly long at the neck and kept it slicked back in place with just a touch of gel.

It had just turned 1 a.m. and a faint line of shadow traced his razor-sharp square jaw. It made him look dangerous and Sara liked that. She liked it very much.

His arms hung down by his sides, held tight against his body. 'I… I should really go,' he said softly. 'I have to—'

'Shh… just relax,' Sara whispered, dropping her hands down to hold his. She stood up on tiptoes and lifted her face up. He pressed closer and their lips brushed together. Again. And then… a full, passionate kiss. Cole groaned and then she knew he felt it too… an electric bolt of attraction that zinged through every inch of him. 'Come on.' She took him by the hand and led him across the lounge.

'Wait! Where are we… what are you—?'

'I just want to show you the rest of the apartment. Don't be nervous.' She giggled, pulling him through to the bedroom. 'See – it's the same view in here, too!'

'Wow.' He gave a long, low whistle as he scanned the panoramic glass and the shadowy movement of the river beyond. Sara flicked a button on the wall and the room filled with mellow chillout sounds.

Behind him, Sara stepped out of her shift dress, revealing the tiny lace Victoria's Secret lingerie set she'd picked out of her collection for the evening. She knew she looked amazing with her lightly tanned slim and taut body and natural, perky breasts. 'You can turn around if you want to see the best view of all,' she said softly.

'Oh my…' Cole stepped forward and she tangled her fingers in his hair as they kissed. She fumbled with the buttons on his shirt and felt just the slightest hesitation before he all but ripped his shirt away and got fully undressed.

She unclipped her bra strap and felt Cole harden against her. She pulled him over to the super king bed, closing her eyes as she felt the weight of him move on top of her.

'Wait…' Cole mumbled. 'I haven't got a—'

'Shh,' she purred. 'I'm on the pill.'

His eyes were slightly unfocused and his movements a little clumsy. He lay back, a self-satisfied look on his face. He'd already lost interest in taking care of the detail. She shivered with satisfaction. At one point, she'd thought he might resist her advances, but her worries had been groundless.

And now she felt a new confidence. She had him where she wanted him.

CHAPTER 22

MILLER

He sits on a beanbag in the corner of the room, looking round at all the faces.

Gran is here and Aunt Ellen. Damian, too, although he still won't meet Miller's eyes… as if he even cares about that. Then there's Sylvie and his mum.

It's all a bit weird. But then a lot of stuff that's happening around here is weird.

Miller had been in his room watching Messi's goal highlights on YouTube when his mum tapped at his door. 'Five minutes, Miller, and I'm going to need you downstairs. No arguments.'

'Huh?' He'd scowled when she popped her head around the door. 'I've just started watching this, can't I—'

'Five minutes, downstairs please.' He'd seen the determined line of her mouth.

'Why? What's up?'

'I've called a family meeting.'

'A *what*?' They'd never had a family meeting before.

'I need to speak to everyone together about something that's going to happen. Something important.' She'd looked around his bedroom, at the socks and undies discarded on the floor. She'd frowned at the crumbed toast plate he'd left up here from this morning.

But she hadn't said anything at all, which was another weird detail.

'What's this all about, Mum?'

'Five minutes and you'll know everything,' she'd said and then given him a small, sad smile before she'd turned and left the room.

When Miller got downstairs, he'd been surprised to see everyone gathered in the living room together.

Now, his mum clears her throat and looks directly at him.

'I've called everyone together because I have some news. I've invited an old friend of mine, Sara, to come and stay at the house with us for a while.'

'Stay *here*?' Miller's ears prick up at the name he'd seen on the secret texts. 'Why?'

'Because she's new to the area and I thought it would be nice for her to be with people rather than in a flat alone with a small baby.'

'She has a baby?' Sylvie's face lights up.

'Yes,' his mum says. 'A baby boy.'

'Can I help look after him?' Sylvie begins to bounce around the room. 'I'll give him his bottle and brush his hair. I'll even change his nappy! What's the baby's name?'

Miller is tingling everywhere. His arms, legs, the back of his neck and his ears. It's his mum's face, the way she's trying to be all bright when her eyes look so sad.

'His name is Rory, love,' his gran says.

It's her and his dad's baby son.

Time stands still. He stares at his unsmiling gran. He takes in Aunt Ellen's dark eyes. It's not just him; they don't want her here either.

'I'll say again, before it's too late. I think you're making a massive mistake bringing her into this house, Jennifer,' his aunt

Ellen says coldly. 'She's poisonous. Surely you can see it after... everything she's done.'

'What's she done?' Miller bites the inside of his cheek. Does his mum know? She can't do. She'd never bring her here, if so.

'Ellen. That talk isn't helpful in front of the kids,' his mum snaps.

'In front of the kids? They've got to *live* with her... she's a complete stranger to them! You could be putting them at risk, do you realise that? She's a liar and a—'

'Enough! What choice have I got?' his mum screeches and when she stops, the room falls deathly silent. Sylvie melts into his gran's arms and won't look at anyone. 'I'm sorry. Sorry, Sylvie, darling. I'm just...' His mum looks at Aunt Ellen. 'I'm just trying to make the best of a terrible situation, OK? Every decision is fraught with problems.'

'The only way to do that is to let it go. Get yourself and your kids out of here and leave her to it,' Ellen says quietly. 'This can only end in tears.'

'The woman... Sara. She's coming to live *here*?' Miller says, standing up now and taking a step towards his mum. 'She'll be here, in our house?'

'Yes,' his mum says, giving him a smile that is so shallow it barely creases the corners of her mouth.

'Who is she, Mum?' For a few moments, Miller thinks he's pushed his mum too far and she's going to break down in tears.

But she sits up a bit straighter and says, 'I told you, Miller. She's an old friend.'

Miller looks at her once more and then he walks out of the room, ignoring everyone when they try to call him back.

Lies, lies, lies... all they do is tell more and more lies.

Well, he can tell lies too. See how they like that.

CHAPTER 23

SARA

THURSDAY

She hasn't brought that much over with her in the car. She's hired a removals company to pack up her stuff in the apartment. Everything will be ferried over to the house tomorrow morning.

Sara has had removals on standby since the day after the accident because she'd already decided she was moving in here whether Jennifer 'decided to accept' or not. The fact she had appeared to give the other woman a choice had been carefully thought out to give them the best chance of getting on. The truth of the matter was, if Jennifer had refused to move out, Sara had a lawyer ready to start eviction proceedings with immediate effect.

She'd visited the house again and Jennifer had given her a tour around it.

As Jennifer had led her upstairs, Sara had glimpsed framed photographs of Cole with her and the children.

When they'd reached the landing, Jennifer had turned to her. 'There are five bedrooms. You can take one of the two spares.'

'I'd like to see them all if that's OK,' Sara had said. 'To get a proper overview of the house.'

Jennifer had hesitated before showing her the kids' rooms and the spare rooms. Then she'd said, 'And this is my room.'

Jennifer had opened the door to allow Sara a glimpse of the

master bedroom. She'd begun to close it when Sara had slipped past her and stepped into the room. She'd looked around, at the open wardrobe door that showcased Cole's shirts lined up, crisply laundered in the pastel colours he'd liked to wear. Her eye had been drawn to the elaborately framed wedding photograph above the bed showing Jennifer and Cole staring lovingly into each other's eyes. Sara had looked at the untouched pillows one side of the bed.

Her heart had squeezed in on itself. Her dream family hadn't materialised in the way she'd hoped but what was the use in living in the past? She had always survived the difficult times in her life by looking to the future.

She heard Jennifer's feet shifting behind her. 'If you let me know which of the spare rooms you'd like, I can—'

Sara had screwed up her nose. 'Thing is, the spare rooms are both really tiny,' she'd said. 'Too small for me and Rory. I'd like the one next to this one. Miller's room.'

'Oh no… Miller loves his room, Sara. You know what teenagers are like. Their bedrooms are their castles.' Jennifer had given a nervous laugh. 'I don't think it's a good idea to disrupt his safe place so soon after he's lost his dad.'

Sara had appraised her coolly. 'What do you suggest instead?'

Jennifer bit her lip. 'Well, Sylvie's princess bed is fixed to the wall so that's not practical. That only leaves the two spare rooms.'

Sara had looked at her and waited.

'What?' Jennifer had frowned.

'Well, there's your room, too,' Sara had said.

'What?'

'Rory and I need a decent space. Miller's room is a decent size and so is yours.'

Jennifer's face had reddened. 'Are you saying you want me to move out of our bedroom?'

'I'm not saying that,' Sara had calmly replied. 'I'm saying you have a choice. I'd be happy with Miller's room.'

Jennifer had dropped her head and closed her eyes briefly before turning to Sara.

'I don't want Miller to be upset, so I'll move out and into the spare room and you take the master.'

'That's fine,' Sara had said. 'If that's what you've decided.'

Now, she pulls out her favourite white silk pyjamas from The White Company and lays them on her pillow. Completely impractical with a young baby to care for, she knows, but it's important she shows Jennifer exactly what Cole saw in her. Sara had managed to be everything to him. His lover, mother and the person who'd saved his business. Jennifer, on the other hand, had allowed her standards to slip and Cole had looked elsewhere.

She walks around the room. Jennifer has removed most of her belongings and put fresh bedding on. Sara plucks various items still remaining from the dressing table and tosses them into the corner of the room. Half a dozen cheap and nasty ornaments, a mangy teddy bear, half-used candles and a couple of hand-stitched cushions that have seen better days.

Sara looks around and her mouth tightens when she sees the wall behind the headboard. She slips off her shoes and stands on the bed, lifting down the wedding portrait that Jennifer has so thoughtfully left there. She climbs back down again and unceremoniously dumps the photograph in the corner too, facing away from her.

Sara opens the jewellery box she's placed on the dressing table and slips on the delicate gold and diamond bracelet Cole had bought her for her birthday, and just then hears a noise outside the door. She freezes, her head jerking up when the tricky fastener clicks into place. The door is slightly ajar and wobbles just a fraction.

'Hello? Who's there?'

No answer. Sara moves quickly across the floor of the large bedroom and pulls the handle. A tiny figure jumps back.

'Hello, Sylvie.' She smiles. 'Have you come to say hi to us? That's nice.'

Sylvie presses her lips together and nods, shyly turning away slightly without moving her feet. 'Are you Sara, Mummy's friend who's come to stay with us?' she says, looking at the wall.

'That's right, I am.' Sara can see the similarity in her features to Rory. This child is Rory's sister and she smiles warmly at her.

'Why are you in Mummy and Daddy's bedroom?' Sylvie says, her mouth pinching together sadly.

'We've done a swap, sweetie. See, I've got Rory sleeping with me and this is the biggest bedroom, so your mummy said she'd move into one of the other bedrooms.'

Sylvie regards her solemnly and doesn't respond.

'Any time you want to come and see baby Rory, you just come and tap at the door, OK?'

Sylvie's eyes brighten a little. 'Can I see him now?'

'He's sleeping now,' Sara says and Sylvie's face drops. 'But if you're very quiet, you can take a quick peek at him. Would you like that?'

She nods quickly and comes inside the bedroom, looking around, her eyes settling on the pile of ornaments and personal items Sara has heaped in the corner. 'I bought Mummy that little Care Bear,' she says carefully. 'And they're the cushions Gran sewed.'

'Yes, they're all lovely.' Sara smiles. 'I've put them there with your mummy's other things so she can take them to her new bedroom. Rory is asleep in his cot. Go and have a little look, if you like.'

Sara is touched when Sylvie considerately tiptoes over and bends slightly forward to look at Rory through the bars of the cot. Her profile is so like Cole's and Rory's. Her heart pulls.

'Do you like babies, Sylvie?' Sara asks her softly, moving closer.

'Yes,' she says, a little bolder now. 'Mia in my class has a baby brother and her mummy brought him in one day.' She bends forward to see Rory better. 'He was cute but I like Rory better.'

Sara smiles. 'I think Rory will really like living here with you too, Sylvie. It will be like he has a big sister to play with!'

Sylvie beams. 'I'll play with him every single day!'

'If you like, you could help me look after Rory. Help feed and change him. Would you like that?'

'Yes, I can help you look after him right now!'

'OK. Well, we'll let him sleep now and later, you can help me organise his things.'

'I'll tell Mummy!' Sylvie can't keep the joy from her face. She runs to the door and claps, before darting off down the landing.

Jennifer's kids already seem enchanted by Rory. Miller had sat next to his bouncy chair for ages, just staring at him when she first arrived. It's been just her and Rory most of the time for so long and yet here, Rory has a ready-made family. Children who are actually related to him and share his bloodline. It's a gift she wants to give her son. It's the reason she's putting herself through hell.

A few minutes later, Sara finishes her unpacking and, after checking Rory is still sleeping soundly and ensuring the baby monitor is turned on, she sets off downstairs.

She can hear Jennifer talking on the phone. It's probably her mother, Kris, or Ellen, her spiteful-looking sister. When Sara had first arrived at the house, Ellen had made it abundantly clear to Sara and everyone else that she did not like her or approve of her moving in.

The woman is a bit of a doughy lump with dark, mean eyes. Sara knows her type. There were plenty like her at the private schools she'd attended: plain, talentless girls who hated anyone who reminded them there were important things in life their parents' money couldn't buy. Being attractive or smart, for instance.

Sara has always possessed an innate ability to get the measure of people quickly. To know instinctively what they want most from life. That can be very useful.

She already knows what Jennifer wants. She wants to get Sara out of the house, even though she's just arrived. Jennifer is tolerating the situation for the sake of herself and her children but the first chance she gets to double-cross her, she'll seize it with both hands. Sara can sense that Jennifer thinks that she can, given time, somehow get rid of Sara. Airbrush her and Rory from the history of her family and her doomed marriage.

But Jennifer doesn't yet realise just how bad things are going to get.

Sara steps out on to the landing to check nobody is around and then pulls her bedroom door closed behind her. She takes the small drawstring bag out of the suitcase under the bed and removes her medication. She's checked it's safe to use while breastfeeding but she is hoping she won't be taking it for much longer. She's started feeling so much better lately!

Let Jennifer do her worst. She smiles, reaching for her water and swallowing the first tablet. Sara has nothing to fear now she's in the house with them.

Nothing can stop her now.

CHAPTER 24

JENNIFER

On Thursday afternoon, we sit down with the children and Sara takes out two brown-paper-wrapped packages from her oversized handbag.

'One for you.' She hands the small one to Miller. 'And one for you!' The other, a larger box, she gives to Sylvie. She addresses the two of them. 'Just a little thank you gift from me for letting me stay in your lovely home.'

Sylvie tears the paper without further ado and beholds the contents with a gasp. 'Oh Mummy, look… it's proper make-up!'

I watch as Sylvie opens the shimmering pink and silver beauty case that's packed with Disney princess eye make-up palettes and lipsticks. It must have cost a pretty penny, the kind of thing I'd only buy Sylvie for a birthday or Christmas gift.

'That's so kind of you, Sara,' I say, aware she's waiting for my reaction. 'You really shouldn't have! What do you say, Sylvie?'

'Thank you, Sara, I love, love, love it!' She beams, regarding Sara with new, admiring eyes.

'You're welcome, lovely. Now it's your turn, Miller.' Sara looks at the smaller, neater package that Miller has placed, unopened, on the floor next to his feet. She grins. 'You can only keep it if you open it right now!'

'Miller?' I recognise the militant look on his face. He doesn't want the present and has no qualms showing his disapproval. I don't know why he's being like this with Sara; perhaps he senses something strange. After all, she's supposed to just be an old friend of mine. Granted, one that has never visited and whom I've never mentioned. 'Open Sara's gift, please.'

Miller picks up the package and rips off the paper without enthusiasm. His sullen expression is transformed when he sees the game cartridge in his hands.

'Isn't that the one you're saving up for, Miller?' I frown and peer closer at it. So far as I know, it's the latest big release and not even in the shops yet.

'Yes! And it was going to take me another month of saving my pocket money, but... how did you... I mean, it's not out until next week,' he exclaims.

Sara taps the side of her nose. 'You can get hold of anything when you're in the know.' I look at her questioningly. 'I have a contact. Someone who's high up in the gaming industry. He owed me a favour.'

Miller tears his eyes away from studying the graphics on the plastic case. 'Thanks. I... I love it.'

I look at the scene before me. My two children more upbeat than I've seen them in the days since their father's death and Sara sitting there watching their delight. Far from trying to put on an act to cover up the grief and upset she claims to feel that the man she loved is dead, she looks more like the cat that got the cream.

CHAPTER 25

NOTTINGHAMSHIRE POLICE

FRIDAY

Brewster heads towards Helena's desk, a baffled look on his face.

'I've just spoken to Jennifer Fincham, boss. I explained we need to speak to her regarding her husband's accident. She said it's fine for us to go over there this morning but… well, frankly, it sounds a bit complicated.'

Helena puts down her pen and gives him her full attention. 'I'm all ears.'

'Turns out Cole Fincham only had a secret life with a young woman called Sara Nordstrom and she has a six-month-old baby by him.'

'What? And his wife knew all about it?'

'She didn't know about it until Nordstrom called at the house the day after he died to tell Jennifer about her existence and now—' Brewster shakes his head as if he's trying to make sense of it '—she – Sara – and the baby have just moved into the Fincham family home.'

Helena lapses into a few seconds of stunned silence before gathering herself. 'You're telling me that less than a week after Cole Fincham died, his girlfriend and her baby son have moved in with his wife and two children?'

'Yep, that's about the size of it. Mrs Fincham said she'll explain more when we get there but, apparently, she didn't have much choice in the matter. Not sure what that means but unsurprisingly, she sounded a bit frazzled.' Brewster runs his fingers through his springy red hair. 'I reckon we might do well to speak to both women separately. I don't fancy getting in the middle of a spat.'

'That sounds like a very good idea, Brewster. I imagine they'll be guarded in what they say anyway, in the company of each other. Sounds like they're basically complete strangers.'

'I said we'd be there early afternoon. They've got removals there this morning, bringing over Cole Fincham's other woman's furniture,' Brewster says, bewildered.

'Hmm, well, far be it from me to speculate, but it sounds like we've got our first two ready-made suspects to make a start on. Fincham's head injury might not be quite as mysterious as we first thought.'

*

When they arrive at the house, Helena makes their introductions and Jennifer Fincham leads them through into an enormous, light-filled kitchen. She is a short, chunky woman in her mid-thirties with an attractive freckled face. Helena can see the toll recent events have taken by the weariness in her eyes, but she greets them in a friendly, open manner.

When they've walked a few paces inside the room, Helena sees another, younger woman, sitting quietly on a green sofa near the big windows. She is slim and stunningly attractive with high cheekbones and piercing blue eyes. Her short hair looks expensively highlighted with at least four varying shades of blonde and Helena instantly recognises the distinctive green and red Gucci stripe on her fine wool sweater.

'This is Sara Nordstrom,' Jennifer says stiffly. 'And Sara, this is DI Price and DS Brewster from Nottinghamshire Police.'

'Hi, welcome.' Sara stands up and walks over to the kitchen counter, standing there proprietorially. 'Can I get you both a tea, coffee… or perhaps a glass of water?'

Helena notices that Jennifer looks taken aback and there's no wonder. Sara is clearly the newcomer here and yet she's assuming the lead role.

'Water is fine, thanks,' Helena says.

'For me, too,' Brewster adds and starts as an ear-piercing squeal comes from another room.

'Just so you know, my mum is looking after three kids in the other room while we have our chat, so please ignore any noise.' Jennifer gives a weak smile.

'Please, take a seat.' Sara indicates the cluster of comfy sofas by the windows. Jennifer follows meekly. When they're all sitting comfortably and Sara brings over the drinks, Brewster clears his throat.

'When we spoke earlier, Mrs Fincham, you explained that Miss Nordstrom is living here now. I assume you're happy for us to speak freely in front of her?'

She nods. 'Call me Jennifer, and yes, as I explained, I've recently discovered Sara was in a relationship with Cole too. We've decided to try and move on from that situation and put our children first.'

Helena notices Jennifer's flushed cheeks and fidgeting fingers, indicating the unusual arrangements have perhaps not been as easy to accept as it might first appear.

'Cole was the father of my six-month-old son,' Sara says. 'You probably ought to know that I'm the legal owner of this house, too. So please do feel free to involve me in your conversation.'

For a young woman, Helena considers her to be remarkably confident and self-possessed.

Helena says, 'Thank you both for explaining your arrangements. We have some news about findings after the accident, which my colleague will explain in a moment. Then we'd like to speak to you both individually if that's OK.'

'Why not together?' Sara says immediately.

'It's just to simplify matters. Your individual circumstances before Mr Fincham's death were probably quite different, so it will help to just separate that out so we can get a clear and accurate picture of his whereabouts and routine.'

Sara doesn't respond but Jennifer says, 'I suppose that makes sense.'

'So, we have some news.' Brewster laces his fingers together and looks down at his hands. 'I'm very sorry to tell you both today that there has been a significant development. During the post-mortem examination, Mr Fincham was found to have suffered a blunt force trauma injury to his skull. We believe this was inflicted before the accident where his vehicle left the A453 and rolled down the embankment.'

'Could there have been someone else in the car?' Jennifer asks faintly. 'Someone who attacked him?'

'There was no evidence of any passengers in the vehicle. It's far more likely Mr Fincham was attacked *before* he got into his car.'

The two women look at each other. 'Someone hit him?' Jennifer says, a look of abject dread spreading across her face.

'It was a very serious injury,' Helena confirms. 'The pathologist compared the force as similar to being hit with a baseball bat.'

'Oh God!' Jennifer Fincham's hand clasps her chest.

'But how could he drive if he'd been hit so hard?' Sara says calmly.

'Not everyone loses consciousness. Sometimes people can act normally for a short time before the brain starts to swell,' Helena explains. 'It's only later that the secondary injury comes into play and that can be fatal.'

'There was no obvious reason for the vehicle to leave the road at the scene of the accident,' Brewster adds. 'And the injuries Cole sustained during the accident did not kill him. The ante-mortem injury – inflicted before his death – not only incited the road traffic accident, it was also the probable cause of his death.'

'Essentially, someone hit Cole so hard it killed him,' Jennifer repeats, slightly dazed. Helena notes her pale face and slightly shaking hands.

'I'm afraid it's looking that way, Mrs Fincham, yes,' Brewster replies grimly.

CHAPTER 26

Jennifer agrees to speak with the detectives first and leads them back into the hall and off to a room on the left. There seems to be no shortage of spare rooms in this place, Helena thinks to herself, as the door closes behind them. She notices that once Jennifer had moved away from Sara, she suddenly appeared very low, as though she didn't have to put on an act any more.

This room is smaller and appears to have little function other than to house a quirky small table, six chairs and a sideboard.

'Cole enjoyed playing cards and he planned to have friends over for games in here.' Jennifer lifts a table leaf to stroke the green felt beneath it. 'But he never got around to doing it,' she adds sadly.

'Jennifer, we're so sorry for your loss,' Helena begins. 'I would imagine that Sara's visit the day after your husband died added a tremendous burden on top of all the existing shock and grief.'

She nods and looks down at her fingers twisting a tissue. 'I can't describe the shock. I mean, I suppose everyone wants to think well of their husband, believe he is faithful, but I honestly would have bet my life Cole would never do this to us. But when I realised he'd sold me down the river financially as well, it was a thousand times worse than him having a secret life and a baby son. I honestly thought my heart might just stop, there and then.'

Helena glances at Brewster. She isn't aware of anything financial and, by the look on her colleague's face, neither is he.

'Could you explain a bit more about the financial stuff, Jennifer?' Brewster says gently. 'Sara mentioned she owns this house and… I don't mean to pry but it's vital we have a full picture of your husband's life and that includes every aspect of it.'

Jennifer sits quietly for a moment, seeming to gather strength before she begins to talk.

'When Sara told me she was in a relationship with Cole the day after he died, I asked her to leave. She refused and said that, if she wanted, she could insist the children and I left the property. That's how I found out. When she told me she owns this house, our cars… in fact, that she owns every asset I have because she was Cole's sole investor. She'd basically acted like his personal bank and he'd obviously been so keen to get his hands on the money, he'd agreed to punishing legal agreements. Probably thinking he'd eventually make enough money to get out of them.'

'Sara was funding your business?' Helena says.

Jennifer nods. 'Cole's accountant came over here on Sunday and explained everything to me. About a year ago, Sara bailed Cole out with a massive loan to save him from going bankrupt. I didn't know anything about it and yet the accountant showed me I'd signed all the papers.' She covers her reddening face with her hands. 'I've been such a fool. I'm so embarrassed, but it's the truth of the matter and now I have to face it. In legal terms, I knew all about their deal.'

'We really appreciate your honesty, Jennifer,' Helena says. 'This can't be easy, I know, but it's essential you tell us anything that could be relevant to the case.'

Jennifer continues. 'The accountant tells me the loan agreements we signed appear to be watertight. Anyway, Sara basically gave me a choice. We all live together here, in this house, so her son can be raised in a family environment with his half-siblings, or me and the kids are out on the street.'

To Helena, it sounds like Jennifer had been given an impossible choice. 'That must have been unbelievably difficult for you.'

Jennifer pulls out a tissue and dabs the damp corners of her eyes. 'I'm still not sure if I've made the right choice. Ellen, my sister, is furious with me. She thinks I'm behaving like a doormat but she doesn't realise how dire my financial situation is as it stands. I literally have nothing. No money and no resources to start again with. When I was a teenager, I lived on the streets for a while and I promised myself that my own children would never know what it feels like to be homeless. I will never allow that to happen to them, no matter what I have to do.'

'How much of all this are your children aware of?' Brewster probes gently. 'I know your daughter is still very young.'

'They both know their dad died in the accident, but neither of them knows that baby Rory is their half-brother. Sara and I agreed it was best not to say anything for a while, until we know if this arrangement is going to work. As far as the kids and anyone else is concerned, we're saying she's my friend from long ago who has come to stay with us. Sara has agreed to play along with that story for now.'

'Your mum and sister are aware of the truth, I presume?' Helena asks.

'Oh yes, we've had a family meeting.' Jennifer rolls her eyes. 'Hence their refusal to accept what I'm doing.' Her voice drops lower and she glances at the door. 'I just need some time to get my life back on track. Think about how I'm going to support myself and my children.'

Helena can see the other woman is under a tremendous amount of pressure. Plainly, she hadn't many choices.

'Thing is, I've been really worried about Miller, on top of everything else. He had some trouble at school back in the spring term and he's only just settled down again.' The tissue in her fingers now lies in shredded pieces on the table. 'The school counsellor said stability was of the utmost importance to him and we should do everything we can to keep things on an even keel. I honestly don't think he'd cope losing his dad *and* his home.'

'I'm sorry to ask, but please understand there are simply boxes that must be ticked in a serious investigation such as this,' Brewster says, his pen hovering over a notebook. 'Can you tell us where you were at the time of your husband's accident?'

'I was here, at the house,' Jennifer says without hesitation. 'We had a marquee company here the whole day setting up for our annual Halloween party. It was an elaborate affair this year. It was supposed to be a celebration of our new home and a chance for Cole to entertain some important business clients for a key contract he was keen to secure.'

'You didn't leave the house at all?' Brewster confirms.

'No. Apart from… I popped out late morning to pick up the fancy-dress outfits after the dressmaker's van broke down, but that was it.'

'So the last time you saw your husband on the day of his death was…'

'I think it was about eleven. He'd been "working away".' Scornfully, Jennifer hooks her index fingers in the air around the phrase. 'He told me he'd been travelling around the country estimating for jobs, so he'd stayed out a couple of nights, coming back each morning. He came home about nine-thirty Saturday morning and then around an hour or so later he left the house without telling anyone.'

'So he left the house before you went to collect the outfits and you've no idea where he might have gone?' Brewster says. 'You didn't see him again?'

'No. I mean, it wasn't unheard of for him to go out at short notice, usually to iron out some work issue.' Her lips give a little ironic twist. 'But he'd always tell me usually before leaving. Luckily Miller heard him go.'

'You must have felt concerned as time went on and he hadn't returned.'

'Yes. I kept ringing and texting him, but his phone was off. I thought he must be meeting with a client, or something like that, but I was worried he wouldn't have enough time to prepare for the party starting at seven.'

'Did you have the slightest inkling Cole was having an affair?' Helena asks her. 'Even just a feeling something wasn't quite right?'

'No, nothing. But I'll be straight with you, it's not the first time he'd played away.' Helena resists glancing at Brewster, but this revelation is unexpected. 'He moved out about six years ago now to be with someone he met at work.'

'An employee?' Helena ventures gently.

Jennifer nods. 'Her name was Rhea Brace. She was young, pretty, early twenties. It fizzled out within a few months. Cole really came to his senses then, realised he loved his family and, once we'd decided to reconcile and save our marriage, he was really committed.' She hesitates. 'At least he seemed to be. I truly thought we were very happy. You know that saying, "What does not kill me makes me stronger"? Well, that was us. I'd have trusted him with my life. Ask anyone who knew him, they'd all say Cole was a real family man.'

'But then he met Sara and she was unaware he was married with children?'

Jennifer wrinkles her nose. 'So she says. Sara insists Cole told her we were divorced and he didn't see the kids. She said they were planning to live together permanently within a few months. I refuse to believe that. He might have been unfaithful, fathered another child and made disastrous financial decisions, but he adored his kids. Call me naive, but despite everything, I honestly still believe he loved me, too.'

CHAPTER 27

Jennifer leaves the detectives and returns to the kitchen. It seems to Helena that Jennifer is telling herself a story that helps to ease the pain. Isn't that what everyone does, to cope with heartbreak? A minute or two later, Sara comes through.

'Please, Miss Nordstrom, take a seat,' Helena says, noting she does not offer the informal use of her first name.

Sara sits down and places her hands in her lap. She looks calm and relaxed but her thumbnail chafes repeatedly on her palm. If Helena were to place a bet right now, she'd probably hazard a pretty accurate guess that Sara Nordstrom is hiding something. Sara avoids meeting her eyes and Helena can feel a gaping distance between them that she doubts she'll be able to bridge during the time they have available.

'Can you tell us briefly when and how you met Cole Fincham?' Brewster begins.

'I met him last summer at a private networking event,' Sara says efficiently.

'And you embarked on an affair right away?'

'That's right.' Curt. Confident. Not in the least bit intimidated... bar the chafing nail.

'Were you aware Mr Fincham was married with two children, Miss Nordstrom?'

'Cole told me he was divorced and that his family lived abroad.'

'Did he tell you about his children, or where he lived when you weren't together?'

'He said his kids lived abroad now and that Jennifer wouldn't let him see them. He travelled all the time with work and stayed in hotels around the country, but he was renovating this house for us to live in together with Rory.'

'And did you personally have any input to the renovations at all?'

'He discussed general plans with me, but he'd told me progress was slow, that there had been various hold-ups with the building works.' She coughs. 'I've found it tough, having Rory to cope with all on my own with Cole being away so much. I think he probably didn't want to bother me with it all.'

'It must have been frustrating, the house taking so long… or so you thought. I expect you visited the renovation project several times to see the progress, make joint decisions about the design aspects and that sort of thing?'

Sara shifts in her seat. 'Well, no… Cole had very set ideas about what he wanted and… well, I think he wanted it to be a surprise for me.'

'I see,' Brewster says. 'That was quite accommodating of you. Did you think it was quite a strange approach, though? To keep you so completely in the dark?'

Sara sniffs. 'I knew Cole loved me and he'd promised we'd live together as soon as it was finished.'

'And yet here it is, fully complete and he'd still not managed to deliver on that promise,' Brewster says lightly.

'There was other stuff to sort out,' Sara says, a tad defensively, Helena feels. 'The business for one thing.'

'Exactly how much money did you loan Mr Fincham?'

Sara frowns. 'I'm not sure that's any of your business or relevant to what's happened.'

Brewster shrugs. 'It's relevant to the background of the case and that's what we're trying to establish here. We'll be contacting

Mr Fincham's accountant, so if you prefer, I'm sure she will be able to furnish us with the required information in due course.'

'However, your cooperation would be appreciated,' Helena adds.

Sara runs her tongue under her top lip. 'I lent him two hundred grand to clear his business bank loans. There was enough left to give him a director's loan to tide him over until business picked up again.'

'Mrs Fincham has informed us that you also own this house.'

'That's correct. I funded all the renovation costs.'

Brewster gives a long, low whistle. 'That must stack up to quite a substantial figure. How old are you, Miss Nordstrom?'

'I'm twenty-eight.'

'You've amassed quite a fortune,' Brewster presses her. 'Are you in business yourself?'

'No, but my father left me a good inheritance including a substantial trust fund, if that's what you're getting at.'

'I have to ask myself why you'd want to squander that trust fund on a man who was clearly in financial straits. The risk of him going bankrupt must have been quite high.'

'I'm not an idiot.' Sara bristles. 'It wasn't just about the money. I loved him, I'd just fallen pregnant with his son. I wanted to show him I supported and believed in him. That I wasn't going anywhere.'

It's an interesting answer, but Brewster isn't having much luck piercing that steel shell.

'You seem like a very astute woman.' Helena takes up the questioning. 'I'm sure you thought long and hard before you decided to fund the consolidation of Mr Fincham's various business debts.'

'You're right, I did,' Sara says tightly. 'I'm no fool even though people have tended to underestimate me my whole life.'

'Well, the joke is clearly on them. It sounds as though you ensured everything was done legally and above-board.'

'Absolutely, and Cole was very happy with me doing that. It was one of my conditions in helping him out.' She looks at Helena. 'When I heard he'd died I was devastated, but I thanked my lucky stars I'd taken care of myself by doing things properly in terms of the finance.'

'Indeed,' Helena agrees. It occurs to her that Sara hasn't shown a glimmer of emotion about Cole Fincham's death since the first moment they met her. 'As I understand it, you would have been legally within your rights to ask Jennifer and her children to vacate the house. Instead, you decided to come to an arrangement with her. That seems a very generous offer under the circumstances.'

'There are benefits for me and my son, too. We have no family. I came to England aged eight, when my mother passed away. I lived with my father, a surgeon, but I was raised by nannies because he was so busy. I don't want that lonely life for myself again, nor for Rory.'

'I understand that would be a powerful motivation, but it has to be said, most people would rather be lonely for a while rather than live with their lover's wife and all the aggravation that might entail.'

Sara smiles. 'I'm not threatened by Jennifer, DI Price. I don't know why Cole lied but they clearly had no relationship to speak of, even though she's in denial about that.' Helena is struck by her evasiveness. Sara might make a good politician.

'Can I ask where you were at the time of Cole Fincham's accident, Miss Nordstrom?' Baxter says.

'I was at home, feeding my child and wondering when the situation I was in was going to end,' she says. 'I suppose I've got the answer to that now, but it wasn't the one I'd hoped for.'

. . .

Brewster raises an eyebrow when they get outside. 'Blimey. I've never seen an arrangement quite like that one. Do you think it'll work?'

'Who knows?' Helena purses her lips. 'Miss Nordstrom seems quite astute at setting up situations that are difficult for people to walk away from.'

'Like loaning Cole Fincham the money?'

Helena nods. 'Loaning him the money and tying him up in so many knots he hadn't a hope in hell of ever walking away from it.'

'Meaning he had to stay in the relationship whether he wanted to or not.'

'Exactly, Brewster. All speculation, of course, but in bankrolling him as she did, she definitely tipped the balance of power. I can see the logic behind that arrangement although I don't understand it but…' Helena hesitates. 'I still can't really see what Sara is getting out of moving in with Jennifer and her children.'

'Most people would run a mile from an arrangement like that,' Brewster agrees.

'They both seem to think they're putting the needs of the kids first but what if it screws them all up? It's a risky solution and it wouldn't be my choice, that I do know.' They reach the end of the short driveway and head over the road to the parked car. 'If there's one thing this job has taught me, it's that there's no "one size fits all" when it comes to the ways in which people live their lives.'

'You can say that again. It was a revelation that our Mr Fincham had previous extra-marital relations, too. A serial offender, it seems,' he murmurs, opening the car.

'Hmm, we'll need to speak to that woman, Rhea something-or-other.'

'Rhea Brace,' Brewster provides.

'Could be she never quite got over him and decided to clout him over the head after all this time. Unlikely, but we've seen stranger things happen.'

'Agreed. What did you think to the two women's reaction to the news about Fincham's cause of death?'

'Hard to tell,' Helena says, sliding into the passenger seat. 'Jennifer seemed upset but I thought Sara was probably hiding her shock. They're understandably quite guarded with each other. What about you?'

'Sara Nordstrom seems a bit of a cold fish to me,' Brewster says, checking the mirror and driving off down the leafy street. 'But the truth of the matter is that somebody gave Cole Fincham a killer whack over the head shortly before he died and both women had a strong motive even if it doesn't seem apparent at first glance. His wife might have discovered his affair before his death, for instance.'

Helena considers this. 'Or maybe Sara *did* know about his family all along, and he told her he'd decided not to leave his wife and kids despite her financial stranglehold on him. After all she'd done to bail him out, she could have snapped and attacked him. No evidence to support it whatsoever, but at this early stage it's important we keep in mind both women could have had their reasons.'

'I can't help but get the feeling there's something we're missing, boss. Some crucial piece of information.'

Helena looks out of the passenger window. 'You might be right, Brewster. If so, we'll do what we always do: keep plugging away until we find it.'

CHAPTER 28

SARA

FIFTEEN MONTHS EARLIER

After they'd made love, they lay together in Sara's bed, Cole spooning her, his muscular arm draped over her body. She stared out of the wall of glass at the dark sky and the lights of the city skyline beneath it.

His breathing slowed and became heavier. She waited and watched the glowing red digits on the bedside clock. When another ten minutes had elapsed, she gently slipped out from under his arm, replacing herself with a pillow to ensure he wouldn't stir.

He lay naked on top of the covers and she stood for a moment admiring his muscular, strong body. She padded around the side of the bed and picked up the trail of clothes he'd discarded only thirty minutes before.

Their passion had burned strong and bright, but thanks to the booze, it hadn't lasted long. Next time it would be less frantic, less alcohol-induced and altogether gentler. Still, she wouldn't change tonight for anything.

It had started out as a strictly planned arrangement and then quickly morphed into something very special. Sara had felt electrified by their instant deep, strong connection.

She had to have all of him.

. . .

When she opened her eyes the next morning at seven-thirty, Cole had already left the flat. Sara's chest burned with disappointment.

She looked in the bathroom, on the kitchen counter, in the hallway but there was no note. Nothing. After coffee, she showered and got dressed before driving across town. When she reached the offices of Cameron Beesley, she sat in the car and waited.

Right on cue, a five-year-old black Audi slowed and turned into the car park. It parked in a space a couple of rows in front of her. Cole Fincham got out of the passenger side, dressed in a black suit and white open-necked shirt. He looked handsome and fresh despite the late night they'd shared.

It was hard to think she'd been snuggled up in bed next to him only a few hours ago. Her skin prickled with pleasure at the thought of being with him again.

She opened the car door. 'Cole… hi!'

He turned, startled and then when he saw her, he faltered. 'Oh, Sara! Are you… OK?'

The driver of the vehicle, a man, slowed his walk and stopped. Cole waved to indicate he should carry on into the building without him.

'I was disappointed to wake up to find you gone this morning,' she said lightly when he walked over to her. 'I thought you'd at least stay for breakfast.'

'Sorry, I… I had to get back home.' Then, hastily, 'To prepare for today's meeting, you know?'

She nodded slowly, closing the car door behind her. 'You forgot to leave me your number.'

He bit his bottom lip. 'I… I didn't know if you'd want it and—'

'Oh, I definitely want it.' She stepped closer, and she saw him react at the physical spark that instantly re-ignited between them.

He glanced at his watch and then at the office building. 'Sara, I'm really sorry, but I have to—'

'I know. You have to get to your appointment with Beesley. I'm the one who got it for you, remember?'

He looked sheepish. 'I know. And I'm so grateful, really I am. It's just that... well, you should know that things are complicated for me, Sara. I mean, what we did. I shouldn't have... I'm actually—'

She pressed her business card into his palm. 'No need to explain now, Cole. No pressure.' His face relaxed a little. 'Call me later, yeah? We really need to see each other again, and soon. You know it makes sense.'

He looked down at her card and then nodded, slipping it into his pocket.

Later, he called her. And the following morning, too.

The next day Cole came back to Sara's apartment, and this time, he brought an overnight bag.

CHAPTER 29

SARA

FRIDAY

When the detectives have gone, Sara checks to see how Rory is. Kris is playing a colourful board game on the floor with Sylvie. The child seems subdued, which is unsurprising after losing her father only a week ago. Sara's heart pulls as she recognises the same strain of loneliness she felt as a child.

'He's fine, still sleeping,' Kris says, slightly offhandedly. Then, looking towards the baby, her voice softens a little. 'He's so well behaved.'

'Thanks for watching him while I was in with the detectives. I'll take him back upstairs with me now.'

Sara could swear that Kris is looking at her strangely. 'If you've got stuff to do, you can leave him down here,' she says slowly.

'I can look after Rory.' Sylvie looks up hopefully from her game. 'I know how to change his nappy.'

'Thank you, Sylvie.' Sara smiles. 'And… if you're sure, Kris, that will be great. Thank you.'

Kris shrugs as if it doesn't matter to her either way but she keeps her eyes on Sara, inclining her head slightly as if she's trying to get the measure of her. 'Seems a shame to disturb him for no reason.'

Sara thanks her, feeling scrutinised by the older woman. She knows Kris is suspicious of her, but it's also clear she's already becoming fond of Rory. Sara feels sure that if Jennifer wasn't around, she and Kris could come to an understanding for the sake of the children.

Then she has a wonderful idea and turns back to Kris.

'Say, it's Bonfire Night tonight... we could take the kids to a local display. Would you like that, Sylvie?'

Sylvie looks up at Sara and then glances at her granny. 'I don't think that's appropriate, do you?' Kris says witheringly. 'It's not a time for celebrating and socialising. At least not in this house.'

'Course, yes. I wasn't thinking,' Sara mumbles and turns, heading for the door. She's sure she can feel Kris's eyes burning into the back of her head.

Sara goes upstairs to continue with her unpacking. Jennifer was itching to discuss what Sara had said to the detectives, but she isn't in the mood for talking.

Sara had been worried, when she first started speaking to the police, that they knew something. At the same time, she knew that couldn't be the case because she'd been careful. Very careful. Turns out it was something else altogether; the news that Cole had a head injury inflicted before the accident was a shock. According to the pathologist, someone had practically caved his skull in. Sara imagined that proving it beyond doubt was another matter altogether.

She keeps thinking about her tablets. She hasn't taken any today at all... there's been too much happening. She will, though; she'll take the half-dose she's promised herself she'll continue with for now. Until everything is sorted out, at least. Until she gets what she wants, she needs to keep her wits about her.

But upstairs on the landing, Sara stops walking and opens the door to her right. Previously a spare room, but now Jennifer's new bedroom.

The room is quite a bit smaller than the master bedroom Sara and Rory have now commandeered. There is a hanging rail in there full of clothes as well as a small built-in wardrobe. The curtains are pulled to, so the room is dim. The bed is unmade and there are clothes and wet towels strewn over the floor.

Sara glances behind her, but all is quiet. She steps inside the bedroom and walks quickly over to the chest of drawers near the window. She opens the curtains to let in a little more light and then pulls open the top row of three small, deep drawers and pokes through the tangle of underwear in each one. What she is looking for isn't there. She looks in the bigger drawers full of T-shirts and sweaters but finds nothing.

It's still quiet outside so she moves to the bedside drawers and checks in there. She sighs with frustration. It's not there.

She closes the curtains again and leaves the room. Two doors down she hears low music that sounds as if it's coming from a television. She taps on the door and the music stops. Silence.

Sara pushes down the handle and opens the door before closing it again behind her. Miller is lying on his bed in the dim space. The floor is covered in crap and she wonders why Jennifer lets him get away with it. The television is on but muted and he's scrolling through an iPad.

'Hello, Miller,' she says.

He sits up and sets the iPad aside, his eyes widening and darting around but not settling on her. 'What do you want?'

'I'm looking for something,' she says. 'And I thought you might be the person to help me find it.'

'Huh? What is it?'

'Your dad's silver iPhone. I don't suppose you've seen it, have you?'

Miller bends his knees and wraps his arms around them. 'I don't know what you're talking about.'

'Oh, I think you do.'

'I... I haven't got it. Dad would've had it with him when he had the accident.' Sara watches as two spots of deep pink bloom on his pale cheeks. 'Maybe it fell out of the car when it rolled. Or Dad might've opened the door and it fell out, or—'

'And yet his other phone was recovered, wasn't it? His normal phone. The police said they'd combed the scene of the accident. Every single inch of it. So, what I'm thinking is, perhaps your dad didn't have his silver phone on him for some reason. Maybe he'd left it behind, here at the house.'

'I don't think he did,' Miller said quickly. 'I haven't seen it. I'd say if I had.'

She walks across the room and sits on the end of the bed. Miller inches back against the headboard, pulling his feet closer in as if he's trying to make himself smaller.

'There's some extremely private stuff on that phone, Miller. Stuff I wouldn't want your mum to see because it might upset her. Do you understand what I'm saying?'

Miller nods vigorously. 'I know. I mean, I know she'd be upset if she saw... the private stuff.'

'Your mum would also be very upset if she knew you've been lying all this time, Miller. I think it would break her heart after everything that's just happened. I really do.'

'I... I...' He gulps for air like a stranded fish.

Sara takes time to inspect her short, shell-pink nails before looking up.

'You know, if you could find that silver iPhone I'd really owe you.' She stands up, brushes down her jeans. 'I'd make sure your mum never finds out the truth about those nasty text messages you sent me or... the other stuff you haven't shared with her.'

'I – I didn't—'

'Save it, Miller. We both know the truth about what you saw.' He looks at her, his eyes wide and pleading. 'Hopefully she won't need to find out. Get me the phone and we might be able to forget about it, OK?'

He thinks for a moment and then slides off the bed. She watches as he opens his wardrobe and pushes aside a few items before retrieving the phone and handing it over without once looking at her.

'There. That wasn't too hard, was it?'

He drops his head and stays silent. Sara turns and leaves the room. Just as Cole had complained to her on more than one occasion: his mother has treated the boy more like an adult. It's a trait that's doing him no favours, nor anyone around him because everyone knows that children need boundaries.

If anything were to happen to Jennifer, Sara would feel responsible for Sylvie and Miller. They would live here – all four of them together – in this house. Things would be very different then. Miller would be forced to toe the line.

If something were to happen to his mother.

CHAPTER 30

JENNIFER

TUESDAY

For the next few days after Sara moves in, I purposely keep busy. Bonfire Night celebrations pass at the weekend without acknowledgement in our house. The kids are certainly not bothered and, apart from lying in bed several nights with the sound of bangers exploding until nearly midnight, terrifying local dogs and keeping folks awake, I wouldn't have remembered the celebration at all.

Mum is preparing stew for the slow cooker and giving me earache about Sara. 'I'm telling you, Jennifer, the day the detectives came over, she was spaced out when she came into the living room to check on Rory.'

'To be fair, Mum, I felt a bit spaced out myself after their questions and learning that Cole had an existing head injury.' It isn't that I want to defend Sara, far from it. But Mum has a lively imagination, and I could do without her making a bad situation worse by seeing stuff that wasn't there.

But Mum persists. 'I'm not talking about that kind of reaction. She seemed… well, just odd. I don't know, it's hard to put my finger on it.'

I already feel so uncomfortable with the new living arrangements, I don't need anything to worry about. But I can't help wondering if Sara is distracted because the police have discovered Cole had a head injury prior to his accident. Could she have something to hide?

Mum glances at the clock. 'I've got to go over to Ellen's later for when Damian gets home from school.'

'Where's Ellen?' I lean across and pinch a slice of carrot.

'She's had to pop out.'

'Where to?'

Mum keeps chopping. 'To see someone.' She pauses briefly and frowns. 'At the hospital, I think. To do with a job.'

I raise an eyebrow, still chewing. 'Thought she was going for something different next,' I say, remembering her dissatisfaction with working as a temporary auxiliary nurse after she was let go in summer.

'Well, she changes her mind like the wind. You know that.' Mum sighs and picks up an onion.

I've noticed Ellen stays as far away from the house as possible since Sara moved in, but that's up to her. She should count her lucky stars: at least she hasn't got to live with Sara like I have.

Miller and Sylvie went back to school yesterday. Their respective schools have been brilliant, arranging additional support in the form of the shared school counsellor and offering Miller some assistance in catching up on the school work he's missed.

Sylvie came home last night full of talking about her day, that the teacher had chosen her to collect in the artwork at the end of class – a big honour, apparently – and her little friends all sat with her at lunchtime and never left her side. But Miller refuses to engage with anyone. He went to school without a word yesterday morning and his form tutor rang at lunchtime to say Miller had decided, at the last minute, he didn't want to see the school counsellor that day, after all.

Since the news about his dad's death, he has barely emerged from his bedroom at home apart from when I insist he comes down for his meals. I know it's completely understandable on the one hand. He is crushed with grief and guilt. He and Cole had their problems – his father didn't always deal with Miller's moods in the best way – but his isolation worries me because it had already started before his dad died. I never managed to get to the bottom of why.

Miller does seem fascinated by baby Rory on the rare occasions he comes downstairs. A part of me wonders if he sees any of his dad's features in Rory but I doubt that. I think babies tend to all look the same to teenage boys. I'm desperately hoping this whole situation will be short-lived.

I called Corinne this morning to keep her up to date with developments, the fact that Sara had moved in. 'Any progress with the loan agreements?' I asked.

Corinne made a noise of frustration. 'Not yet, but I'm working through, interrogating every word they've written in those contracts. As you know, the documents were prepared by Sara's own legal team, so there's always that possibility I missed something the first time around. If that's the case, I'll be the first to put my hand up.'

'Well, rest assured I'll be delighted if you find something did escape your eagle eye, Corinne. I'll be thanking, not criticising you.'

We agreed to touch base again in a few days' time when I pray she'll have good news for me.

Despite my best intentions to talk to Miller before school this morning, he skipped breakfast and slipped out of the house, calling a hasty goodbye as he slammed the front door. I took Sylvie to school and, although she was quiet on the way in, she perked up a bit when a couple of her friends ran over as we arrived.

The small gathering of mums that I'd usually stand with and pass the time of day with for a few minutes are standing there, in their usual spot. Sam, the mum of one of Sylvie's closest friends, calls me over. I feel like running the other way, not yet ready to face a barrage of questions about exactly what had happened to Cole. I drag myself over there and feel surprised when they form a little supportive huddle around me. Instead of shying away from the attention, I find myself opening up a little, absorbing the condolences and affectionate touches to my arms and hands.

'Anything you need, you must let us know,' Sam says. 'We'd love Sylvie to come for a sleepover one night, when you feel she's ready, that is.'

'Thanks, Sam,' I say gratefully. 'She'd like that, I'm sure.'

The other women join in with sleepover offers. Then someone says, 'It can't be easy for the children at the moment. I don't know how you can do it, having that woman there, right under your nose.'

I freeze and there's a few moments of awkward silence as the other women cringe at her forthright manner.

I look up and meet the woman's eyes. She's the newest mum in our group; her child only started the school partway through the last term.

She immediately starts to backtrack. 'Sorry, I didn't mean that to sound like I'm blaming you for the situation. I mean, I don't know all the details, I just heard—'

'It's your own business, Jen,' Sam interjects, cutting the other woman off. 'Nobody here is judging you. Believe that.'

A murmur of agreement.

'Absolutely not. That's not what I meant,' the woman babbles on. 'Sorry.'

I nod, showing there are no hard feelings. I don't feel angry at her. I know if I was on the outside looking in, I'd be wondering what was happening, too. They aren't to know Sara owns the house and gave me a Hobson's choice.

'It's a very difficult situation,' I say. 'There are extenuating circumstances I can't speak about at the moment.'

'Of course not,' Sam says. 'It's nobody's business but yours, Jen. Just know I'm here any time you want to talk or fancy a coffee… anything at all. And we'll get that sleepover sorted for Sylvie; you only have to drop me a text.'

'Thanks, Sam. I appreciate it.' Hugs all round and then I am able to scurry off back to the house with my shame and sadness fully intact.

Sara had insisted on doing the food shopping this morning. We're running low on lots of basics and, although I'd offered to do an online shop, she said she wanted to get out of the house. I gave her a list of stuff for me and the kids that she agreed to buy alongside her and Rory's items.

'If I'm not back in a couple of hours, send a search party!' she'd joked when she saw the long list of items I'd requested. Then she'd popped Rory into his car seat and left for the supermarket. That was about ninety minutes ago, so I expect her back anytime soon.

I walk into the kitchen and open the fridge to get one of the creamy hazelnut yogurts I love. I frown, scanning the shelves. I know for a fact I had two left yesterday and the kids don't eat them. Sara must have had them, which is fine…

she wouldn't have realised they were my guilty treat and I've noticed she doesn't seem to have a problem asserting herself in the house. To be fair, we hadn't really got around to the finer details of joint occupation, like shelf allocation in the fridge. In the wake of all the upheaval and upset, stuff like that still seemed irrelevant.

It suddenly strikes me that the fridge looks emptier than it should be, even though supplies have got low. I bought Sylvie a pint of full-cream milk yesterday from the local shop and she's only used a bit of it… that's not here either. Nor are the Babybel snack cheeses or Miller's favourite chocolate mousse pots.

Curious, I open the larder cupboard. The shelf that's usually full of crisps and snacks is completely empty. In fact, it looks as though it's been physically cleaned; there's not a crumb to be found. The shelf below that – usually home of the bread and pasta and cakes – has been decimated too with just a pack of brown spaghetti and wholewheat penne left.

I walk over to the bin and look inside. It's half full with the missing items. I stand staring for a moment, nonplussed. The only person who could have done this is Sara.

I hear the front door open and I walk into the hallway.

'Any chance you could bring the shopping in, Jennifer?' Sara says. 'Rory's fallen asleep in his car seat so I'm going to bring him in and try to settle him in here.'

'No problem.' I walk past her to the driveway where her brand-new car stands with the boot already open. I'll bring the bags into the house and let her get Rory sorted out. Then I'll address the food situation.

There are so many bulging shopping bags, it takes me several trips to empty the car. I close the front door and go back into the kitchen to start unpacking. I glance into the bags, trying to find all the things I put on my list. Sara said she'd put my stuff through separately, so I'd know exactly how much I owe her. But none of these items look familiar.

'That's lucky,' she says, coming into the kitchen, smiling. 'Rory's stayed asleep so I can help get everything unpacked now and feed him when he wakes up.'

'I'm trying to find my shopping,' I say. 'Did you keep it separate?'

'Yes, I did. Let's see.' She peers into several bags. 'Yep, it's these four here.'

Two of the bags I've already inspected. I begin to take out the items. 'Low-sugar beans? Miller hates those and he won't eat them. I did put "*not* low sugar" as they tend to stack them together and it's easy to pick up the wrong ones. You must have missed it.' I pull out more things. 'Oh, I didn't ask for natural yogurt, I wanted fruit yogurts. I don't think this is my bag.'

'Yes, that is your stuff.' Sara stops pulling out her own shopping, lowers her chin and looks at me. 'Jennifer, do you realise how much salt and sugar they pack into stuff like baked beans? They do it with almost everything, in fact! Take the yogurt. The brand you asked for is one of the worst offenders. It's far healthier to add proper fruit to natural yogurt.' She goes back to unpacking her bag. 'There's this really great website I can show you that has printable—'

'You changed my shopping list?' My throat is burning. 'You've no idea the trouble this is going to cause. Miller's food preference list has literally under a dozen items on it, and Sylvie is the pickiest kid you've met when it comes to food. They simply won't eat this stuff!'

I up-end a bag on the worktop, revealing all manner of super-healthy alternatives my kids won't touch.

'Don't take this the wrong way, Jennifer, but if the food I found in the fridge is an example of what you've been feeding them, you really need to change your approach.' She is clearly affronted, and turns back to her own shopping.

I punch my hands on to my hips. 'I'm so glad you decided to bring the food in the fridge up,' I say. 'You had no right to throw it away! The food in the larder cupboard, too. What were you thinking?'

She continues to unpack as if I haven't spoken, a smug look on her face. I feel infuriated by her lack of concern at my annoyance. Finally, she answers. 'Did you know that right after you've eaten white pasta, bread or potatoes, they release a spike of sugar into your bloodstream? This triggers a cycle of food craving. In other words, you and your kids will just want more and more of this refined stuff.'

'That's not all we eat! I make sure the kids have lots of fruit and veg and we eat plenty of wholewheat stuff too. But that's by the by. It's not your decision what I keep in my cupboards. You can't just walk in here and take over, Sara.'

She sighs and shakes her head, as though I'm too ignorant to realise my mistakes. I feel like if she gets away with this, she'll move on to something else. Exercise, or turning us all into vegans whether we want to or not. She's already got the balance of power thanks to the unreasonable financing agreements. I have to nip this in the bud or my life will be hell.

I grab my jacket and car keys and turn to her. 'I'm going to the supermarket to get the things I need,' I say. 'I won't be long.'

'Huh?' Now I have her attention. She points to the four bags. 'What do you want me to do with all that?'

I know precisely where I'd like to tell her to deposit it, but in the interests of being the better person, I say calmly, 'That's entirely up to you. But whatever you decide to do, I'll need half the fridge free when I get back so do bear that in mind when you unpack it.'

I'd like to think I've just gained the upper hand, but the way I feel now, like a stranger in my own home, nothing could be further from the truth.

In the car, I breathe out and try to wind down. I'm not someone who likes confrontation, but the food issue seemed too important to let go. Maybe, underneath, it wasn't really about the food at all.

I start the engine and turn the radio on, hoping for distraction. But as I turn the corner at the bottom of the street, one question rattles around my head, refusing to be ignored.

What the hell have I done, letting her into our lives?

CHAPTER 31

By the time I get to the supermarket, my thoughts have calmed a little. Once I begin a therapeutic meander up and down the aisles, the piped muzak fills my head and the colourful displays lure my gaze. Finally, now I'm away from the house, I can breathe again.

When the kids were at school, I'd often come here to get the ingredients for a special meal if Cole was returning home after a 'work' trip away. I took pleasure in planning every stage of our evening including the music and the wine we'd drink. There were lots of occasions when I'd get a text or harried phone call from Cole to say he'd been delayed, or would have to stay over another night to deal with yet another work issue on site. I'd swallowed every one of his excuses without question.

Was I a fool for believing Sara when she said she didn't know about us, Cole's family? Or is she a victim too? A woman who loved him and believed the lies that slipped so easily from his tongue, like I did?

I pick up a bottle of wine as a peace offering, already feeling a bit contrite over the disagreement with Sara. What she'd done was infuriating, but I ought to pick my battles. My only hope of avoiding the decimation of our life is to buy myself some time. Still, I've realised it's in my nature to blame myself just as I'd blamed my own shortcomings when Mr and Mrs Phipps wouldn't take me in all those years ago.

When Cole left home six years ago to move in with Rhea, I went through a gamut of emotions. First there was fury but that gave way to denial, sadness, grief. Then I turned on myself. What could I have done differently? Had I ignored the signs Cole was getting restless? Inexplicably, it was only when he came back to us that the fury returned.

A new track starts on the supermarket's rolling playlist and it sounds reassuringly identical to the song before it. The trolley is filling slowly but surely with the items I wanted in the first place. I'm thirty-four years old and the mother of two kids I've managed to successfully raise despite feeding them ruddy baked beans with sugar in them! Sara shouldn't have done what she did with the food but, at the end of the day, now I've calmed down, I suppose I can admit it wasn't anything *that* terrible.

I look down at the bottle of wine again and almost put it back on the shelf. Sara probably won't drink it unless it's made from organic grapes, which, at this offer price, it most definitely won't be. Still, I leave the wine in the trolley. The way I'm feeling, if Sara doesn't want any, I'll drink it all myself.

I'm struggling, seeing Sara and the baby every day. It's the physical embodiment of Cole's treachery right here, under my nose, that's amplifying my grief and pain. I'm finding the best way to keep strong is to remind myself several times a day why I'm doing this. Not because I'm a pushover, but because I'm trying to hang on to what we have, to find a way to build a future for me and my children.

When I get back to the house, Sara opens the front door before I'm even out of the car. She walks over to me.

'I came to help you bring in the shopping,' she says sheepishly. 'And… to apologise. I was out of order throwing out your food and hijacking your shopping list. I thought I was helping but… I guess I'm too set in my own ways.'

'I'm sorry I just took off like that,' I offer.

She smiles, lays a hand briefly on my arm before walking to the boot. 'Let's get this stuff inside, eh? Then I'll make us a cup of coffee and you can have one of my organic, sugar-free cookies as a treat.'

'It's a deal.' I laugh, feeling my shoulders drop just a touch.

Maybe I can persuade her to have a glass of wine after all. You never know what she might let slip.

I suggest opening the wine later when the kids are all in bed. Sara accepts a glass and talks a bit, but seems guarded and doesn't really reveal much about herself.

When I ask her about her career, she skims over the last few years in scant details.

'I've worked mainly temporary jobs in PR,' she says vaguely. 'Organising networking meetings, that sort of thing.'

That's as close as she comes to talking about Cole. She seems determined not to share any real details in that regard. She's even reluctant to give precise details of her previous address, citing only the area, Lady Bay.

I do catch one piece of information she inadvertently gives up: the name of her landlord at the flat she and Cole lived at when he wasn't being husband and father to me and the kids. A Mr Friedmann, apparently.

I still feel a frisson of shock and denial when I think about how close Cole's treachery took place to our family home. When they'd been in bed together, making love and I'd been at home playing the dutiful wife, there had only been a couple of short miles between us.

CHAPTER 32

SATURDAY

At the weekend, Sara suggests we take Sylvie and Rory to the park.

While we're getting ready, it occurs to me how the strangeness of our living arrangements is already starting to feel like the norm. Not in a good way at all but in a new, awkward way where I'm forgetting how it felt to enjoy contentment and security in my own home.

A text comes through from Sam, suggesting we set up a playdate for Sylvie this weekend. I decide it's too soon and send a return message thanking her but explaining Sylvie isn't quite ready to stay away from home.

The park is relatively busy but there's plenty of play equipment here so Sylvie doesn't have to wait long to take her turn. I watch my daughter as she periodically jumps from the slide or the swing to run over and talk to Rory. She's so caring, explaining to him in detail what all the different play equipment does, as if she believes he can understand every word she says.

My heart squeezes when I think about her being so fond of him already, but not realising he is her little baby half-brother. It feels wrong to keep it from her and yet it's far too much, too soon to tell her now, after all the upheaval.

I sit on a wooden bench, content to watch Sara pushing Sylvie on the swing, Rory nestled close to her in his papoose.

Sylvie is laughing, throwing back her head and squealing with pleasure and a tinge of fear. Sara is pushing her too high… too high and too fast for a little five-year-old girl.

I think about Mum's recent insistence that Sara seemed a bit spaced out and not quite with it.

I jump up and rush over. 'I can take a turn,' I say. 'Must be hard work, carrying the baby, too.'

'No, it's fine!' She turns to look at me, sees the expression on my face and her wide smile fades. She takes a few steps back and I stand in her place, barely touching the swing when it reaches me, in an effort to slow it down.

Sylvie grips the chains and twists around. 'Not you, Mummy! I want Sara to push me.'

I ignore her and, again, miss out a push to slow down the swing.

'I don't want you, Mummy! Auntie Sara? Can you push me instead?'

Auntie Sara? When did *that* become a thing?

It's just a little kid wanting the thrill of a scary push but hearing her openly call so affectionately for Sara instead of me makes me feel like bursting into tears. Despite his treachery, I'm missing Cole so much and I need the love of my kids more than ever.

Sara approaches and I shake my head. 'It's fine. I'll do it.'

She walks back to the bench and sits down. Sylvie starts to cry. 'I want Sara to push me, not you!'

I grab hold of the back of the swing, forcing it to stop, and then I lift Sylvie from it. She's yelling and shrieking and when I try to grab her, she throws herself to the ground. Other parents over by the roundabout and the climbing frame look over, concerned.

I reach down for her hand to pull her up to standing. She clenches her fingers so I can't get a hold, so I grip the top of her arm instead. She's twisting and turning, refusing to stand up as she yelps in indignation and I realise, if I carry on gripping her arm, I'm going to hurt her. So I'm forced to let go.

She jumps up, throws me an angry scowl and runs over to the bench, rubbing her arm and sitting next to Sara.

'Let me see, darling.' Sara slips Sylvie's arm out of her coat and rolls up the sleeve of her jumper and cries out loud enough for other people to hear. 'Oh no, you've really hurt her, Jennifer!'

Sylvie starts to cry in panic at Sara's reaction. She twists her neck and upper body back and forth in her efforts to see the red, angry marks on the fleshy part of her arm where my fingers dug into her skin.

'It's OK, Sylvie,' I say, calmly, throwing Sara a look. 'It's only where Mummy pulled you up off the ground. The marks will be gone soon.'

Sylvie has always bruised easily. Her legs are usually dotted with little marks where she's scuffed herself on hard surfaces even in the house. I already know these marks will develop into angry bruises that will take a week or two to fully disappear, and I feel sick with guilt I inflicted them in an angry reaction to her behaviour.

I feel bereft when Sylvie ignores my outstretched arms and nuzzles into Sara's side instead. Sara kisses the top of Sylvie's head and hugs my daughter in closer to Rory.

'Don't worry, darling. The nasty bruises Mummy made will soon be gone,' Sara coos unnecessarily.

Sylvie reaches a hand to stroke Rory's cheek. 'Your mummy is nice but mine is horrible,' she tells him.

'Oh Sylvie, your mummy is lovely too. I'm sure she didn't mean to hurt you,' Sara says with obvious satisfaction.

Inexplicably, I feel tears prickling at the back of my eyes. I turn away, keen not to let Sara see that Sylvie's behaviour is bothering me. Before I do, I glance at her and Sara fixes her pale blue eyes on me.

I'm convinced there's a faint smile playing on her lips and yet… I can't be sure if that's the reality, or if I'm imagining it.

CHAPTER 33

On Saturday afternoon, I watch as Miller prowls around the kitchen. He reminds me of a caged tiger, stalking back and forth for no apparent reason. It will be the stress manifesting, of course. The grief of what's happened is tainting every part of him.

When he paces past me for the umpteenth time, I grab his arm and pull him to me. 'Come on. Let's have a cuddle.'

'Mum,' he grumbles, pulling away. 'I'm fine. I'm just… thinking.'

'Well, you don't look fine.' I let go of him. 'Whenever you want to talk, I'm here, Miller. Day or night, it doesn't matter. OK?'

'I know,' he says.

Sara comes into the kitchen and Miller slopes off without speaking to her.

Earlier, I'd cornered Miller at the bottom of the stairs as he'd headed up to his bedroom with a glass of milk.

'Hey, you don't mind Sara and her baby staying for a while, do you?'

I'd expected him to shrug ambivalently, but his face had darkened. 'I don't care any more,' he'd said. 'Do what you want.' He'd pushed past me to run upstairs, a big splash of milk spilling out at the top.

I'd mopped up the spill with a damp cloth from the bathroom. I was going to have to watch Miller like a hawk. I was afraid his grief might turn to depression, and that I'd soon have so much to think about I'd somehow forget to check on him.

'I'll make some coffee,' Sara says now, taking two stoneware mugs out of the cupboard. Something glints on her wrist, and I peer closer.

'Oh,' I say, touching my own wrist. 'We have the same bracelet!'

She glances at my forearm as I raise it in the air to show her and at that exact moment, a shiver travels down my arm as I remember. Cole gave me this bracelet for our tenth wedding anniversary five years ago. He told me he'd had it custom made by a jeweller at Hatton Garden in London. 'It's one of a kind,' he'd said as he'd fastened it around my wrist. 'You'll never see another like it.'

It's so fine and delicate, I mostly forget I'm wearing it.

Our eyes meet. 'Was your bracelet a gift?' I say softly.

She nods, extending her wrist towards me. 'Yours?'

'Yes. For our tenth wedding anniversary. You?'

'When Rory was born.'

There's a few moments of silence as we both glance down at our identical gold chains, each with a bezel-set, single round diamond. 'It's to signify our love,' Cole had whispered as he'd nuzzled my neck.

Sylvie runs into the kitchen and we spring apart. I pull my sleeve down roughly over the bracelet.

'Rory's awake!' She beams, her bright little eyes looking expectantly from Sara to me.

'I'll go and see to him,' Sara says, her voice suddenly dull and quiet.

'I'll make the drinks,' I say. First, I follow Sara and Sylvie into the living room. 'Coffee, Mum?'

'Not for me, love.' She groans and rubs her knees when she gets up. 'I'm going to get going, I think. It's been a busy few hours.'

'Thanks for all you've done today.' I kiss her soft, warm cheek.

'Yes, thanks for watching Rory, Kris,' Sara says, bending down to scoop the whimpering baby up into her arms.

Mum gives her a stony glance, gathers her things and I walk her to the front door. 'You OK, love?' she whispers, her eyes watching the hallway behind me. 'You seem a bit subdued.'

I nod. 'Just been a busy day, like you said.' I pull up my sleeve and the gold bracelet drops loose around my wrist again. 'This is all going to take some getting used to.'

Mum nods and lowers her eyes. I follow her to the front door. When we're in the hallway, Mum leans in close and whispers in my ear. 'When you were in the kitchen, Sylvie rubbed her arm and said, "Mummy got angry and gave me some bruises for being naughty, Gran." No prizes for guessing who's put those words in her mouth.'

I press my fingers to my forehead. 'Oh no. That's awful. I feel so bad, Mum.'

'You shouldn't. You just pulled her to her feet to stop her hurting herself on the floor,' Mum says. 'But other people don't know that. Maybe you should have a word with her teacher in case she's saying the same thing at school.' Mum hesitates. 'You should tell Sara to watch her step, too. Nobody with any sense would say that kind of thing in front of a little girl.'

Unless they had a hidden agenda.

I wait at the door while Mum walks to her little silver Fiat parked on the driveway and wave her off.

On my way back to the kitchen to finish making the coffee, I pause in the living room doorway. Sara sits feeding Rory and Sylvie kneels before her, entranced.

'Sylvie,' I call. 'Come and get a glass of juice.' Sara looks up at me. 'Sorry she won't leave you alone,' I say. 'She's just curious, I think.'

'She's fine here with me,' Sara says. 'She's going to help me wind him after his feed in a few minutes.'

I turn back to the hallway, leaving Sylvie where she is. I've every intention of going back into the kitchen when another thought occurs to me instead. I walk quickly and quietly up the stairs in my socked feet and down the landing. I open the door softly and step inside the master bedroom that used to be mine and Cole's, pushing it to behind me. I don't know what I'm looking for specifically – something that might tell me a bit more about this woman we're now living with.

The bed is in the same place but she's moved my dressing table and the small accessories I left in here… a few cushions, the odd vase, a rug and some candles are piled up in a corner, waiting, I presume, for me to remove them. Our framed wedding photograph is also there. I couldn't resist leaving that in situ when I moved into the spare room.

On the dressing table there's a jewellery box. I open the lid and a couple of the little drawers, but I can't see anything else like the bracelet.

I see she's hung quite a lot of clothing up already in the wardrobe. I flick through the garments. Sara is a big fan of natural fibres, cashmere, wool, pure cotton, as I am. My heart starts beating a little faster when I catch sight of an exquisite white beaded material covered in a stiff protective polythene case. I pull out the bottom of the dress and hold it there, my fingernails gripping so tightly I leave tiny half-moon indentations in the plastic. I have an identical evening gown hanging in my wardrobe although it's at least two dress sizes bigger than this one. I wore it for a dinner-dance at a swish restaurant with some of Cole's business associates.

I remember I'd fretted what to wear for months before and one day Cole had held up his iPad and showed me a picture of the ridiculously expensive dress. 'You'd look stunning in this, Jen. I'm going to treat you. Any objections?' I'd been ecstatic. Now, I wonder, had he also treated Sara?

After pausing close to the door and ensuring all is still quiet, I move over to the chest of drawers and pull open the top one. Folded yoga bottoms in here, very similar to the ones we've both already worn. In the second drawer, a tangle of comfy, soft knickers and bras. My hand flies to my mouth when I open the third and final drawer and I take in the neatly folded matching sets of lingerie, several of them exact replicas of the sets in my own collection.

I close the drawer, feeling sick. It's just stuff, I tell myself. Anyone can buy it. But could it be coincidence that there's so much of it?

I turn to leave and that's when I look at her bed, specifically her pillow. Folded neatly on there are the identical white silk pyjamas Cole treated me to for Mother's Day this year from the kids.

What does it mean? Cole bought me some of this stuff, but other things, like the lingerie, I've chosen and bought without his input.

I hear a creak on the stairs and freeze. The top three steps all creak in different places and, unless you know exactly where, it's almost impossible to avoid making a noise. Somebody is upstairs… but who can it be?

It's not Sylvie, who bounds up like a galloping pony.

It's not Miller because he's already in his bedroom with the door shut.

I stand rigidly, looking around the room, wondering, ridiculously, if I can hide behind something. A shuffling sound outside… I watch as the door is pushed slowly open, and Sara stands there.

She laces her fingers together and stretches her arms above her head before lowering them again. Her face is as blank as a mask.

'Have you found what you're looking for, Jennifer?' she says.

CHAPTER 34

'I'm sorry, I shouldn't have come in here without asking. It's just… it seems so strange this not being my bedroom any more. I just wondered how you were getting on with your unpacking,' I say quickly, walking over to the door, keen to leave. I swallow down bile, in denial I've been caught in the act. Her silence forces me to fill the gap. 'I was passing… and, I thought I could collect any washing you needed putting in.'

'I see,' she says, unconvinced. 'So, which one is it?'

'I'm sorry?'

'I mean, did you come in here to hunt for my dirty knickers… or to monitor my unpacking?'

I feel heat channel into my face. 'I… I shouldn't have come in at all. It was rude and I apologise.' How many ways can I say it? I've been caught out big time and I stand there squirming, desperate to escape her incisive gaze. She's blocking the doorway and shows no sign of moving. 'I'll get back downstairs and make our coffee.'

She folds her arms but doesn't move. She's smaller than me: slightly shorter and quite a bit slimmer. At first glance she looks so pretty and perfect but standing here with attitude, it seems like all that is just a veneer. Now, all I can sense are moody, dark vibes emanating from her. I find myself wondering if Cole saw this side of her very often. He wasn't one to put up with moods; he'd always find some reason to leave the house if I 'got one on me', as he called it.

'You know, I've only been here a short time, but I'm struck by how similar you and I are, Jennifer,' she says, a strange, vacant look in her eyes that reminds me again of Mum's earlier concerns.

'Oh, really?' I give a nervous laugh, thinking about all the identical possessions I've just seen in her bedroom. 'In what way?'

'Well, we like the same things, right? The same clothes, jewellery, the same interior style.' Her voice drops, low and husky. 'We even like the same type of man.'

I take a sharp breath in, shocked. I glance behind her to make sure the kids aren't hanging around, listening.

'We should be careful what we talk about in the house. The children are never far away,' I say stiffly, looking at her empty arms. 'Where's Rory?'

She was feeding him just a few minutes ago, which was why I felt safe to come up here snooping. The baby can't be asleep again so soon.

'Sylvie's watching him for me.'

'Sylvie's too young to watch him!' A thread of alarm lifts my voice higher. Sara is a new mum, I know, but most people would have the sense not to leave a five-year-old alone with a baby. Neither should Sylvie have the weight of that responsibility placed on her young shoulders. 'My advice is to bring Rory with you if you need to come upstairs for a few minutes. It's a big house and so you can't always hear if—'

'Thank you... for the advice!' she sings out bizarrely. Her bright tone feels incongruous in the middle of our tense exchange. Not for the first time, I wonder if she's a bit unstable.

A slow smirk crawls across her mouth and I step forward, suddenly desperate to get away. 'Excuse me, Sara. I need to check Sylvie is OK down there.'

Silently, she steps aside, and I rush out. I can't live like this. Something's got to change. Just as I start walking back downstairs, Miller appears at the bottom. He bounds up, two steps at a time before I can reach the bottom. I flatten my back against the wall. 'Hey, careful! What's the matter?' His eyes look wild as he whooshes past without answering me.

A second later, his bedroom door slams shut just as Sylvie's sweet voice calls out, shrill and alarmed. 'Mummy? Mummy! Come quick!'

I belt downstairs, almost falling down the last step, and rush across the hallway. I hear Sara call out, her feet thundering across the landing, just a few seconds behind me.

'Sylvie, what is it... what's wrong?' I cry, rushing into the living room.

My blood runs cold when I see Sylvie is standing very still by Rory's bouncy chair, staring down in horror.

'Let me see!' Sara pushes me roughly out of the way and dashes across the room. Her hand flies to her mouth. 'Oh God, he's not breathing... he's not breathing!' She snatches the baby up and holds him tightly in her arms, frozen in panic. 'He's not breathing!'

Rory's face is turning blue. 'Give him to me.' I reach for him but her arms hold him fast, like a vice. 'Sara! Give him here!' She snaps out of her trance, and I take him, lay him on the floor.

Sylvie moves away, whimpering softly.

'Ring for an ambulance!' I cover his nose and mouth with my own mouth. I lift his chin, keep his head tilted and give a controlled breath. His tiny chest rises and he coughs and splutters almost immediately, his eyes springing open. I wait and when I'm sure he's breathing again, I place him in the recovery position and look up at Sara's stricken face. 'Ring for an ambulance!' I shriek and she physically jumps, pulls her phone out of her pocket and makes the call.

Rory's colour normalises and Sara sits beside him on the floor, stroking his head. 'Will he be OK?' she whispers.

I stand up and squeeze next to Sylvie, putting my arm around her. 'Well done for shouting for me, darling.'

She nods and sniffs, her eyes pooling. 'Is Rory alright, Mummy?'

'What the hell happened?' Sara glares up at us and I feel Sylvie stiffen beside me.

'Leave this to me, please,' I tell her curtly. I soften my voice. 'Can you tell me what happened, Sylvie? Did you see what happened with Rory?'

'I just went in the kitchen to get a Fruit Shoot,' she says in a small voice. 'Miller said he'd watch Rory and I—'

'Miller was here?' Sara sits up straight and looks around. 'I thought he was in his room. Where is he now?'

'He passed me on the stairs,' I say calmly. Inside, my chest is swirling.

'He must have crept down here when we were in my bedroom.' Her face darkens. 'Why would he do that?'

'Perhaps he needed something. He's back in his bedroom now.'

'He came downstairs, saw Rory wasn't breathing and did absolutely nothing about the situation?' Sara demands.

'I – he must have panicked,' I stammer.

She glares at me and shakes her head. 'You think you know everything about your son, but you're mistaken. I don't think you know him very well at all.'

I leave the room, shaken by Sara's cryptic comment about Miller. I sit in the hallway, reflecting how oddly my son has been acting recently. I've put everything down to the death of his father but… maybe there's something else bothering him. This extraordinary situation at home can't be helping. This is what Ellen has been so concerned about.

Sylvie comes out of the living room and sits next to me, pressing her face to my arm. I cuddle her, whispering reassurances.

I'm relieved when Sara calls out from the other room. 'The ambulance is here!'

I kiss Sylvie on the top of the head and stand up. 'Don't worry, darling. Rory is going to be fine, and the paramedics are here now to check him over and make sure.'

We walk back to the living room and Sylvie curls up in a foetal position in the chair and slides her thumb into her mouth. I drape a waffle blanket loosely over her.

Sara stays with Rory while I go to the door and let the ambulance crew in. I point them to the correct room, briefly outlining what had happened. I close the door and turn to follow the medics when I hear a noise at the top of the stairs. A sort of faint whimper.

Miller is standing there, staring down at me over the banister with dark, troubled eyes. I climb halfway up and look at his pale face. 'Miller, what happened with the baby?' I whisper.

He shakes his head. 'I don't know, he just stopped breathing,' he says, looking away. 'I didn't do anything, Mum. I just watched him, and then he went a funny colour. Is he… is he going to be OK?'

'Yes, I think so. He's breathing again and they'll give him a good check over. Go and rest and I'll come up when the ambulance crew have gone.'

I start to walk back downstairs when Miller makes a strange, strangled noise before hissing, 'Mum?'

I stop again and look up. His face is screwed up now, tears streaming down his cheeks. I run upstairs and grab hold of him.

Miller rarely shows any emotion these days. He'd rather shut himself in his bedroom for hours on end than reach out. 'What's wrong? Please don't worry, Rory will be fine and—'

'I... I've got something I need to tell you!' he cries out, his voice stretched and high. 'It's all my fault...'

'Shh, it's OK.' I glance downstairs. I can hear the paramedics talking. 'What's your fault?' My heartbeat is pounding in my throat, dreading his confession.

'I'm sorry, Mum. I'm so, so sorry.' He buries his wet face in my neck. His words are muffled and hard to hear.

What is he about to say? That he tried to smother the baby?

A wave of panic hits me and I step back. 'Tell me, Miller,' I whisper. 'What did you do?' I push him back slightly so I can look at his face, but he won't meet my eyes. He's already said he didn't touch the baby, that he'd just watched over him for a very short time. My son couldn't do anything terrible to a tiny child, could he? He's had his problems, yes, but at his core, he is a good, kind boy. I know it.

'Listen to me, Miller. You did nothing wrong.'

'I did! That's just it... I *did* do something wrong, Mum.'

My knees weaken and I lean heavily against the banister rail. What will I do if he confesses to hurting the baby?

'Tell me,' I say, my voice little more than a whisper now.

His reply hits me for six.

'I knew Dad was seeing Sara. I followed them this one day... and he saw me.' He looks at me, takes my hand. 'And... I did something bad, Mum. Something really bad.'

I feel my knees begin to buckle. I lower my eyes, trying to prepare myself before croaking, 'What did you do?'

He squeezes my hand so tight I automatically try to pull away. But he won't let go. He waits until I finally meet his eye.

'What did you do, Miller?' I say again.

He stares at me, a light sheen glistening on his forehead and upper lip.

And then, very slowly, he says, 'I think it might have been me who hurt Dad's head before the accident.'

CHAPTER 35

NOTTINGHAMSHIRE POLICE

Helena looks up from her paperwork at the sound of someone calling her name. She's been absorbed in studying the spreadsheets Corinne Waterman, Cole Fincham's accountant, had sent over at their request, and she has diverted calls to her direct line to Brewster for an hour or so while she grapples with the numerical content.

Brewster stands up now, waving the phone in his hand. 'Call for you from Roland Rat, boss. I'll put it through.'

Her phone rings and she picks up. 'Afternoon, Rolly. Didn't expect to hear from you on a Saturday afternoon.' She greets the pathologist brightly. 'What can I do for you?'

'I'm trying to catch up; we've had a busy few days. And I think it's more a case of what I can do for you, DI Price,' McAfee says drily. 'I've just had the toxicology results in for Cole Fincham.'

Toxicology reports are considered standard in post-mortems of sudden death and fatal accident enquiries so there is nothing unusual there. Still, Helena's heart begins to beat just a little faster because the only reason McAfee would call her himself is if there is something significant to report in the results.

'I appreciate you calling, Rolly,' she says, grabbing a pen. 'Ready when you are.'

'As you know, blood and urine are routinely analysed to establish whether any toxic substances – drugs, alcohol and other chemical substances – contributed to the victim's death. And in the case of Cole Fincham, the toxicologist found something unusual.'

Impatience pecks at Helena. McAfee has always liked to dangle the carrot, dance around a bit before imparting the nugget of information that has the power to change a case.

'Let me guess,' she says, knowing he'll appreciate her participation in his game. 'They found alcohol after all?'

'Guess again.'

'Cocaine, then? Maybe he used it to cope with the stress of his financial and personal situation.' During her time in the force, Helena has witnessed the most ordinary of people relying on cocaine to get them through their daily lives. The drug is no longer restricted to celebrity use as it had once been.

'Nope.' Then, 'But you're not a million miles away, Helena. A significant amount of a drug called lorazepam was found in his bloodstream. The brand name is Ativan. It's a benzodiazepine tranquiliser and a Class C controlled drug.'

'Interesting,' Helena murmurs, although she's not familiar with this particular prescription drug. 'Why would someone take lorazepam?'

'Usually for anxiety, or for sleeping problems that are related to anxiety.'

'Right.' With everything Cole Fincham had going on in his life, there is every possibility he fits the patient profile. 'As a restricted drug, I'd assume it's probably an offence to drive when taking this medication?'

'If the medicine makes you drowsy, then yes,' McAfee agrees. 'But it should be remembered that not everyone experiences this side effect.'

Helena thinks about Jennifer Fincham's description of her husband's demeanour the last time she saw him. The disorientation, distraction. His stumbling around the patio area, witnessed not by her, but by their teenage son.

'Would it be possible, in your opinion, that Fincham could have taken the lorazepam while he was still at home, left the house and then somehow, due to the effects of the drug, fallen over and hit his head?' Helena thinks for a moment. 'Or, could he have sustained the fatal skull injury in some other accidental way before he got back in his car and headed on to the A453?'

McAfee's response is instant. 'Certainly, it's perfectly possible he might have taken the drug at home before going out. It's usually taken by the patient in tablet or liquid form and there's about a twenty-minute lag until it takes effect. But the full sedating benefits can last around six to eight hours.'

'And the injury?'

'Ahh, I'm afraid that's where your theory rather lets you down, Helena. You started off so promising, too,' McAfee says with some satisfaction. 'As I said before, the severity of this antemortem linear fracture wasn't something that could be caused by a stumble or accidental injury. This was a targeted blunt force trauma that was purposely administered to the victim – in my opinion – via an external object such as a baseball bat or similar.'

'I reckon I'd need a double daily dose of lorazepam if I was juggling two lives like Cole Fincham,' Brewster quips when Helena brings him up to speed with McAfee's call. 'While you were on the phone, I got a call back from a colleague of Rhea Brace. Apparently, she left Fincham's employ when they split up and went to work at a temping agency specialising in placing administrative staff. I'd been trying to get a lead to her and left a message there.' His face darkens. 'She just told me Rhea Brace is dead.'

'What?'

'She took her own life, a few months after her relationship with Cole broke up.'

'That's sad,' Helena says. 'She was only in her early twenties, had the whole of her life to find someone more worthy of her affections than Cole Fincham. How did it happen?'

'Overdose of prescription pills, apparently. I checked and there was an inquest. The coroner recorded a verdict of misadventure, but Rhea's family weren't happy because there were signs Rhea hadn't been alone. Her flat door was unlocked although she was known to be paranoid about security, and the tenant below her thought she'd heard more than one set of footsteps up there but couldn't be absolutely sure when questioned.'

'Interesting. Was there a note about how Rhea had been in the days before her death?'

Brewster nods. 'Her friends and family said she'd been depressed over the relationship break-up and they'd feared something like that happening. On balance, with the other tenant not being one hundred per cent sure if she'd heard two people, and without any solid evidence, nothing came of it.'

Helena thinks for a moment before saying, 'We'll definitely need to mention this to Jennifer Fincham, hear her take on it. Strange she never mentioned it when she told us about Cole's affair with her... maybe she doesn't know what happened.'

'Maybe. This came through, too.' Brewster waves a printout. 'Using data from mobile phone masts, we can see Cole Fincham stayed in the Nottingham area for nearly an hour after leaving the house at ten-thirty. He didn't join the A453 until around eleven-forty-five.'

'So the question is, who did he see, or where exactly did he go that was so close to home during that hour?' Helena murmurs. 'I guess our next move is to chase vehicle numberplate recognition data.'

Brewster nods. 'I've already sent an urgent request through to the ANPR team so with any luck, we'll have some results back pretty quickly.'

'I think we need to speak to Jennifer about this. Sara Nordstrom claims she didn't see him at all on the day of his death, so Jennifer is our starting point. We'll need to speak to the son, too…' She checks her notes. 'Miller. Obviously in the company of his mum.'

'I'll get that organised.' Brewster starts to move away.

'I don't want Sara involved in these initial interviews, Brewster. Cole Fincham might have had two women on the go, but I think we'll continue with our habit of talking to just one person at a time.'

'Boss.' Brewster grins and returns to his desk.

CHAPTER 36

JENNIFER

I slide my arm around Miller's shoulders and lead him back into his bedroom.

'Come on, sit down.' He's shaking like a leaf, his face so pale and drawn. I sit next to him on the bed, my hand rubbing the top of his back to calm him as I used to do when he was a little boy. 'Tell me what you meant, Miller. About your dad.'

'We... we had an argument.' His words are punctuated by sharp, shallow breaths as he forces the words out.

'When was this?'

'On the day he had the accident. After he came home in the morning.' He takes a breath before continuing. 'You were down the garden with the marquee people and Dad came up to my room. He always used to wait until you weren't around and come up to me.'

I look at him, baffled. To my knowledge Cole barely ventured into Miller's room. When I complained about the mess up there, Cole used to tell me I should just stay out and leave Miller to it. 'He's the one who's got to live in his own mess,' he'd say. If I asked Cole to get Miller down for his tea, he'd just bellow upstairs. He'd hardly ever go up there.

'You don't believe Dad came into my room, but he did.'

I think I might have hurt Dad's head. I can't repeat the words out loud.

'I do believe you, Miller,' I say. 'I need you to tell me what happened and why you think you've done something wrong.'

'Ever since he knew I followed him and saw him with her...'

'With Sara?'

He nods. 'Ever since then, he never left me alone. He used to come upstairs when you weren't around and threaten me that, if I told you, you'd leave us and it would all be my fault.'

'Oh no.' I cover my mouth with my hand, tears prickling my eyes. I can't believe Cole would ever be so... so *cruel* to our boy.

'He kept saying it wasn't what I thought. That she wasn't his girlfriend, which I know is a load of lies.' He uses his sleeve to wipe his eyes. 'I've seen evidence it's all lies.'

'When did it happen, Miller? When did you first see them?'

'It was just after last Christmas, I think.' All that trouble he'd had at school. That had started around that time, too. 'I... I heard Dad on the phone one night when you had some friends round. He was talking to someone on his secret phone.'

'His *what*?'

'He had a silver iPhone that he kept hidden. That's what I saw him using that night.'

A secret phone? My hands are shaking. Mandy had brought a bag of Cole's personal belongings from the hospital. There had been his crushed black phone in there but no silver iPhone! It was lie after lie after lie.

'And who was he talking to on this secret phone?'

'Talking to *her*! He said something like, "You shouldn't have rung me," and then he said, "I'll come over later but I've been drinking, so I'll have to get a cab".'

Now, I remember. We'd had a few friends round for a late New Year celebration and Cole had to take a call out in the hallway. I think he might have said it was someone ringing in sick.

Anyway, he'd come back in, and we'd continued with our night, but then Cole had to cut it short because of an emergency flood repair at one of the building sites his company had the contract for. *You guys carry on. I'll grab a cab and stay at a local hotel. I'll be back in the morning, Jen.*

Everyone had had plenty to drink and, frankly, we'd hardly noticed he'd gone.

'And after you heard him on the secret phone, you decided to follow him?' I say.

'Yeah. One day, I heard him tell you he had to pop over to a local house build, so I hopped on my bike before he'd even left the house. I waited a couple of streets away and then followed him. There was lots of traffic, so I was able to keep up with him.'

'Where did he go?'

'He went to Lady Bay retail park.' I know it well. A small cluster of shops set around a car parking area just about a ten-minute drive from our house. 'Dad sat in his car and then *she* arrived about five minutes after that. She parked right next to him, got out of her car and into Dad's Range Rover.'

I feel gutted Miller had been forced to witness his father's deceit and betrayal so overtly. It's the kind of thing that could stay with him the whole of his life.

'They were talking for ages,' he continues. 'I chained my bike up and moved closer on foot to get a better view. That's when I saw she had her head on his shoulder, sort of nuzzled into him. Then suddenly, Dad turned in his seat and looked straight at me and she saw me, too.'

'Oh my, what did you do?'

'I felt scared, I couldn't move, and then Dad undid his seatbelt and opened his door and that shocked me into doing something. I just turned and ran. Dad got out and ran after me, shouting my name.' Miller's eyes look wild as he relives the moment.

'I'd chained my bike up, so I couldn't just take off on it. I was trying to unlock it but the chain just kept slipping through my fingers. Then Dad grabbed me.'

'And that's when he told you not to say anything to me?'

Miller nods. 'He was so mad at first, I… I thought he was going to punch me. Then his face went really pale and he almost started to cry. I said, "Are you cheating on Mum?"'

I squeeze his shoulder. I feel so touched by his loyalty but sickened that he had to align himself to either me or his dad.

'And what did your dad say to that?'

'He said he wasn't cheating on you! A few minutes earlier he'd been sitting in his car with her cuddling into him, and the next minute he's lying to me, like he thinks I'm an idiot.' Miller's cheeks inflame. 'Dad said, "You've got it all wrong, buddy. It's not what you think," and I looked back at her. She was smirking and craning her head from inside Dad's car to see what we were doing, and I thought, *Yeah, right.*'

'Did you see them kiss?' I can't help myself. But he shakes his head and, pathetically, I feel glad. Sara has given birth to his son! What the heck does the lack of a kiss prove, anyway? Miller hadn't got it wrong. Cole had been just trying to force him to doubt himself. I would never have thought he would do that to his own son.

'Then what happened?'

'Dad looked sad then. He begged me not to tell you.' Miller's face crumples. 'He said it would kill you if you found out and if I really loved you, I would never hurt you like that.'

'That was so unfair of him,' I say softly. 'He had no right to use emotional blackmail on you like that.'

Miller shakes his head and looks down at his feet. 'Anyway, I finally managed to unlock my bike and I just left him standing there. I avoided him at home as much as I could after that.'

I think about all those times I hadn't been able to get Miller out of his room. Then the occasions he'd finally come downstairs for dinner and would barely look up from his food or answer his father if he spoke to him. I'd scold him for his bad manners and all that time… I shake my head. I can't bear to think about it.

'When I stopped coming down when he was home, that's when he started coming up to my room,' Miller adds.

'When I wasn't around?'

'Right. He'd come up and pretend to be interested in school, or my gaming levels or something. But he always brought it around to what I'd seen that day. He kept saying it was all in the past, that they weren't together. If he'd just left it, I might've tried to push it to the back of my mind but he went on and on so much, it made me think about what he might be trying to hide. And that's when I decided to follow him again… the day before the accident.'

'You *did*?' I feel dazed all this stuff had been happening without me even noticing. I thought I knew my husband and had been proved wrong, but I would have bet my life that I knew my son inside out.

'I followed him to this fancy house that I think had been made into apartments in Lady Bay. *She* met him at the door. I screamed at him from the road, shouted out everyone should know he's a liar before riding off again.' Miller's voice grows quieter. 'Next morning when Dad came home, he came up to my bedroom, trying to smooth things over, swearing it wasn't what I thought again.' He squeezes his eyes closed. 'I didn't understand what had happened, why my dad had turned into such a massive liar.'

So Sara *had* known about us. She'd seen Miller twice. She couldn't have failed to make the connection he was Cole's son, not least because he's the image of his father. Miller had even been to the apartment she'd mentioned. She'd said her landlord's name in passing and I'd duly filed it away in my head. *Mr Friedmann.*

'The day Dad had his accident, he tripped up on the patio when he shouted up to my bedroom window.' He looks down at his hands. 'He dropped the silver iPhone but didn't realise 'cos he was stressed out big time. I saw it happen and when he'd left the house, I ran down to get it.'

He grips my hand, his body shaking as he tries to control his emotions.

'Mum, I know Dad had another son… and he n-never told us.' His stammer is back. It first appeared a year ago when I thought his only problems were connected to school. After a few sessions with a speech therapist, he got it under control. My heart breaks as he tries to take in big gulps of air. 'I saw all the evidence on the phone with my own eyes. Dirty pictures she s-sent Dad and everything.'

'It's OK, Miller, you're not to worry, do you hear me? It's going to be fine.'

'I hate her, Mum. I really hate her,' he whispers in my ear. He sounds so certain, so full of vitriol and it prompts me to look back nervously at the stairs in case Sara has somehow crept up again without me hearing.

My eyes widen. 'So you have this secret phone?'

Miller shakes his head. 'Sara came to my bedroom and m-made me give it to her.'

'What?' A swell of rage rises from nowhere and I swallow it down. The audacity of her, intimidating my son in his own bedroom…

But there are more important things to ascertain while Miller is in the mood for talking. Things that may have far more dire complications for my son.

'Miller, what did you mean when you said you were worried you might have hurt your dad?'

'He… he hit his head in my room.' He squeezes his eyes shut. 'I heard you telling Gran the police said he had a head injury even before the accident and… it might be my fault.'

I feel as if I'm going to throw up. I take a breath. 'Did you hit him?'

'I didn't hit him, but I wanted to hurt him, make him feel the pain I was feeling every day because of him. So when he came into my room on the day of the accident, I ran at him and pushed him really hard. He wasn't expecting it. He fell backwards and hit his head hard, on here.' He walks over and gingerly touches the sharp corner of his desk.

If a head hit a sharp surface like that hard enough, I felt sure it could cause a serious injury.

Maybe, it could even kill someone.

Miller and I sit quietly. I hold him close, reflecting on our conversation and waiting for my fury to die down a little.

Sara has lied to me repeatedly. She had seen Miller – who people say is the image of his dad – and she'd seen Cole trying to pacify him at the retail park and at her flat.

It's now crystal-clear Sara knew Cole had a family. Miller's revelations prove she also knew his kids weren't abroad.

I can't ignore the things my son has told me. If I lose our home tomorrow then so be it. Nothing is as important as Miller knowing I have his back and will fully support him. I have no option but to speak to Sara about her lies and about Cole's secret phone that she is now in possession of.

I won't move out of this house until Corinne tells me those financial agreements are watertight. I won't just give our home away, but if it's proven she has full ownership, I *will* give it up without any further ado.

There is a lot to say to Sara but if I go down there screaming like a banshee, that's going to get us nowhere.

My suspicions have been proven correct. I hold my hands up: Mum and Ellen were spot on. Sara Nordstrom is a liar and I know I've not uncovered the full truth yet.

It's just a feeling but I have this conviction that there's something I'm just not seeing.

I'm only going to get a little closer to finding out the full truth if I get Sara to open up. And I'm fast running out of time.

CHAPTER 37

SARA

FOURTEEN MONTHS EARLIER

Sara had set out to ruin Cole Fincham. That had been her sole intention when she'd engineered bumping into him at the networking meeting.

Yet she'd known within hours that he was the one. He was handsome, successful, and kind. The sort of man she'd been waiting for her whole life. It sounded trite but she could tell, by his kind eyes and manner, that he was a thoroughly decent guy.

Sara had ways and means of finding out everything about Cole. On the afternoon they met, Sara already knew about his family. She knew Cole's rented address back then and also the address of the house on Dovedale Road that he had recently received planning permission to renovate. She knew who his clients were and what the bottom figure on his business balance sheet said.

This was a man who adored his family and that, for Sara, did not put her off. In fact, to her, it made him worth pursuing all the more. He'd been married to his wife for fourteen years. They were probably content, but were they happy? It became apparent they were not happy enough to withstand the temptation she presented to him.

The hungry look in his eyes in the bedroom when he'd seen her standing nearly naked in front of him. The surge he could not hide when she pressed her body close to his. With all the will in the world, it would be a tough ask for his wife to maintain a house on a shoestring and look after two kids while still trying to keep the romance and excitement in their marriage alive.

Sara was counting on the fact Jennifer Fincham struggled on that front, at least. She'd seen her from a distance once at a local shopping mall. Sara could imagine she used to be very attractive but now, the extra weight had crept on, the weariness had taken up residence in her face. She'd seen it all before.

On that first afternoon, Sara had gambled on the fact their marriage was probably on the downward spiral and one thing was almost certain: Cole Fincham was ripe for the picking.

She'd told him she was pregnant just a month after they met. He'd happily fallen into a nice cushy arrangement whereby he'd rock up at the apartment with his weekend bag – sometimes giving her no more than a few hours of notice – and stay for one night, sometimes two.

One night she'd booked Restaurant Sat Bains, bought a fancy new cocktail dress and worn her killer Valentino heels. His face when she'd told him about the surprise dinner!

'Oh my God, you look sensational!' he'd exclaimed when he'd seen her. Then his face had fallen. 'But… I wish you'd told me we were going out, Sara. I've literally nothing to wear. I just brought my—'

She'd touched his lips lightly with her index finger. 'Look inside your wardrobe.'

She had cleared a double wardrobe out for his use. He'd walked over and opened the doors, his mouth dropping open when he'd spotted the tailored Paul Smith trousers and silky shirt.

Hugo Boss shoes and leather belt completed the sophisticated look.

'Sara, I… I'm speechless!' He'd fingered the rich fabrics, rubbed the silky shirt between his fingertips. 'What's all this in aid of? I mean, what did I do to deserve you?'

She'd smiled widely. She'd stripped naked and soaped his back in the shower but laughingly pushed him away when he'd begged her to join him.

'I've spent hours on this hair, this make-up,' she'd scolded him playfully. 'But tomorrow morning's shower? Well, that's a different story.'

By the time they'd got to the restaurant, Sara had seen that Cole was buzzing, high on the adrenalin of good living. He suited well-cut clothes. He had the air of a very successful businessman, but he'd already confided his financial problems to her. She'd played along even though she'd already known how bad things were.

Somehow things hadn't quite worked out for him and she intended to change all that.

They'd ordered drinks. She'd feigned a headache and ordered only sparkling water but Cole had chosen an expensive glass of red wine to kick off the evening.

When they'd ordered food and the waiter had left them alone a while, she'd reached over and held both his hands. 'I have the best news for you,' she'd said, watching his every reaction. 'News that is going to change your life.'

He'd laughed and squeezed her hands. 'Now this I can't wait to hear. Go on, surprise me.'

'I'm pregnant.'

His fingers had instantly loosened around hers. The colour had drained from his face within seconds. 'What did you say?' he'd whispered.

'I'm four weeks pregnant, Cole, with our child.'

'But, how… I mean, we've always been so careful. You said you were on the pill.'

'Accidents happen.'

He'd pinched the top of his nose, run his hand through his hair. 'I don't… know what to say. I mean… oh God, Sara. I'm sorry to be like this, I'm just in shock. It's a shock.'

He'd pushed a fist to his mouth, and she'd wondered if he was going to be sick here at the table.

He'd looked at her. Looked away again. Then he'd said, 'I'm sorry to ask this, but… do you intend keeping the baby?'

She'd stared at him. She'd need to put an end to this before he went any further.

'Of course I'm keeping the baby. I want us to be together. I want to invest in your business… I believe in you, Cole.' She'd reached across the table again and stroked the top of his hand. 'Say you want the same thing?'

That's when he'd held her and cried. He'd cried for joy.

She'd started cutting down on her medication that night. She felt so happy, there really was no need for it any longer.

CHAPTER 38

SATURDAY

The paramedics had completed the checks on baby Rory and, satisfied, they'd left the house ten minutes ago. Sara has been sitting staring out of the window, but Jennifer still hasn't come downstairs to ask how the baby is.

Sara's eyes slide around the room and she asks herself what she's doing here, living with people who don't want her around. The story of her life. The ordinariness of the room feels incongruous after the life-or-death drama of thirty minutes ago. Over in the chair, Sylvie is still curled under the pale-lemon blanket. Her thumb is in her mouth, her eyes closed.

It's deathly quiet in here. Rory has fallen into an exhausted sleep and after the busy efficiency of the paramedics, the silence seems even more pronounced. The medics said it is quite normal for a baby to stop breathing for no reason. That seemed a very odd thing to say, to Sara, but apparently, they see the condition all the time.

'Infant apnoea is classed as a pause in breathing for under twenty seconds,' the woman explained matter-of-factly, as she checked Rory's heart. Satisfied with the reading, she added, 'The fact he turned cyanotic – the blueish colour he had when we got here – well, that's normal too.'

'Gosh,' Sara said softly. 'Hard to believe it's a common thing.'

'I know it's very scary but it's nothing you've done, so don't worry.' She began packing up the equipment while her colleague went out to the vehicle. 'They usually outgrow the apnoea phase by the time they reach a year old.'

Sara hadn't mentioned to the paramedics that she had left her baby in the sole supervision of a five-year-old, or that a troubled teenage boy had been alone in the room with him at the time of the incident. The last thing she wants is to attract the attention of the authorities, having them raking around in her personal life. Who knows what they might find.

But Jennifer doesn't need to know that. Sara will deal with this in her own way.

At last, she hears the soft pad of footsteps coming down the last few steps and moving across the hallway. When she looks around, Jennifer is standing in the doorway.

'I heard them leave,' she says, looking over at the baby. 'How is Rory?'

'He's sleeping,' Sara says. 'How's Miller?'

Jennifer walks across to the chair to check on Sylvie. 'That's why I stayed upstairs a bit longer. Not surprisingly, he's very upset.' It occurs to Sara that Jennifer's manner is slightly offhand.

'He's upset, you say?' Sara feels a twist of resentment in her chest. She waits a few moments and says nothing more until it settles. It's important she plays this the right way. 'I'd like to speak to Miller about what happened earlier.'

'He can't tell you any more than he has, Sara,' Jennifer says, instantly on the defensive. 'He stood by the baby's chair to make sure he was OK while Sylvie got herself a drink. That was all, he said, and it was just for a couple of minutes or so. He didn't know anything was wrong until Rory began to turn blue.'

Sara studies the other woman's face. Something is different about her, something Sara can't quite put her finger on. Her cheeks are slightly flushed, her mouth tight and puckered, but it's not just the impenetrable expression. It's her eyes that have changed. They look a shade darker and are trained on Sara with a new, laser-like focus.

What has that brat son of hers been saying upstairs?

CHAPTER 39

JENNIFER

Sara stands there, staring at me as if she's trying to weigh up my mood.

Sylvie is obviously exhausted, still curled up in the chair, dozing under her blanket.

'There's something else I need to speak to you about, Sara,' I say at last.

'About what?' She clasps her hands together in front of her and looks over at Rory. He's fast asleep in his baby bouncer chair with its little row of toys stretched across the front that Sylvie loves to spin and shake to make him chuckle.

'Miller's just got really upset upstairs.' She opens her mouth to speak and I hold up a hand. 'Not just about what happened to Rory. He told me he knew you and Cole were seeing each other.'

'Really?' She blinks.

'Yes. So I know you were fully aware that Cole had a family despite you swearing you thought we were living abroad.'

She stares at me. Her left eyelid gives an involuntary twitch. 'I didn't know you were… together, together as such. Cole did tell me you'd returned from abroad.'

I sigh and shake my head. 'No more lies, Sara. You knew. I always suspected it but the other stuff Miller has told me is even worse.'

She laughs. A mean, harsh sound. 'Oh, I can't wait to hear what other tales Miller has concocted. He's quite the storyteller.'

'Don't speak about my son like that.' I jab my finger at her, unable to shrug off the rage. 'This "arrangement" you somehow managed to talk me into isn't working. I want you to leave the house.'

'The arrangement that was for your sole benefit, you mean?' She wrinkles her nose in distaste. 'I think you know I won't be going anywhere, Jennifer. This is my house, don't forget.'

'I know you intimidated Miller into handing over his father's secret phone. That wasn't your property to take.'

'Secret phone?' She frowns.

'Yes, I'm sure you remember. The silver iPhone his father used to communicate with you.'

'Jennifer, I honestly don't know what you're talking about!'

I can feel my face heating up. This is not the reaction I expected. Her sitting there, all calm and collected. I could call Miller downstairs to add weight to my words, but I really don't want him getting embroiled in what's warming up to becoming a full-blown argument.

I take a breath and keep my voice level.

'You went into Miller's bedroom and demanded he gave you the phone or you'd tell me he'd known all along about the affair you were having with Cole. What kind of a person does that to a thirteen-year-old?'

'I don't know anything about a secret phone and I certainly haven't been in Miller's bedroom.' Sara looks incredulous. 'I really like Miller, I do. But I do think he needs help. Has he told you about the text messages he sent me?'

'What?'

'On the day of Cole's accident, he sent me several abusive text messages. I could have gone to the police there and then but I didn't. And I haven't mentioned it to them during our interviews.'

My blood runs cold. 'Miller would never send anything like that,' I say faintly.

'And yet he did exactly that.' She sits up straight and pulls out her phone with a flourish. 'Why don't you call him downstairs, now? I'm very happy to tell you in front of him.'

'No need for that. I'll ask him myself.' The fire evaporates from my belly. Miller wouldn't lie about Sara going into his bedroom and demanding a phone. I mean, why would he? What would it serve? And yet… he's kept so much from me. All that stuff about confronting his dad and Sara. He's only just told me about Cole hitting his head after Miller had run at him in anger. I'd never admit it to her, but my son has been very selective in what he's told me before now.

Sara holds out her phone triumphantly. 'Here they are! Take a look. I deleted the texts as they were upsetting but I took a photograph first in case I decided to involve the police.'

I take the phone and read the texts on there. Vile, troubling messages about death, demanding naked pictures and calling her a bitch.

I'm shaken. 'There's no number shown on here. I can't see who sent them.'

'The messages came from Miller,' she says curtly, folding her arms and recovering her composure. 'Just ask him. In fact I'd like to speak to him myself about what happened to Rory.'

'He won't be coming downstairs again today,' I say firmly, as I fuss unnecessarily with the ribbon-bound edges of Sylvie's blanket. 'I've told him to stay in his bedroom and rest. It's been quite a shock for him to see the baby in distress like that.'

'The paramedics gave me a number to call for social services,' Sara says lightly, unsuccessfully trying to mask her irritation. 'If

I'm in the least bit concerned about what happened, they said I should ring to discuss it.'

I feel my face sag. 'What do they mean by *concerned*?'

'Who knows? But I *am* concerned, Jennifer, and that's why I want to speak to Miller… to try and put my mind at rest. I want to avoid involving social services for obvious reasons. I'm sure you understand.'

'What do you mean?'

'Any sniff of a problem and they'll get the police involved. They'll see a boy of thirteen, having had some serious problems at school, and who knows what will happen… they're well known for taking kids into care, aren't they? And if they find out Miller sent me abusive text messages, well…'

I look at her through narrowed eyes. 'Are you threatening me?'

'I could have told them there and then, couldn't I? Described how Miller was alone with Rory and that he acted suspiciously, running upstairs, and shutting himself away in his bedroom, leaving his five-year-old sister to raise the alarm.'

'He was upset. He—'

Sara speaks stridently above me. 'He left an innocent baby – who had stopped breathing and who was turning blue – to fend for himself. It's shocking, Jennifer. Indefensible, and I think if it was someone else's son who'd behaved in this way, you'd be appalled and demanding something be done.'

'His father just died, remember? He's struggling, he wasn't thinking. He didn't hurt the baby… he'd never do that.'

We lock eyes for a few long seconds until Sara breaks the silence.

'I want to speak to him, today. It's not an unreasonable request especially with all these accusations and lies he's aiming my way.'

'Well, he's not coming down.'

Sara stands up. 'You leave me no alternative but to contact social services then. And while I'm speaking to them, I might just mention the injury you caused to Sylvie's arm.'

'Injury? She had some accidental bruising!'

'Not *had*. The bruises are still there.'

I feel sick because she's right. The five small bruises are still there, tracing my impatient grip at the park. Ugly, livid blemishes that mar her delicate skin.

'It's your call, Jennifer. This has all got to be resolved one way or another. If Miller is old enough to make such serious allegations then he's old enough to discuss them.' Her tone turns regretful. 'If it comes to the worst-case scenario, you can't say I didn't give you the chance to nip this in the bud.'

Upstairs, I tap on Miller's bedroom door. 'Just me.'

'Come in, Mum,' I hear him say.

I walk in and sit on the edge of his bed. For once, he puts down his games console without being asked. 'Miller, I've spoken to Sara about everything you've told me and now I have something to ask of you.'

A muscle flexes in his jaw but he says nothing.

'I'm going to ask you a question, Miller, and I need you to tell me the absolute truth.'

He sniffs. 'OK.'

'Did you send some text messages to Sara the day your dad had the accident?'

'I—'

'Think carefully before you speak, Miller,' I say sternly. 'You need to tell me the truth. Sara has shown me the messages that she says you sent her. Texts that call her a bitch and demand naked photos.'

He bends his knees and wraps his arms around them, burying his reddening face. 'She deserved it! She *is* a bitch and I've seen pictures of her on Dad's phone. She had no clothes on and… and… they were disgusting. They made me sick!'

'Miller, did you lie about her coming into your room and taking your dad's phone?'

'No! That was the truth. I swear it!'

I close my eyes. I feel beaten down by it all. Trying to unravel the truth, the lies and whatever comes in between.

I love my son with all my heart, and I want to believe him. But Miller has kept so much from me already. The trouble at school, stealing money from younger kids and now all this…

'You don't believe me!' he yells suddenly, jumping up from the bed. 'I can't believe you've taken her side!'

'Miller, calm down. I'm not taking her side at all. I just need to know the truth.'

He stands very still and looks at me. When he speaks, his voice is considered and sounds older than his years. 'She can say what she likes because nobody knows the truth about her, Mum. Nobody but Dad.' His voice cracks. 'And he's dead.'

My son might seem like a sullen teenager with attitude to other people, but underneath all that he is vulnerable and lonely. The inescapable fact is that, together with Cole, Sara has played a full part in making him feel so insecure. She can't begin to know the real boy and therefore she's not in a position of deciding what's best for him.

'What I'm about to say is going to be hard for you to understand, Miller. You may have some questions that I can't give you the answers to just yet, but what I'm asking you to do is to just accept what I'm about to tell you. Do you think you can do that?'

He frowns. 'I'll try,' he says reluctantly.

'We're going to play Sara at her own game, OK? For reasons I can't go into with you right now, I can't just throw her out of the house. Yes, I could take you and Sylvie and we could all leave and that's something we might ultimately have to do. But it's a last resort because this is our home and we don't want to leave it unless we have no choice.'

'Why can't you just kick her out?'

'That's one of the questions that I'm not able to answer at this point in time. You just need to trust me and know there are good reasons. That's all I can say for now, Miller. OK?'

'OK,' he mutters, sounding unconvinced.

'There's something else.' I pause for a moment. 'Sara wants to speak to you about what happened to Rory earlier.'

'N-nothing happened!' His eyes widen. 'I didn't do anything. I told you that.'

'I know, and I completely believe you, but there's something very important that you need to understand. Sara can make trouble for us. She can insist that you tried to hurt Rory on purpose and that could cause some serious problems for us. For you.' He opens his mouth to object and I hold up a hand. 'I know you didn't do anything, Miller. I just need you to tell her that yourself. Confidently and politely, even though I know you're very angry inside. Do you think that's something you can do?'

'I don't know why, but she hates me,' he says, his bottom lip wavering like it used to do as a child when he'd done something wrong. 'But I don't care 'cos I hate her, too!'

I can't let him become stuck in this rhetoric. 'Can you do that, Miller? Look her in the eyes and tell her that you didn't touch Rory? I'll be there, so you don't have to speak to her alone. You just need to tell the truth, and if she gets too stroppy, I'll put an end to the conversation.'

He thinks for a moment. 'OK,' he says, sounding beaten. I hate that I've had to cajole him into doing something he obviously feels so uncomfortable with.

But it's vital he tells her himself, face to face. And then it will be her turn to go under the microscope.

'There's one more thing, Miller.' He looks up. 'I need the address of her flat.'

CHAPTER 40

FOURTEEN MONTHS EARLIER

For as long as she'd known him, Cole had been what her dad might have called 'a steady sort'. Not one for big swings in mood, he remained constant and reliable. But for the last few weeks, his steady countenance had faltered. At first, he'd seemed buoyant and excitable when there was no obvious cause for it.

'Is there a new contract in the offing?' she'd asked him on more than one occasion. 'You've got a spring in your step.'

'Now that would be telling.' He'd grinned.

He'd taken to grabbing her and pulling her to him when she headed past him to the fridge or had come out of a room to find him watching her from the doorway.

'What is it with you, just lately?' she'd complained half-heartedly when he'd hijacked her outside the bathroom.

'What? I can't cuddle my gorgeous wife now without a reason?' he'd complained and she'd relaxed into him, enjoying the attention.

But then during the last week, the impulsive cuddles had abruptly stopped and Cole had grown quieter, seeming to spend a long time staring out of the window or into empty space in apparent contemplation.

'How's the new contract coming along?' Jennifer asked him one day. 'I assume there *is* a new one you've been working on?'

'It's... tricky,' he said without offering any details. 'I'm hoping I've practically got it in the bag.'

She stared at him, sitting there looking all morose. Usually, a new contract would have him smiling, humming to himself as he tapped away at a calculator trying to establish the potential profit margins. Today, though, he was flat as a pancake.

'I know something is wrong with you, Cole, however many times you deny it.' Jennifer sighed, sitting down next to him at the breakfast bar. 'I'm always here if you want to talk about it.'

Then something impossible happened. At least Jennifer would've *thought* it impossible until now. Cole's eyes brimmed with tears and he stood up, looking directly at her.

'There's nothing you, or anyone else can do, Jen,' he said, his expression pained. She was speechless but embraced him. 'I've let you down. I've got myself in a fix.'

'Cole! What is it?' She held him tighter as he pressed his face into her neck. Fear traced its way up into her throat as Rhea Brace's face drifted into her head. 'Tell me... what's happened? If you're honest with me, we can get through anything. We can do it together.'

As quickly as he'd broken down, he seemed to gather himself back to full strength. He pulled away from her, stood up straight and threw back his shoulders. 'It's nothing. Sorry. I was... it's just work getting on top of me.'

She felt a flood of relief it was work-related. He wasn't having an affair.

'What work stuff? Talk to me. Whatever's upsetting you... you can talk to me, Cole.'

'It's nothing. Truly.'

She grasped his hand. 'It obviously is *something*. Please, we need to talk about—'

He shook her hand free. 'No! Just leave it, will you? Please, Jen, I know you mean well but... I just need some time alone. Sorry.'

And with that, he stormed out of the house, slamming the door behind him.

CHAPTER 41

MILLER

When he gets downstairs, his mum is sitting in the armchair with Sylvie on her knee. Sylvie is sucking her thumb and does not look at Miller.

Sara sits on the sofa and he's careful not to look at her. Instead, he glances over to where baby Rory is sleeping.

'Sit down, Miller.' His mum indicates the other chair. 'Thanks for coming down. I know you're still upset.'

Miller sits in the chair and taps his fingertips together. He doesn't want to look at Sara's cheating, lying face.

'Sara's going to have a little chat with you, OK?'

'I just want to ask you a few questions about what happened earlier,' Sara says. Her voice sounds kind, but Miller isn't fooled one bit. She sounded nothing like that when she'd come into his bedroom. 'As you know, it was very serious that Rory stopped breathing. It's vital we find out exactly what happened, and you were the only person watching him. That way, we can make sure it never happens again, OK?'

Miller glances at his mum and she nods her encouragement. Sylvie begins to brush her Barbie doll's hair.

'When I left the room to go upstairs to see your mum, Sylvie was sitting by the baby and you were over there, in the chair,' Sara says. 'Is that right?'

Miller can feel the words tangling together in his throat, so he says nothing.

'How did you come to be next to Rory's chair?' she presses him.

'Sylvie wanted a drink, so I stood next to him while she w-went in the kitchen,' Miller struggles to say. When Sara doesn't comment, he adds, 'I wanted to make sure Rory was OK.'

'Although you could see him perfectly well from where you were sitting. But when Sylvie went into the kitchen, you decided to move right next to his chair,' Sara says, as if she just wants to help Miller remember.

Miller takes a breath and pushes the words out, the way the speech therapist taught him. 'I stood there so I could see him and m-make sure he was OK.' He knows she's trying to trick him and it's making him more nervous. He knows from watching real-life cop shows, you have to be very careful what you say, so nobody can twist your words.

'I see,' Sara murmurs. 'So, what did Rory look like when you first went to stand next to him?'

Miller glances over the other side of the room. He avoids his mother's eyes and watches his little sister. The doll's hair is very smooth and shiny now, but Sylvie keeps on brushing.

'He looked... normal. He was breathing fine,' Miller says. 'I could see his chest m-moving up and down.'

'So at that point, he was a normal colour and breathing?' Sara says.

'Yeah.'

'Then what happened?'

'His face just changed. It went a funny colour and he st-stopped breathing.' Miller bites the inside of his lip until his mouth tastes like metal.

'So, as you watched, Rory turned a funny colour and stopped breathing. Have I got that right?'

'Yeah,' Miller says. 'He went a b-bluish colour. Even his lips.'

'How did you know he'd stopped breathing?'

'His chest wasn't moving up and down any more,' Miller says, pulling at the neck of his T-shirt. It is warm in here and the bottom of his back feels a bit damp.

'You never took your eyes off him for one second?'

'I might've looked round to see if Sylvie was coming back, b-but I was mostly watching him.'

'Why were you watching to see if Sylvie was coming back in the room? Were you worried she might see you doing something?'

'Don't put words into his mouth,' his mum says in her warning voice.

'Miller, did you touch the baby?' Sara says.

Miller shakes his head.

'You never touched him to see if he was alright when you realised he wasn't breathing?'

'N-no.'

'I saw Miller poke baby Rory,' Sylvie says, laying down the doll's hairbrush.

'I n-never!' Miller rounds on her, his eyes dark.

'Did so! I saw him do it, Mummy.' Sylvie turns, burying her face in a cushion.

'Hey, come on now,' his mum says, jiggling Sylvie on her knee. 'Perhaps you thought you saw him, sweetie, but you were in the kitchen and you can't see Rory's chair from there.'

Miller reminds himself that Sylvie doesn't mean to get him into trouble, she's only little. She doesn't know what a lying witch Sara is.

'My leg knocked his chair when I m-moved away and I reached to stop it rocking with my hand,' Miller says. 'That's what Sylvie means.'

'But I saw you,' Sylvie says again, her words muffled and low.

'This was at the point you left the room, was it?' Sara says, her eyebrows knitting together.

'Yeah.' Miller's forehead feels damp and warm. 'C-can I back go up to my room now, Mum?'

'I have a few more questions,' Sara says. 'When you realised the baby was in trouble, did you leave the room to call me or your mum for help?'

'I ran up to my room,' Miller says, so quietly he can barely hear the words himself.

'Sorry?'

'I ran upstairs,' he says, louder now. 'I saw Mum, so I knew she was on her way d-down.'

Sara glares at his mum. 'Have you got anything to say about that, Jennifer? Your thirteen-year-old son runs upstairs leaving a helpless baby in crisis?'

'We've already discussed this, Sara. He was clearly in shock. Plus, he knew I was already on my way downstairs.'

'Only because Sylvie had the sense to shout for help.' Sara's blue eyes are blazing. Miller almost expects tiny sparks to start flying from them at any second. She is wearing a tight white T-shirt and when she twists in her seat, Miller can see the lace of her bra underneath. 'We're talking about a tiny baby, who'd stopped breathing and needed help. A helpless baby who—'

'He's my b-brother!' Miller yells suddenly, standing up. 'I know he's my brother, so you can just shut your filthy m-mouth, you lying bit—'

'Miller!' His mum's mouth drops open. 'That's enough.'

'Miller nearly said a very bad word, Mummy,' Sylvie says gravely.

'And here he is, at last!' Sara cries out triumphantly. 'The *real* Miller. The boy with a temper that can flare in a matter of seconds. What might he be capable of when he loses it?'

Miller stands stock still. Every inch of him feels frozen. His fists are balled, his teeth are locked together. Sara stands up, takes a step towards him.

'You found out Rory is your brother and that sent you into a jealous rage. When Sylvie left the room, you thought you'd try and snuff him out. Is that what happened?'

'That's enough!' Sylvie hops down as his mum faces Sara. 'Don't you dare try and frame my son for something he had nothing to do with. Don't you dare!'

'You really need to stop treating him like he's a little kid,' Sara growls. 'He's a teenager with an anger problem. It's time you faced up to that and got him some help.'

'This conversation is done.' His mum turns to him. 'Miller, you can go back up to your room, now.'

Miller doesn't move.

Sara scoops the still-sleeping baby into her arms. 'I'll be upstairs if you need me. I think, if we can't sort this out, it's time for me to speak to social services and possibly the police. Looks like our living arrangement isn't going to work after all.' She looks at Miller's mum. 'Finding your own place might be for the best.'

CHAPTER 42

JENNIFER

Finding myself homeless at the age of fifteen wasn't something that had been coming for a long time. It had been an instant, jarring shock.

My life fell apart in the space of one night when a horrible noise I couldn't identify woke me up in the early hours. It was pitch black in the bedroom I shared with Ellen as I jumped out of bed, snapped on the light and shook her awake. We rushed out on the landing to find Mum haemorrhaging in the bathroom, the toilet bowl full of her fresh, bright blood. We helped her to her feet and she coughed again, spraying blood everywhere. We ran around to the neighbours' house screaming and they called an ambulance as Mum lay unconscious on the kitchen floor.

Right away, the paramedics saw Mum was seriously ill and would have to be taken to hospital. They said because Ellen and I were both under sixteen, we'd need to be looked after by someone or they'd be left with no option but to call the police, who would alert social services.

Our neighbours, Mr and Mrs Phipps, agreed to take Ellen in.

'Regrettably, we can only take one girl,' Mr Phipps told the paramedics. 'We haven't the room for Jennifer as well.'

We'd both cried and begged them to let us stay together but Mr and Mrs Phipps had eyed me and shook their heads. They were probably remembering the incident just three weeks ago when the police brought me home for my part in vandalising a row of local shops. I'd been with a group of teenagers with nothing to do but hang around. I hadn't thrown stones at the shop windows like some of the others, but I had been the slowest runner. Before that, I'd had two exclusions from school and a scrape down the side of the Phippses' car that Ellen had made with her scooter handle but that they'd blamed me for.

When Mr Phipps said that, they'd all stood there looking at me. The paramedics, Ellen and the Phippses. I felt hollowed out inside, mortified at the rejection.

I ran away before social services could take me into care. I'd woken in my bed, at home with my sister and Mum, and by teatime, I hadn't got a place to live. That was OK, I'd thought. Better than going into care, better than standing there like a faulty possession nobody wants to claim.

But what was waiting for me on the streets turned out to be far worse than I could ever have imagined. The freezing nights that seemed to last forever and the cold that bit into my bones with razor-sharp teeth. The men with hungry eyes and creeping hands who said they wanted to look after me, to keep me safe... and then gripped my arms hard until I managed to pull away and run yet again.

I started trying to sleep during the day so I could stay awake at night, hiding amongst the bushes in the park, or dark, dank places most people stayed away from, like behind the stinking garbage bins the shops on the High Street used.

I'd spent six weeks on the street when somebody told me that Mum had been discharged from the hospital.

Those six weeks changed my life. I ditched the dodgy mates. I asked my teachers to give me another chance and took advantage of after-school study classes to bring up my grades and I stopped hanging around on the streets and cared for Mum the best I could.

The day I returned to the safety of home, I promised myself one thing. One thing that was non-negotiable, that I knew I must never compromise on again. I swore out loud I'd never allow myself to get into that position again and, years later, that promise has extended to my family, too.

I don't really know whether Miller was telling me the truth or lying about Cole having a secret phone. He'd certainly lied about the text messages because I'd seen the evidence with my own eyes. I would have bet my life he'd never send something like that.

If Sara goes to social services or the police, Miller could end up in the sort of trouble that will follow him into adulthood and I can't allow that to happen.

I know what I have to do. I need to play for time, and more importantly, I have to do a little digging of my own. I close my eyes and take a few breaths, pushing my true feelings down deep.

I can do this. I have to do this.

I ask Miller to sit with Sylvie and then I go upstairs and knock at Sara's bedroom door. When there's no answer, I tap again and open it slowly.

'Sara? It's me. Can we talk?'

She emerges from the en suite bathroom, carrying Rory. 'What is there to talk about?' she says tartly. 'You've made your feelings clear.'

'Everything has got out of hand,' I say. 'I really want to sort this out and make our living arrangement work, Sara.'

She sits on the end of the bed and bounces Rory on her knee, saying nothing.

'I know it's shocking, Rory stopping breathing like that. It was so scary for us all.' I continue, treading carefully. 'You seem convinced there was foul play but the paramedics didn't take that view.'

'They weren't there; they didn't see what happened,' she shoots back instantly.

'None of us were there, just Miller. And he swears he never touched Rory.' I sigh. 'Look, I'm just asking you to acknowledge the possibility that it was a natural cause, the reason Rory stopped breathing. Can you do that?'

She frowns, gently placing Rory next to her on the bed and dangling a ribbon above him that he laughs at and tries to grab.

'He's OK, Sara, look at him. Thank goodness he's fine. Please, can you find it in your heart to just allow the possibility that Miller is innocent into your reasoning?'

'Sylvie said she saw him poke Rory.'

'Sylvie is just five years old, Sara. Miller is adamant he didn't touch him... surely you can see he thinks the world of the baby?'

She sniffs and looks down at her son.

'Can we give it another go... please? Try to talk a bit more, get the kids to bond a little? Cole's memorial gathering is coming up. I could really do with your support on that day.'

'OK,' Sara says magnanimously. 'But any more suspicious behaviour from Miller and we're going to have to revisit our arrangement.'

I look away. If I don't get out of here in the next minute or so, I won't be responsible for keeping my hands from her scrawny throat.

CHAPTER 43

The old stone house is beautiful and stands close to the River Trent in its own grounds behind a tall, wrought-iron gate. I park on the road and press the intercom on the brick gatepost.

Birds chirp among the plethora of trees inside the retaining wall and a peeling sign reads: 'The Old Vicarage'.

An older man's voice crackles through the speaker. 'Yes?'

'Hello, my name is Jennifer. I'm a friend of Sara Nordstrom who lives in your—'

'At last! I've been trying to contact her for days. Come through.'

There's a buzz and the gates start to slowly open. There's just one car parked outside the stone house. The building stands well with its square bay windows framed with grey stone mullion pillars. The circular driveway is gravelled and my shoes crunch as I approach the ornate fountain that sprays artistically in front of the door.

As I draw closer to the entrance, a winter coat of the gnarled, tangled branches of wisteria reveal themselves sprawled across the left side of the house. It must look glorious in spring when flowering. To the side of that I notice a shiny black orb fixed high on to the wall. It suddenly moves one half-turn so it's facing me, signalling I've been spotted by an all-seeing eye: CCTV.

The heavy wooden front door opens and a short, thin man in his mid-seventies appears. He is dressed rather scruffily in grey trousers and a striped shirt with rolled-up sleeves revealing pale, bony forearms. The garments look as if they're hanging off his scrawny frame but he has a good head of cropped white hair and an impressive bushy grey beard.

'So, you're her friend, are you?'

I swallow and nod, worried he somehow suspects I'm here specifically to try and get information. But this is my best and only chance to try and find the missing pieces to Sara's past and, now I'm here, I have no choice but to front it out.

'I'm Jennifer and you must be Mr Friedmann. I'm pleased to meet you. Sara and Cole have mentioned you.'

'Never heard of a "Cole", but Sara, yes. Of course.' He shakes my hand half-heartedly and, when he frowns, my heart rate begins to gallop. He doesn't know my husband, which means Cole might have given a false name to cover his tracks. 'Do you know where Sara is? She told me she wanted to keep her tenancy but she seems to have forgotten all about this place. I've emailed and telephoned her numerous times. I've had people turning up here for appointments, all sorts of things.'

'I'm in contact with her, so I should be able to pass any message on,' I say. 'I can explain why you haven't heard anything from her; in fact, that's sort of why I'm here.' I don't say any more because I need him to invite me inside.

He looks at me for a moment or two. Seemingly satisfied I can be trusted, he says, 'Well then, you'd better come in. Straight along the hallway through the open door at the end.'

I follow his instructions, walking through a narrow but beautifully preserved Victorian hallway with what look like the original mosaic floor tiles and oak wooden panelling. The effect is dark but authentic. I like it but can't help thinking this place is probably the furthest from Cole's tastes as it could be. He's always liked modern, airy and light. I can imagine him calling this place a mausoleum, but I can't imagine him living here.

I walk through the open door into what is clearly Mr Friedmann's own apartment. It's decorated very much in keeping with the foyer. Authentic but drab. As I pass, I glance through an open door to a dark office packed with bookshelves. A monitor divided into four clear sections shows CCTV footage from various vantage points of the property.

'First door on the left,' he says, suddenly behind me. He moves quickly for an older man. He indicates me to sit on a threadbare sofa while he settles back into a padded leather recliner. He doesn't offer me a drink but that's OK; I'm not here to socialise. 'Where is Sara, then?' he says bluntly. 'Has she said anything about the second half of her annual service charge being due for payment?'

'She's had some bad news, I'm afraid, Mr Friedmann. That's why I'm here, to tell you. I'm sure it won't be long before she settles her bills.'

'Has she been ill again? I know she gets... a little low at times.'

Interesting. She's never seemed particularly downbeat to me. On the contrary, she's always confident and seemingly in control. 'No, she's quite well.'

His face softens slightly. 'It's not the baby, is it?'

'No, no, baby Rory is fine. It's her partner. I know him as Cole. I'm afraid he died suddenly a few weeks ago in a car accident. I know they lived together here and—'

'Sara and the baby lived here,' he corrects me. 'Nobody else.'

I realise he must have got confused because Cole was here only part-time. I'm not about to explain that my husband had lived a dual life. If Sara paid all the bills, Cole probably wasn't even on the tenancy agreement.

'I understand he only lived here a few days a week because he worked away,' I explain.

Mr Friedmann frowns. 'I can assure you that no man has ever lived with Sara in this house, even part-time. The young couple who rent the other apartment across the hall have another home in London, so are hardly ever here. Most of the time it's just me, Sara and the child. I'd know if there was someone else up there.'

'Well, I confess I'm confused. He's the baby's father, you see.' Something occurs to me. 'I know he kept unusual hours. Arriving late, leaving early… that sort of thing. You might have just missed him.'

'Listen.' He cups his ear and I fall silent. 'Hear anything?'

I shake my head.

'Exactly. This house, although soundly built, was not constructed to house tenants in separate apartments. I'm particular about the tenants I accept because there is no soundproofing. You can literally hear every footstep when someone is upstairs.' He looks up at the ceiling. 'Sara's bedroom is directly above here. If I so wished, I can tell you what time she goes to bed and what time she rises.'

'I see,' I say, careful not to offend him. 'I'm sure I don't know what to think, then.'

'There's something else, too.' He shuffles to the edge of the padded seat and pushes himself up to standing, grimacing as he shakes out his rickety legs. 'Follow me.'

He leads me back to the small office I glanced into when I first came inside the apartment. I follow him inside the room and he points behind the door where there are more shelves. They're also stacked, not with books, but with small cassette tapes.

'CCTV!' Mr Friedmann declares triumphantly, sweeping his hand towards the shelves. 'Meticulously stored after I've monitored any movement over the previous twenty-four hours. I keep a whole year's worth before I start to tape over them again.' He turns to look at me. 'Once I had the police come here investigating a burglary five months earlier. You should have seen their faces when I was able to give them footage of a car – complete with registration plate – passing the vicarage the very night they were querying.' Mr Friedmann beams. 'Led to an arrest, they told me later.'

'That's very impressive,' I say.

'As you can see, there is no way anybody can get within a country mile of this place without me knowing about it. Much less live upstairs without me noticing.'

Finally, I get his point. I pinch the top of my nose, more confused than ever and Mr Friedmann seems to take this as another sign I'm doubting him.

'Sit down, miss.' He indicates the chair behind the desk. 'Go on, sit. Now, let's see… bear with me a moment.'

He tugs at his beard while perusing the shelves, before pulling out a few tapes. He inserts one into a machine on a small table in the corner and a monitor leaps into life.

'Here's a little taste of the upstairs apartment activity. A montage, if you will, of arrivals and departures during October.'

He sets it playing at speed. Clips of Sara arriving home, leaving the house, making several trips to carry in bags. She has Rory with her in most of the clips and every single time, without fail, she is alone. 'Stop!' I call out, spotting another figure. 'There… a man.'

Mr Friedmann rewinds and plays at normal speed. A man walks up the driveway and rings the front doorbell. My heart sinks when I see he's short and tubby. Clearly not Cole. 'The plumber,' he announces with a flourish. 'Her washing machine started leaking on the…' He peers at the screen. 'Twenty-fourth of October.'

I take my phone out of my jeans pocket and, opening my photos folder, I select a good, clear, full-length picture of Cole.

The photograph was taken at a dinner-dance last year and he looks handsome in his tuxedo. I press my stomach as I feel a twist as sharp as a blade inside when I realise, that night, as we'd danced and laughed with friends, Sara would have already been heavily pregnant.

'This is Cole,' I say, holding up the phone so Mr Friedmann gets a good look at the screen. 'Have you seen him here?'

He squints, studying the image and muttering to himself. 'Hmm, let's see…'

Dread starts to build in my chest that I'm about to see the final evidence of my husband's betrayal with my own eyes.

He rattles about with the tapes, feeds a couple in and gets a few false starts. Then, 'Here we go, I knew I had it somewhere. Seven months ago, in April.'

Suddenly, there he is, there, on the screen. Cole. He is dressed in jeans and his lightweight navy utility jacket, the one I bought him for Valentine's Day. He walks up to the front door and rings the bell. He waits.

'What time is this, please?' I keep my voice level.

'One second.' Mr Friedmann bends closer to the monitor. 'Ahh, here we go. It was ten twenty-two in the morning.'

Cole would have left the house that morning in April on the pretence of going to some meeting or other. The kids would have been at school and I'd have been busy doing something in the house, or rushing around trying to get out to go someplace or other.

The tape rolls on and I watch as the door opens and Sara appears, still clearly pregnant at that point. She folds her arms, seems to be unfriendly. Then Cole turns around and she reaches out to him, tries to put her arms around him, which he resists. She stretches up as if to kiss him and he turns away, steps back. Then she's angry. Her face is a little blurry but she's jabbing her finger at him, obviously yelling.

Cole breaks away from her and walks back down the driveway.

'Have you got any more footage of him coming to the flat?' I ask, looking at the plethora of carefully stacked tapes on the bookshelves.

Mr Friedmann frowns and pulls at his beard. 'I don't think so but... we have a few more months to view so we'll soon find out.'

Then with a jolt, I remember the time. 'Sorry, sorry. I have to pick my daughter up from school.' I've no choice but to leave in the next five minutes. 'Would you mind if I came back another time and went through more of the recordings? It's any tapes we haven't seen in the past year I'm interested in.'

He hesitates before answering. 'If it would help, I can give you the tapes to take home. I've got a spare player you can borrow. There's a wire attached so you can hook it up to your television screen.'

My heart thuds. I can't quite believe my luck. 'Thank you so much, that's very kind of you.'

'Just make sure you bring it back in one piece. This older equipment is a devil to get hold of these days. There is one thing.' He raises an eyebrow. 'If you're her friend, why don't you just ask her if this fellow you're so interested in visited her?'

'I don't want to bother her when she's grieving,' I say easily. 'But I'm very grateful for your help. Thank you.'

He nods and hands me a small scrap of notepaper. 'There's my phone number. Give me a bell if you need anything.'

'Thank you. Just one more thing, Mr Friedmann. If you do see Sara, I'd be very grateful if you wouldn't mention I came here. She can get very... agitated and—'

'Paranoid!'

'Sorry?'

'That's the word you're looking for. She can easily become paranoid and, as I'm sure you know, she's not always as disciplined as she could be in taking her medication. I could always tell when she neglected it. Once, I caught her telling the postman she owned this place and I was just the tenant and as such he should theoretically be giving all my mail to her.' He chuckles. 'Fortunately the chap had been coming here years and he knew I—'

'Do you know what was wrong with her? Why she was taking medication?'

Mr Friedmann looks at me strangely. 'You claim to know her well. Perhaps you'd be better asking her something so personal.'

'Of course, yes. Thank you for your time; I'll be in touch soon to arrange the return of your equipment.'

And with that, I take the bag full of tapes and equipment and head for the car, my heartbeat pounding in my throat.

CHAPTER 44

I get to school five minutes before the bell. Sam waves from across the playground and I saunter over to meet her halfway.

'How's things?' she says. 'Don't forget that sleepover invite is still open for Sylvie.'

'I know, thanks, Sam. I'm sure it won't be long before we can arrange something. Everything is OK…' The words stick in my throat. Who am I kidding? 'Everything is pretty rubbish, actually. We're just trying to get through each day.'

'I'm so sorry, Jen.' She touches my arm affectionately. 'If there's anything I can do, you only have to say. I hope you know that.'

'I do. Thanks but… well, it's just an impossible situation really. I don't know where it's all going to end. I'm worried Miller will go off the rails again, but I can't seem to reach him. At least he's agreed to go to football practice tonight after school. It's been so long since he's shown any interest.'

'Oh, that's great news. Joel's going, too. He's been asking about Miller, so hopefully the two of them will have a catch-up in the changing rooms.'

Sam's son is Miller's age and he plays for the school team. They're in different tutor groups but they've always shared a love of football and been good friends before Miller's problems earlier this year. They've drifted apart as Miller has become more insular, but Joel never turned against him as most of his other friendship group did.

The bell rings and we look towards the classroom doors,

waiting for the explosion of our little ones, eager to tell us about their day.

I say goodbye to Sam and spot Sylvie running across the playground, her face bright and energised. I hold out my arms, gratified to see her so happy but the smile slides from her face.

'Oh! I thought Auntie Sara and Rory were coming to pick me up,' she says, disappointment dulling her tone.

'Just me, I'm afraid!' I say, keeping my voice upbeat.

Huffily, Sylvie hands me her lunch box and reading folder, a scowl settling between her eyebrows. 'Auntie Sara said we could go to the park and have ice cream,' she says grumpily.

'Ice cream in November? It's a bit cold for that.' I grin but Sylvie doesn't crack a smile.

She cheers up a bit when I suggest we go to the park anyway and she's soon running around happily between the slide, the climbing frame and… the swings. I try not to think about the upset last time we were here as I push her to yells from Sylvie of: 'Higher, Mummy. Higher!'

As soon as we get home, Sylvie rushes into the house, shouting for Sara. In the hallway, I call out to her. 'Shoes off in the house, please!'

There's no response and when I've taken off my own shoes and coat and stashed the bag Mr Friedmann gave me under the stairs, I walk through to the kitchen. Sylvie is cooing and tickling Rory in his bouncy chair and Sara is already pouring Sylvie a small glass of juice.

'Hi,' I say tersely. 'Sylvie seemed to think you were collecting her from school today?'

Sara looks puzzled. 'Oh? I don't remember saying so.'

'We were going to have ice cream. Remember, Auntie Sara?' Sylvie looks up. When Sara doesn't respond, Sylvie adds quickly, 'But it's OK because I'll just play with Rory here, instead.'

I get changed upstairs and then, back in the kitchen, I make Sylvie a cheese sandwich and chop up some tomato and cucumber to go with it. I suggest we all go into the living room.

'You can sit with Rory if you like, Sylvie.' I turn to Sara. 'And we can have a coffee and a chat.'

She puts the carton of juice back in the fridge and closes it thoughtfully.

'OK…' She draws out the word, turning towards me. 'A chat about what?'

'Just a catch-up, really. I feel like we rush around and never get a chance to find out a bit more about each other.'

She presses her lips together and walks over to Rory. 'Is he getting a bit restless?' she says faintly. 'I might need to take him upstairs for a lie-down.'

'But you said he'd just woken up, Auntie Sara!' Sylvie says, her mouth full of sandwich.

Before she can do a disappearing act, I make our coffees and then usher everyone through to the other room. Just as I get in there, my phone beeps with a text notification.

I put down the drinks and open it.

Joel just got back home. He said Miller wasn't at footie practice. Hope everything OK. Sam.

I frown and glance at my watch. If Miller didn't go to football then where has he been for the last hour? On cue, the front door opens. I hear him kick off his shoes and start up the stairs.

'Miller?'

I rush into the hallway and he's already nearly at the top of the stairs.

'Yeah?' He stands still, looking down at me. His face looks dark and brooding.

'Everything OK?' I say lightly.

'Fine. I'm just sweaty after footie. I need a shower.'

And with that, he's gone.

Back in the living room, Sara is fidgeting. Twisting the hem of her top into a knot before releasing the fabric and starting again.

It's really important I speak to her but I also want to see Miller and find out why he's lying to me.

'I had to pop over to Lady Bay this afternoon to pick up some dry cleaning,' I say casually, picking up my mug. 'You used to live there, didn't you?'

'Yes,' she says carefully. 'In an apartment.'

'It's a nice area.'

'Yes. I loved the apartment when I first saw it but then I decorated it too industrial, and it felt a bit cold and isolated.'

'What did Cole think?' She looks up sharply at the mention of his name. 'To the apartment, I mean?'

'Well, he... I think he felt the same way I did.'

'Cole loved interior design. We worked on the look for this house together, but he had very set ideas on how things should be done, and he had a good eye.' I glance across at Sylvie, who is combing Rory's wispy hair and crooning softly to him. 'I always remember one of his pet hates was the industrial chic look. He said it belonged in a warehouse, not a home.'

We look at each other and neither of us speaks for a few seconds.

'Cole let me do as I liked,' she says. 'He trusted my judgement.'

'You didn't have set days when he'd stay at the apartment? I'd imagine you must have felt quite lonely at times. After all, when he was here at home, he couldn't be there with you.'

She shrugs. 'We worked it out,' she says, her eyes pinned to Sylvie and Rory.

'Are you keeping the apartment? I expect you've left an awful lot of Cole's stuff there.'

She stands up, dusts off her immaculate jeans and walks over to the window, looking down towards the road. 'I don't know what I'm doing yet, Jennifer,' she says. 'I suppose it depends what happens here. With this house.'

She glances at me, waiting for her comment to land, extracting a reaction from me based on what she's seen before. Fear, panic, desperation to keep my home. But for the first time, I don't feel those emotions. Yes, I'm concerned about where we're going to end up but there's a feeling growing in me that tells me we'll be OK, whatever happens. We won't end up on the street and whatever transpires, I will have my children with me. Nobody can change that, not even Sara.

'We had parties!' she blurts out, turning back from the window and causing Sylvie to look up with interest before Rory's gurgles demand her full attention again. 'Big parties with all our friends. Everyone loved Cole. He'd go around the room telling everyone how happy we were, how we were going to get married and live together here.' She looks at me, her face shining and triumphant. 'I was never lonely because he never left it more than a day or so before he was back with me.'

'At your flat?' I say, wondering where all her friends are now.

'Yes,' she replies, quick as a flash. 'At *our* flat.'

It certainly doesn't match Mr Friedmann's account of what went on there.

I open my mouth to respond when my phone rings. I look at the screen and my heart sinks, but I answer.

'Hello, Jennifer, it's DI Helena Price from Nottinghamshire Police here. We're five minutes away from your house. Could we pop in for a word? There's been a development.'

CHAPTER 45

NOTTINGHAMSHIRE POLICE

Brewster stops the car outside the Finchams' home. 'I wonder how they're all getting on in there,' he murmurs. 'Cooped together in one big dysfunctional, unhappy family.'

Helena unbuckles her seatbelt and climbs out of the car. 'I suggest we speak to Jennifer initially, and then bring her son in, if she's happy for us to see him, too. Hopefully we can put them both at ease so they don't feel attacked in any way. They're grieving and must be struggling in the middle of a highly unusual domestic situation.'

'I can only imagine,' Brewster remarks.

He rings the bell and Jennifer Fincham comes to the door. Her hair is scraped back from her face and she looks drained and exhausted.

'Come through,' Jennifer says when they step inside. 'Can I get you a coffee, or some tea?'

They both decline the offer of refreshments, but Helena says, 'Would it be possible for us to speak to you alone, Jennifer?'

'Sure.' Jennifer closes the front door behind them. 'Go through to the little room we chatted in before if you like and I'll just make sure Sara's OK to watch Sylvie for me.'

Helena pushes open the door to the small room down the hall and sits down at the card table. 'She looks tired,' Helena says in a low voice. 'Coping with having Sara and the baby here on top of Cole dying must be beyond tough.'

Brewster nods. 'Added to that is the burden of the financial stuff she's been surprised with. Fincham certainly left her and the kids in the dark and smelly on a number of fronts.'

Jennifer comes through a minute or so later. 'Sara's not happy you're speaking to me alone.' She sighs. 'I said I'd tell you how she feels.'

'Noted.' Brewster softens his voice slightly. 'If it's alright with you, Jennifer, we have more information to impart about your husband's post-mortem and we've also got a few questions we need to ask.'

Jennifer looks taken aback. 'OK.'

Helena watches as the other woman takes a deep breath in to steel herself. She can't help feeling that every time they come here, it is to add yet another lead weight on to Jennifer's sagging shoulders.

'Firstly, we've just discovered that Rhea Brace took her own life. Were you aware of that?' Brewster says. 'It's just that you never mentioned it when you told us about Cole's relationship with her.'

Jennifer squeezes her eyes shut. 'I was aware of that, yes. I didn't see how that was relevant, I suppose, and… well, we never mentioned it after Cole found out from a colleague. I think he felt quite bad about it.'

'Why was that?'

'Well, he finished the relationship and then Rhea took an overdose. He always felt sort of responsible, I think. But like I said to him at the time, we'll never know her state of mind and whether it could have been avoided if they'd stayed together.'

'We understand there was some concern about whether Rhea had had a visitor prior to her death,' Brewster ventures. 'The door was unlocked, which was apparently unusual and, on reflection, the downstairs tenant thought she'd heard more than one set of footsteps up there.'

'I don't know about any of that,' Jennifer says. 'Sorry I can't be of more help.'

It is clear to Helena she doesn't want to talk about Rhea Brace and who can blame her?

Brewster goes on to outline the toxicology report and what it is used for. 'These reports are considered standard in the cases of sudden death and that includes fatal accidents like the one Mr Fincham was involved in,' he says. 'The results are used to establish if any toxic substances contributed to the victim's death and, I'm afraid, in the case of your husband, the toxicologist found a significant amount of lorazepam.'

'Loraz-*what*?' Jennifer frowns.

'Lorazepam,' Brewster confirms. 'It's a tranquiliser and a Class C controlled drug, which means it's prescription-only. The brand name is Ativan.'

Jennifer seems genuinely stumped. 'I... I haven't a clue what that would be doing in Cole's bloodstream. I mean... he wasn't taking any medication...' She falters. 'To my knowledge, that is.'

'The drug is effective for use in the treatment of anxiety,' Helena adds, relaying the information the pathologist has given her. 'Or for sleeping problems related to anxiety.'

'Cole wasn't anxious as such,' Jennifer says, looking at them both in turn. She falls quiet and seems to think for a moment before continuing. 'I mean... sure, he had periods that, with hindsight, would probably make most people sick with worry. Now I know what was happening behind the scenes with Sara and the business, it's not impossible. But a strong drug like that, one that's been prescribed... no way. He told me all about his recent health check and his results, so I've no reason to believe he was holding anything else back.'

Helena nods. 'Thank you, Jennifer. We had to ask you about it, but we've also requested medical information from Cole's GP, so hopefully that will soon shed more light on it and give us a final answer.'

Jennifer's face changes, as if something has just dawned on her. 'Do you think that's why he had the crash? Because he was dosed up on prescription drugs?'

'We're not jumping to that assumption,' Helena says quickly. 'Some people can take lorazepam and their driving remains completely unaffected. But we're obliged to check it out because of it turning up on the toxicology report.'

'Yes, of course.' Jennifer nods. 'I can see why you'd need to do that.'

'When people start acting out of character, that's when we need to start asking questions,' Brewster adds.

Helena checks her notes. 'You've also mentioned that your son commented on his father's disorientation out on the patio shortly before he left the house. Now we have the toxicology report results, it would be very useful to speak to Miller. In your presence, of course.'

A shadow passes over Jennifer's face. 'Miller is really suffering at the moment. His grief for his dad is showing itself in some challenging behaviour, and animosity towards Sara particularly.'

Jennifer's lightning-flash glance at the door isn't lost on Helena. She also thinks she saw a darting movement there.

'He's bound to find it difficult,' Helena says lightly. 'Does Sara understand how hard it is for him?'

Jennifer scowls. 'I don't think she's got a clue. In fact...' She glances at the door again before lowering her voice. 'I just found out Miller knew his father was having an affair with Sara and his dad made him promise not to tell me.' Her face flushes with fury. 'How screwed-up is that?'

CHAPTER 46

MILLER

He follows his mum down the hallway. 'Just answer their questions the best you can like we discussed,' she turns and whispers to him. 'Don't talk about anything else.'

He knows she means his argument with his dad on that last morning and the texts he sent to Sara. But his mum doesn't know the half of it... that isn't all he has to keep from the police. And on top of all that, his embarrassing stammer has made an unwelcome comeback.

When the door opens, Miller sees the two detectives sitting there. A big sloppy-looking man with red hair and a neat woman wearing a navy suit who reminds him of a schoolteacher. Both are smiling at him, but Miller doesn't smile back. He and his mum sit down at the table.

'Hello, Miller,' the woman says after introductions. 'Thanks for agreeing to speak with us. It'll just be a quick chat, OK?'

Miller nods and his mum reaches over to squeeze his hand.

'We're very sorry about what happened to your dad,' the man says solemnly. 'I know it's a really difficult time for you and your family, but it's very important we establish exactly what happened.' He glances down at his notes. 'You were the last person to see your dad before he left the house, is that right?'

'Yeah,' Miller says.

'Could you tell us, in your own words, exactly where you saw him and what he said to you?'

Miller takes a moment to think. 'I was in my bedroom. I had the window open and D-Dad shouted up from the patio.'

'What did he say?'

'He said, "Your mum wants you to look at the party marquee", or something like that.' Miller looks down at his hands. 'I came to the window but I kind of ignored him. I… I wish I'd have come down now.'

'I understand,' Helena says gently. 'Why did you ignore him?'

'Because I didn't even want to go to the p-party, and I didn't want to go down to see the stupid marquee.'

'Miller doesn't really like our parties,' his mum explains. 'He'd got a friend from school coming, though, and his cousin, Damian, hadn't you, Miller?'

'He's not my friend; he was only c-coming because my dad's doing business with his dad.' Miller scowls, then corrects himself. 'Dad *was* doing business with him.' He looks at the detectives. 'I haven't got any friends at school, but Mum doesn't like to admit it.'

'Oh, Miller, that's not true!' His mum gives a forced laugh. 'You had lots of friends, didn't you? And then…'

'And then?' Brewster prompts.

'He's had a few problems at school,' Jennifer says quickly. 'All sorted out now. You know how kids of that age can be with each other.'

'What kind of problems did you have at school, Miller?' Brewster says.

'It happened earlier this year,' his mum chips in. 'It was just a misunderstanding, a—'

'If Miller could tell us in his own words, please.' Brewster interrupts. 'It's important we hear his take on things.'

His mum clamps her mouth shut and Miller watches as her cheeks flush pink. He likes the fact the detectives aren't treating him like a kid. Now he's feeling a bit more confident and his stammer isn't as bad as it was when he had to talk to Sara.

'I got in some trouble at school about lunch money,' Miller mumbles, inspecting his thumbnail before nibbling at the tip of it.

'What kind of trouble about lunch money?'

'I took some lunch money from a few younger kids.'

'He was being bullied himself!' his mum blurts out. 'I know you want him to tell you himself, but he won't.'

'You were being bullied and so you, in turn, bullied some younger kids?' Brewster keeps his eyes on Miller.

'Yeah, I suppose that's it.' He stops chewing on his thumbnail. 'I haven't done it for ages, though. The teachers found out and I stopped.' He lowers his eyes. 'I d-don't know why I did it.'

'He's a good boy at heart. He had a few problems, but we worked through them with the school, didn't we, Miller?' His mum's eyes are silently pleading with him to say the right thing.

'Yeah,' Miller mumbles.

'So, Miller, let's go back to the morning of the accident when you were in your bedroom,' Helena says. 'Your dad shouted up and you ignored him. What did you see next from your window?'

'I saw Dad sort of staggering around. Then he tripped and nearly fell.'

'I see,' Helena says. 'Did you think he might be unwell? Did you consider going down to see if he was OK?'

Miller shakes his head. 'Not really. I thought he was drunk again.'

'Cole had seemed to drink more this past year or so, but he wasn't an alcoholic,' his mum says quickly. 'And it was only late morning, so he wasn't drunk.'

'So, your dad nearly tripped, then what?' Brewster taps the table with the end of his pen.

'He didn't look up again; he just walked into the house and then I heard the front d-door slam and his car start up.'

'Did you and your dad get on well, Miller?' Helena says.

'They had their problems, but they were still close. That's fair, isn't it, Miller?'

'Mrs Fincham. We need Miller to answer himself,' Brewster says more formally.

'I just wanted to... sorry,' Jennifer stops herself.

Miller watches his mum's fingernails pressing into her palms.

'So, Miller. You and your dad... did you get on?' Brewster continues.

Miller shrugs. 'S'pose so.'

'It's just you said you ignored him when he shouted up to your bedroom window, and I wondered if you'd had a disagreement or something?'

Miller stays quiet.

Helena says, 'When he shouted up to you, was that the first time you'd seen him that day?'

Miller feels his face beginning to heat up. 'I... I think I saw him once b-before that.'

'Downstairs? Upstairs?'

'He came up to my bedroom.'

'What was the reason he came up, Miller?' Brewster asks.

'Just to talk. I... I can't remember much about it.'

'Can you try hard to remember? Have a think. It would certainly help us piece together what happened before the accident,' Brewster says. 'Even the smallest detail might help.'

Miller feels his hands begin to shake. He's made a mistake. He wasn't supposed to mention his dad coming up to his room.

'He w-wanted to make sure I was OK. That was all.'

'Why was that? Had you been upset?' Helena presses him.

'I... I was a bit fed up, that's all, and D-Dad wanted to make sure I didn't tell Mum and upset her.' He pushes his hands under his thighs.

'Tell your mum what exactly, Miller?'

'Look, I d-didn't mean to say that.' Miller stands up, his voice louder now. 'He just wanted to m-make sure I didn't get upset. That's all!'

'It's OK, Miller.' His mum stands up and slides her arm around his shoulders. 'Come on, remember what we said. Keep calm.'

'Miller, it's really important you tell us exactly what—'

'I t-told you!' He pushes his chair back hard and it falls over. 'I can't remember.'

'I think we'd better leave it there,' he hears his mum say. 'He's so upset about what happened. About his dad. He needs to calm down and—'

Miller turns and bolts for the door.

'My, he's got quite a temper,' he hears Brewster say.

'Miller, wait!' his mum calls out.

Sara appears in the hallway. She is holding the baby close to her, the top few buttons of her sheer pink blouse unfastened. Miller stops moving for a moment and stares.

'Don't you even look at him,' Sara hisses, cradling her hand protectively over Rory's tiny head as if Miller might try to hurt him.

Miller runs upstairs to his bedroom. The back of his neck feels hot and damp and his heart hammers too hard on his chest wall. What is happening to him? Why has he made such a mess of everything?

He hears the detectives move into the hallway. They are speaking to his mum in low, concerned voices, but he can't quite hear exactly what is being said.

There had been a boy at school, in the year above him. He'd been in trouble with the police for his part in a street assault. Two detectives came to the school to speak to him and a week later the boy had gone. Disappeared. He'd been taken to a facility for young offenders, people said. Stories circulated that he was getting beaten up in there every night by boys much older than him.

Using his sleeve, Miller wipes perspiration from his forehead. Sara is downstairs in the hallway too, and if she tells the detectives about the text messages and what happened to baby Rory – that he'd stopped breathing and that she believes Miller tried to smother him – the detectives could be planning to take him away *right now*…

Bang! The front door slams shut. Miller scurries across the landing into the spare bedroom. He watches from the window as the detectives walk down the short driveway, talking together. When they get to the end, they both turn and look back at the house before getting into their unmarked car and driving off.

They might be planning to return soon with some sort of warrant that will allow them to take him, a minor, to the police station. From there, they could send him to a young offenders' facility. They'd learned at school that you could be arrested from the age of ten in the UK, so there would be nothing his mum could do about it once they had him at the police station.

Miller rushes back to his own room, his breathing rapid and shallow. He stops in the doorway and tries to take some deep breaths when his head begins to spin. The police have ways and means of forcing him to tell the truth, and one thing Miller knows for sure is that the truth will break his mum's heart. He can't allow that to happen.

After a few more moments of thinking, of silently goading himself to act, he dives over to his bed and grabs his football training bag, emptying the unused contents on to the floor.

He might not have long and so he has no choice but to make every second count.

CHAPTER 47

JENNIFER

'What did they want?' Sara demands, her face like thunder when the detectives have gone.

'They had some questions about Cole's past and they wanted to talk to Miller as he was the last person to speak to Cole on the morning of the accident.'

'What did they ask about Cole's past?' She folds her arms, feeling fully entitled in her demands for information.

'They were interested in a period of time before you met him,' I say shortly.

'His affair with Rhea Brace, you mean?'

That takes me aback. I'm struck dumb for a moment. I'd mentioned Cole's earlier affair but I hadn't given her any details.

'Cole told me all about it,' she says, clearly pleased at my surprise. 'He said he wanted me to know everything, so we had no secrets between us.'

This woman is too much. 'Whatever. That's what they wanted to talk about, anyway.'

'Did they mention me, or my relationship with Cole?'

I stare at her, aghast at her ease in being able to openly refer to her duplicity with my husband. Her distasteful narcissistic need to be centre-front in his death as in life.

'No. They didn't mention you at all, Sara. Cole and I had

been married for fifteen years whereas you hadn't yet managed two with him.'

Her mouth drops open and for the first time since this nightmare began, I enjoy a rush of spiteful pleasure.

The next morning, I wake up, my heart even heavier than usual. It's the day of the small memorial gathering that Cole's friends and colleagues have organised with Mum.

'Come on, love,' Mum said when I tried to scupper the plans. 'We still don't know when Cole's funeral will take place because of the police investigation. This will help everyone draw a bit of a line underneath his death, including Miller and Sylvie. They need to be able to say goodbye to their dad and people want to pay their respects.'

I could see Sara wasn't happy but she'd grudgingly accepted she couldn't attend if we were to avoid the obvious questions and possible resentment of Cole's colleagues and friends.

Miller is silent and brooding when he comes downstairs for breakfast. He makes himself a bowl of cereal and takes it back upstairs. I'd gone to his room and tried to speak to him last night about his chat with the police, and to find out where he went instead of footie practice. But he claimed to be exhausted and pulled the covers over his head. I decided our chat could wait, particularly since he needed a good night's sleep to get through today.

Sylvie plays up when I tell her it's time to get ready. 'I don't want to go if Auntie Sara and Rory aren't coming.'

Sara holds out her hand. 'Come on, Sylvie. You can come to my room and Rory and I will help you to get ready.'

Sylvie stops mithering and gives a little nod. Sara slides a fresh cup of tea over the counter to me and I breathe a sigh of relief as Sylvie takes her hand and they head out of the kitchen.

'Thanks, Sara.' I know my comments wounded her last night, but she deserved them. I refuse to feel guilty and, judging by her willingness to help this morning, it might have actually done her good to get short shrift from me for once. Remind her who's the wife and who's the girlfriend.

'You just focus on getting yourself ready and I'll sort out the little princess!' Sara calls as they disappear into the hallway.

After clearing the breakfast dishes, I take a shower and then dress in a robe and return downstairs to take advantage of the good light in the kitchen. I have a small dressing area with a professionally lit mirror in my old bedroom but of course Sara has commandeered that.

Thirty minutes later, my hair and make-up are done and I'm dressed in a black trouser suit with a black-and-white silky striped blouse and black heels. I glance at my watch. Mum, Ellen and Damian will be here in ten minutes in good time for the seven-seater cab arriving.

Miller comes down when I'm finishing pinning up my hair. He looks smart in a pair of black trousers, a white T-shirt and a navy jacket. He's getting so tall and, when he's worried, or thinking, his face has the same brooding expression that Cole had.

'You look lovely, Miller.' I smile at him. 'Your dad would've been so proud.'

'Thanks, Mum. You look nice, too.' He opens the fridge and reaches for the orange juice.

I'm just about to call upstairs for Sylvie when Sara beats me to it. 'We're ready!' I hear her shout. 'Coming down now!'

Miller and I wait in the hall as Sylvie's footsteps bounce along the landing and then descend the stairs.

'Ready, Mummy,' she calls, obviously very pleased with herself. 'Auntie Sara helped me to put on my new Disney make-up!'

Sylvie jumps down the two remaining steps and turns to us, beaming widely.

'Yuk!' Miller makes a derogatory sick sound. 'You look like one of those weird killer dolls,' he says, screwing up his face.

I can't speak. I can't offer Sylvie any comfort as the smile fades from her face. She looks... awful. Like a tiny pageant queen contestant forced to dress up provocatively like a grown woman. Her features are marred by thick blue eyeshadow, a powdered face and red lipstick. And a grotesque drawn-on beauty-spot above her lip. She has big, coiffured hair that Sara must have set in heated rollers or similar, to give it volume. It all looks so wrong against the sombre long-sleeved, navy dress with white lace collar and ribbon belt and dark wool tights I've bought her for the occasion.

My hand clamps over my mouth. 'What the hell... what have you done to her?'

Sara stops walking downstairs and stands halfway, looking down. 'She looks beautiful, don't you think?'

'No, I don't! She looks... all wrong for a five-year-old. She can't go out like that.' I glare up at Sara. 'It's totally inappropriate.'

Sylvie starts to cry just as the front door opens. Mum, Ellen and Damian appear. Sylvie turns towards them, the make-up already beginning to streak, and Mum gasps.

'Jeez,' Ellen exclaims in undisguised horror. 'What on earth were you thinking, Jen?'

Mortified, I stride over to Sylvie and take her hand. 'Come on, I need to take all that off before we can go out.'

'No!' Sylvie screeches, pulling the opposite way and trying to free herself of my grip. 'I don't want to wash it off!'

Mum reaches out to Sylvie and frowns at me. 'She looks like a... it's so wrong to dress a little girl up like that.'

I look upstairs and see that Sara has skulked off. 'Sara was supposed to be helping her get ready,' I hiss at Mum and Ellen. 'I left her to it and then Sylvie came down like this.'

'I don't like to say I told you so,' Ellen hisses back, 'but you shouldn't have let her move in here. What if she's trying her best to break this family up, not keep it together as she claims?'

'Don't,' I snap. 'Just don't.'

'No, Jennifer. You're burying your head in the sand. Who is this person you've moved in with your children? What do you know about her, really?'

'Leave it, Ellen,' Mum snaps, holding Sylvie close. 'Now's not the time or the place.'

Ellen walks off in a huff and I haul a wriggling, sobbing Sylvie to the kitchen sink. But I can't shake my sister's words and by the time my daughter has a clean face again, Ellen's poignant demand has wormed its way into my head where it plays on repeat.

'What if she's trying her best to break this family up, not keep it together?'

We make the start of the memorial service literally with minutes to spare. Sylvie's face is red and blotchy where I've scrubbed off the muck Sara had plastered her with, but people seem to take her puffy appearance as the result of her natural upset.

It's a well-planned service with Cole's colleagues recalling their memories of him and performing various emotional readings.

I decline to say anything. With pain, grief and fury swirling like a brewing storm inside me, I can't trust myself to avoid causing further upset and distress to my children.

Afterwards, a couple of people who work in Cole's office approach me.

'Jennifer, it was a lovely service and we just wanted to… are you OK?'

Mum peers at me. 'Are you feeling alright, Jenny? Your eyes…'

My eyelids feel so heavy I'm struggling to keep them open. 'I'm just tired.' I yawn.

By the way people around me are looking at each other, I know something's not right.

Ellen sidles up to me. 'Have you been drinking?' she hisses. 'You're slurring your words.'

'I haven't! I just feel…'

'Come on,' Mum whispers to Ellen. 'Time to get her home.'

Back at the house, Sara is contrite. She fusses around as soon as Mum opens the front door.

'I'm an idiot, Jennifer. I didn't think… I'm not feeling myself. I keep getting confused and… can you forgive me?'

I feel so exhausted and washed out from the day, I simply nod. 'OK,' I say.

Mum isn't as forgiving. 'Leave her alone,' she says shortly. 'You've done enough damage for one day.'

CHAPTER 48

I feel off-colour until Friday when finally, I wake up with a bit more energy.

'It'll be some kind of virus you've picked up,' Mum says. 'You're so run-down, it's no wonder you feel ill.'

Sara has been attentive while I've felt ill. Mum had a pre-booked trip to the coast organised with her fellow residents at the housing complex, so I was grateful Sara offered to look after Sylvie. I know she's trying to make amends for the make-up incident, which I'm still annoyed about. But resting in bed has given me plenty of time to think and now I have a clear-cut plan in mind that I intend acting on right away.

My chance comes mid-morning when Sara picks Rory up out of his bouncy chair. 'I'm going to take him out for a little walk. Fancy a stroll with us?'

I pull a face. 'I'd love to but I've got lots of jobs that need catching up on now I feel well enough. Maybe next time.'

When they've left the house, I double-lock the front door and go upstairs into her bedroom.

I stand in the doorway and look around. Everything is neatly organised. Her bed is made and it looks like everything has been fully unpacked and put away now. I'm looking for the medication that Mr Friedmann mentioned. She's hardly going to leave it out in plain sight, so I know the kind of places I need to look.

I look in the bedside cabinets, the set of drawers and under the bed. Nothing. I move over to the fitted wardrobes. Cole always used to joke he got exactly a quarter of the space I had for clothes. It was funny because he loved his designer labels, had far more clothes than I did and, if anything, the reverse was probably true.

I slide the door to Cole's wardrobe open and gasp. His shirts have gone, replaced with Sara's clothes. The other side is the same. His suits, shoes, ties and belts… all gone. I look around but there are no bags of his garments to be seen. I rush into the spare room but there's nothing here either.

I feel sick when I remember her words a few days ago. I'd just got back from the school run and she was on her way out with Rory. 'I've loaded the boot with stuff for the clothing bank. Do you need anything taking?'

I feel violated she might have taken it upon herself to dispose of Cole's clothing. It isn't something I've felt ready to tackle yet. And I wanted to involve Miller in deciding what to do with his dad's belongings. If Sara has taken that opportunity away from us then she had no right. No right at all. The worst thing is, I can't say a word or she'll know I've been snooping in her bedroom again.

I march back to her bedroom and I resume my search with renewed determination. I find a bag full of medication at the back of the last wardrobe behind a small suitcase. I tip the contents out on to the floor and look at the array of prescribed drugs, all with names I've never heard of.

And then I see it. For a moment I feel like I can't get my breath and then I shock back to my senses. I take out my phone and take a picture of the packet of Ativan. Under the brand name is the word lorazepam, in brackets. I recognise it immediately as the tranquiliser found in Cole's bloodstream after the accident.

My son has blamed himself for Cole's accident, but it wasn't his fault. Sara could have somehow slipped something into his food or drink. Maybe she also inflicted a head injury while he was sleepy.

I snap more pics of the labels of the other medicine boxes and pill bottles. When I'm satisfied I have them all, I replace the items in the bag and put it back where I found it. Why would a young woman in her twenties need this amount of medication? She must have a serious illness that she's managed to keep hidden since moving in with us.

My imagination is running wild, serving to confirm Ellen's words that have been worrying away at the back of my mind.

'Who is this person you've moved in with your children? What do you know about her, really?'

I imagine Sara will be out walking for at least an hour with Rory, so I rush downstairs to retrieve the bag of CCTV equipment Mr Friedmann gave me.

Just in case Sara returns earlier than expected, I take it up to Miller's bedroom instead of viewing it on the big TV downstairs.

The player Mr Friedmann lent me is simple enough to use. I insert a cassette tape and hook the adaptor cable up to the TV. It works a bit like the HDMI cable Miller often uses to connect his laptop to the living room TV.

Mr Friedmann has cleverly somehow managed, at the beginning of each tape, to put together a montage of any movement during that particular month. It means I haven't got to laboriously forward through hours and hours of time where there is nothing to see. I get through the first three tapes quickly and my heartbeat ramps up as I realise I've viewed months where there is no sign whatsoever of Cole entering the property.

I'm viewing the montage of movement from May last year when an image almost knocks me sideways. I shift to the edge of my seat and punch the pause button on the player. I stare at the person standing outside the front door of the Old Vicarage in disbelief.

I press play. Watch as they wait for the door to be buzzed open and then enter the building. I rewind, press play and watch again. And again, and again until I lose track of how many times I've done it.

I take a few screenshots of various images with my phone and then sit back, my throat dry and tight.

'You evil, lying cow,' I mutter, feeling dazed.

I disconnect the equipment and push everything back into the bag. Then I grab my coat and head out to the car, shoving the CCTV stuff into the boot so it can't be found while I'm out.

The missing piece of the jigsaw that's bugged me ever since Sara Nordstrom moved into our home has just finally begun to shift into place.

CHAPTER 49

CB Associates is a small, modest office located on the top floor of a five-storey building in Wollaton, an upmarket residential area with a few independent shops and pubs that's about six miles away from our home in West Bridgford.

I've only been here once before a few years ago when Cole first started the limited company, and I was required to sign various important documents in front of a witness.

I navigate to the small car park at the rear of the building we used that day, excited and buoyant at the thought of great things to come. How times change.

I use the ground floor lift and emerge on a landing with a frosted glass door bearing the CB Associates insignia in stark black lettering.

A young woman sits at a desk in the tiny reception area and she looks up expectantly when I enter.

'I'm Jennifer Fincham and I need to see Corinne urgently.' The girl glances at the telephone and looks doubtful. 'If you tell her I'm here I'm sure she'll want to see me.'

Her face brightens. 'Oh, she's just this second come off the phone actually. Bear with me a moment.'

She gets up out of her seat and disappears through a door marked *Private*.

I look around the small foyer. It's small but immaculate. Painted cream with low, modern comfy seating, the space features a scattering of real, leafy ferns and tasteful prints. The room reflects Corinne's personality. At least, the one she has always shown to me.

Calm, ordered and genuine.

Two minutes later, the receptionist is back. 'Corinne can see you now. Please, go through.'

I cross a narrow hallway to Corinne's office. I knock and open the door, stepping into a modern room furnished much like the foyer. A few plants, some golf clubs in the corner and a couple of framed photographs on the wall of Corinne accepting awards at open golf matches.

'Jennifer! What a lovely surprise!' Corinne rushes over and air-kisses me. 'Let's sit in the comfy seats. Can I get you some tea?'

'No thank you.' My voice sounds dull and lifeless next to her super-friendly show. 'I'm not here socially.'

She blinks and ushers me to the seating area. 'You'll be wondering if I've managed to make progress with the agreements, I expect.'

'I bet you haven't found a loophole, have you?'

'Sadly, not yet. But that doesn't mean to say there isn't—'

'You told me you'd never met Sara Nordstrom, but you lied. Why is that, Corinne?'

Her face drains of colour. 'What? You're mistaken; I don't know Sara.'

I take out my phone and pull up the screenshots of the CCTV images. 'This is you, I take it? Unless you have a doppelganger in the Lady Bay area.'

She squints at the pictures. 'Where did you get—'

'This is CCTV footage of Sara Nordstrom's flat. As soon as I saw it, I came over here but I bet, if I were to dig deeper, I could find even more instances of you visiting her.'

Two rosy spots begin to bloom on her pale cheeks. 'You're mistaken, Jennifer. When I said I didn't know her, I meant I don't know her well.'

'You actually said "I've never met her", Corinne. If you're going to lie, you could at least remember your own words.'

'OK, OK, you found me out.' She holds up her hands in the air. 'Listen, I said what I said for your own good. You were distraught after Sara's visit to the house. I didn't want to make things worse or complicate matters by telling you the full story.'

'Which is?'

'I'd been very concerned about the nature of the financial agreements Cole was about to sign, so, unbeknown to him, I took the unprecedented step of visiting Sara at home in an attempt to convince her to withdraw the loans.' She sighs and looks at the floor. 'I confess I knew there was little chance I'd be able to find a loophole but I hadn't got the heart to dash your hopes when you were so devastated by Cole's death.'

I feel myself deflate. 'So you're saying we *will* lose our home?'

'All's not lost. I've been very busy with client appointments but alongside that, I've been working diligently through every single word of the loan agreements as I promised I would. Until I've completed the task, we still have a grain of hope remaining.'

'I'm sorry,' I say wretchedly. 'I've been rude and accused you of—'

'Think nothing of it.' Corinne waves my apology away. 'I can't begin to imagine the stress you're under. How are you bearing up?'

'Not well.' I feel my eyes prickle. 'It's like my life is disintegrating right in front of my eyes and there's not a thing I can do about it.'

We both stand up. 'I do understand, Jennifer,' Corinne says. 'I lost my sister suddenly and there's not a day goes by I don't think about her.'

I nod and give her a sad smile. 'Thanks for all you're doing, even if it comes to nothing.'

Corinne nods. 'Take care. I'll be in touch.'

I turn to leave and see a glass presentation unit next to the door. It contains framed qualifications and various corporate awards Corinne has won over the years she's been in business. On the bottom shelf is a silver frame bearing the words 'Sisters Forever'.

It's easy to spot a young Corinne and, with her, a younger woman who I instantly recognise, too.

My breath catches in my throat but I'm careful not to break my step or falter. I walk into the foyer, thank the receptionist, and then run down the stairs rather than use the lift, not stopping until I get outside and can gulp in fresh air, leaning on a wall.

I think about the sign on the office door. CB Associates. *Not* CW. Corinne only got married a few years ago, but she started the business way before that when she'd still have been using her maiden name: Brace.

The woman in the photograph is none other than Corinne's younger sister: Rhea Brace.

CHAPTER 50

Reeling from what I've discovered, I'm not even sure what to do with the information. I still have missing connections. Corinne knows Sara Nordstrom but has given a reasonable explanation why she lied.

But she is also Rhea Brace's sister. That's not a crime in itself, *but* why would she have kept that a secret all these years? I'm certain Cole didn't know about the connection.

What can the police do with the two new pieces of information I have? These days, in our culture of blame, everything must be tied up in a neat ribbon before police officers will even consider questioning someone seemingly unrelated to a case.

I can't tell Mum and Ellen what I've found out because they both share a volatile personality. Either one of them could come over and cause a scene and I have to be cleverer than that. For now, I'll stay quiet and ruminate on the connections I've made.

I did, however, text Ellen the photographs of the medication this afternoon and asked her to find out what they're used for. I could Google it myself, but I know different combinations of medicines can mean different things and Ellen has medical connections from when she worked in the hospital. I don't tell her it's Sara's medication for the same reason as before: I don't want her coming over here and letting anything slip.

Now I'm so close to piecing stuff together, I have to be careful not to blow it. No doubt Corinne has been on the blower to alert Sara to my visit today.

As it's Friday night, we order in pizza and eat it at the kitchen table with an upbeat pop playlist on. Miller says he doesn't feel well so I wrap a couple of slices in foil for him and put them in a warm oven.

My phone rings and the screen lights up with Ellen's name.

'Hi. Can I call you back? I'm just—'

'Who do those drugs belong to, Jennifer?' Her voice is panicked and she's speaking too fast. 'Tell me… are they all hers?'

Sara opens a bottle of wine. Then she stands and watches my face. 'Everything OK?' she mouths.

'I'll call you back. I—'

'No! I need to speak to you right now. Jennifer? Don't ring off.'

'Thanks, then. Bye!'

I end the call and turn my phone to silent. 'Just one of the school mums after a favour.' I roll my eyes.

Sara nods and fetches glasses from the cupboard. I watch her moving around the kitchen when she has her back to me while she pours the wine and I feel tendrils of what can only be described as hatred creeping around my heart.

I'm betting Ellen was going to tell me those drugs are strong and would be dangerous if Sylvie got hold of them. At least they were well out of the way at the back of Sara's wardrobe.

It's possible she slipped an Ativan tablet in my tea the morning of Cole's memorial service. She had every chance and she was angry the police hadn't involved her in their conversation the night before and put out she couldn't go to the memorial. She pulled the unforgiveable stunt with Sylvie's appearance and then possibly administered a drug to me that made me appear drunk. Just like Cole on the morning of his accident.

'Here's to us all. A fresh start together as a family after recent events.' Sara hands me a glass and holds hers in the air to clink. 'What have you been up to today then, Jennifer?'

'Oh, just catching up on errands. I called in to see Corinne Waterman. Just to thank her for her support with the business.'

'Oh yes, Corinne. I think I've met her once on the corporate circuit.'

Liar. Liar.

'Sorry, just need a tissue.' I put down the wine glass and make an excuse to move away from her attempt to jolly things up between us. She goes to check on Rory in the next room and Sylvie sets up her alligator dentist game on the table.

'We can play that in the living room later if you like, Sylvie,' I tell her, wanting to clear things away in here.

'I'm going to play with Auntie Sara,' she says abruptly. She hasn't yet forgiven me for washing off her full face of make-up.

When Sara returns, she sits down at the table with Sylvie while I start clearing away. I watch as they take turns pressing a tooth without the alligator clamping down on their fingers. The game causes much hilarity and Sylvie squeals as she gets caught, making Sara giggle like a big kid.

After Sylvie has instigated another half-dozen rounds of her crocodile game, I say, 'If you both go and get the movie ready, I'll just be ten minutes cleaning up in here.'

'Let me help you,' Sara offers, but I wave her away.

'It'll take me no time at all,' I insist and she doesn't argue, just tops up her wine glass before she leaves the room. 'I'll give Miller a shout when I'm done, see if he'll join us.'

Sara doesn't comment and I know she probably prefers he stays up in his room. But I want him to feel included. I won't allow her to marginalise him while she gets ever closer to Sylvie.

When everyone has trooped out, I close the kitchen door, turn on the radio and start to scrape away the unwanted food and stack the plates. I pick up bits of discarded pizza crust from under the table and wipe up tomato ketchup splashes.

It's become apparent Sara is good at picking and choosing what she wants to do to help in the house and that talent obviously extends to what truths she wants to reveal and those she keeps concealed.

A yelp, then a shrill cry comes from down the hall. I run out of the kitchen.

'Where's Rory?' Sara's voice emerges as a strangled cry. 'Rory's gone!'

I rush over to his bouncy chair and before I get there, I can see it's empty. I look out of the window and my blood runs cold. She looks around at me, her eyes like narrowed slits. 'Where's Miller?'

It's a race to get to the bottom of the stairs but I just about make it before she does. 'Miller!' I yell as I bound upstairs, two steps at a time. 'Miller, are you up there?'

I burst into his bedroom with Sara on my heels. The room is dim, curtains closed. He's not here. She gets to the bathroom across the hall before me but the door is ajar. He's not in there either. Sara's bedroom is empty, as is mine and Sylvie's room. The other spare room is jam-packed full of boxes of Sara's belongings. My son is not in the house.

'He's taken him. He's taken my baby,' Sara wails again and again. She rushes downstairs, almost knocking over an alarmed-looking Sylvie in the hall.

'What's happened, Mummy?' she says in a small, frightened voice. 'Has Miller taken baby Rory away?'

'Wait there, darling. I'll be back in a minute.'

I shadow Sara as she hares through the house, checking all the downstairs rooms and I follow her out into the garden. The marquee has gone now so it's just one big, square, open space and it's immediately clear Miller and the baby are not out here.

Sara pulls out her phone, hyperventilating as she speaks. 'He's gone too far this time, Jennifer. I'm calling the police and nothing you can say will stop me.'

CHAPTER 51

Within minutes of the discovery that Rory has been taken, I follow Sara upstairs, pleading with her not to call the police.

'We can sort this out, Sara. I can find him, just give me half an hour. Please.'

'You must be joking. Anything could happen in half an hour. He's tried to smother Rory once and now he's kidnapped him.'

'Don't be silly. He hasn't kidnapped him; you know that's nonsense.'

'Mummy, Mummy.' Sylvie tugs at my hand. 'Where has Miller taken baby Rory?'

'We don't know, darling, but… he'll be back soon. I know he will.'

Sara turns and glares at me, her face hot and inflamed. 'Why else would a thirteen-year-old boy take a baby? You're the idiot who thinks he's an angel when he keeps showing you, again and again, that he's troubled and aggressive.'

I'm not about to share my concerns with her but I'm racking my brains to come up with a reason of why Miller has taken Rory. He's been so troubled for so long and now I know why. He's been torn between loyalty to me and fear of his dad. He's been so troubled for so long and now he knows Rory is his baby brother. Could he have thought, in some misguided teen way, that he and Rory can escape all the hassle together? Miller has told me in no uncertain terms that he hates Sara. It's clear to everyone she's besotted with her son…

could Miller be motivated by revenge, knowing she'll suffer with Rory gone?

I haven't got an answer to all that, but I still feel convinced Miller would never knowingly hurt the child. But I acknowledge it's not good. Anything could happen to the baby and Miller is ill-equipped to care properly for him.

'Please.' I try again. 'I beg you, just give me half an hour. Trust me, it will be a much quicker way of finding Rory. If the police come here, they'll spend at least thirty minutes interviewing us to get through the red tape before they even begin to search for him.'

My hasty attempt at skewed logic seems to hit home. Sara hesitates. I have this feeling that, for all her threats, she's nervous about getting the authorities involved herself.

'Thirty minutes and that's it. If I don't get a message that you've found him, I'm ringing the police on the dot. In the meantime, I'll be out looking for him myself and you'd better hope I don't find him because if I get hold of Miller, I'll—'

'You'll not touch him!'

Sara turns and closes her bedroom door in my face. I can hear her moving about in there. I've called Miller's phone what seems like hundreds of times and I've left numerous messages. Still, I try it again. Like all the other times, my call goes straight through to voicemail.

Next, I make another call.

'Mum? It's me. Listen... big favour, could you come over to the house to watch Sylvie? We've got an emergency here.'

'I'm at Ellen's watching our Damian. I don't know what's wrong with her but she rushed out in a panic. Can you bring Sylvie across here? What's happened?'

'I'll explain later. Yes, I'll bring her over there now, thanks, Mum.' I end the call. 'Get your shoes and coat on, poppet. Gran's going to look after you for a while.'

'But where's Miller?' Sylvie whines. 'Where's he taken baby Rory?'

'That's what I'm going to find out.' It's all coming to a head. I can feel it.

CHAPTER 52

MILLER

Miller's feet whir around on the pedals as he expertly negotiates the little alleyways and shortcuts he knows so well. He must avoid using the main roads where his mum – and possibly the police – will soon be looking for him.

After another ten minutes of travelling, he stops pedalling and checks on the baby. Rory has somehow gone back to sleep. He lies peacefully nestled against Miller's chest, trusting and calm in his care. Miller feels so capable and strong in his role as a big brother, as if, finally, he's doing something right.

Nausea rises in his chest again and he battles it back. There had been a point, back at the house, he'd nearly cried off and abandoned the plans he'd only just agreed to. But something in him made him plough on ahead, do what was required and now, here he is. He's done it just as he'd promised and now there is no going back. All he can do now is make sure Rory is safe and accurately carry out the instructions he's been given.

The scary bit had been having to wait for his mum, Sara and Sylvie to go off into the kitchen and settle at the table. He'd waited for what seemed like ages on the stairs, listening. After about ten minutes, Sara had come out to check on the baby and once she'd returned to the kitchen, Miller had crept downstairs and into the room where Rory slept. He knew she wouldn't check on the baby now for at least another twenty minutes, or so.

Praying Rory didn't wake up, Miller had gently lifted his sleeping brother out of his chair, making sure his dummy stayed in place. He'd already picked up the changing bag and hooked it over his arms and back like a rucksack. Earlier, he'd tucked two bottles of expressed milk that Sara kept in the fridge in the side pockets.

Miller had strapped the papoose to him. He'd watched Sara do it numerous times and, so long as you ensured the buckles were properly fastened, it held together quite securely. The problem was his hands... they were shaking. He'd made sure his bike was ready and waiting to go at the side of the house.

She had talked Miller through the plan numerous times and had only been satisfied when he'd been able to recite it back to her perfectly. Still, with him being so nervous and wobbly, he'd had to really focus to make sure he'd remembered everything they'd discussed.

'Stick to what we've agreed and it will all go smoothly,' she'd reassured him when Miller had expressed nervousness. 'You know I'm going to have to appear shocked and outraged at first, right? But that's just until everything starts to move into place. The main thing is you don't panic and blurt anything out you shouldn't.'

'I'm worried about Rory,' Miller had said. 'Like, what if he stops breathing again and I don't know what to do?'

'If you carry out my instructions to the letter, nothing bad will happen. Don't worry, Rory will be fine. Just take him to the place we agreed and I'll come soon as I can. The most you'll be waiting is half an hour. If you make sure you've got Rory's dummy and his bottle, he'll soon quieten down if he gets distressed.' She'd looked at him and smiled. 'It's not like he'll be with a stranger, Miller. He'll be with his big brother. You know it's for his own good.'

Miller had felt a warm glow spread in his chest at her words because it was true. He had a brother. A tiny baby brother who needed his protection and love. Nobody could take that away from him.

After satisfying himself that Rory is fine, Miller sets off again and, crossing a small side street, inadvertently pulls out in front of another cyclist.

'Watch where you're going, you great clod!' a man growls as he swerves to avoid Miller's bicycle.

'Sorry!' Miller calls out, but he doesn't stop pedalling. He must keep on going until he gets to the meeting place. He's in far too much trouble to go back now.

The man's nastiness has reminded him of the spat he had with his cousin, Damian. Miller had been unnecessarily cruel, he thinks now on reflection. Those things he'd said about Damian's dad... he'd chosen his words like weapons and they'd had the desired effect. But now, thinking about his own dad and feeling the pain of knowing he will never again be able to spend time with him, Miller regrets his meanness towards Damian. Now, he understands that when your thoughts are taken up with worrying, you often prefer to be on your own and to spend lots of time in your bedroom.

He'd never thought that he and his geeky cousin would have much in common but now things have changed.

Miller takes a left and turns into the small park where he has agreed to take the baby. There is nobody here yet, but she'd said it might take her a while to get there and so he'd just have to wait.

He gets off his bike and props it up against a wooden bench. Then he slips the changing bag from his back. There's no rain but the air is frosty and very cold and Miller pulls his coat closer around baby Rory. He rests his nose and lips on his brother's fine, feathery hair and inhales the smell of talcum powder and something sweet, like almonds. Miller feels so angry and resentful most of the time, it's strange to experience such tenderness for his new baby brother.

He looks up at a sharp noise and instinctively wraps his arms protectively around the papoose. A twig snaps underfoot and the rustle of hedge leaves as somebody brushes against it. A figure steps out from the foliage and his heart begins to pound.

'Hello, Miller,' she says. She holds out her arms, her eyes fixed on the baby. 'You can give Rory to me, now.'

Miller looks down at Rory and then doubtfully back up at her.

'I promise you, he'll be fine. You know this is for the best.' She takes a step closer. 'I'll take it from here.'

Reluctantly, Miller unbuckles the papoose and hands his baby brother over.

CHAPTER 53

JENNIFER

I grab our coats and shoes and lead Sylvie out to the car to head over to Ellen's house, where Mum is looking after Damian.

Sylvie chats all the way and I make the odd response, but I can't really focus on her chatter. All I can think about is the certainty I feel that Sara somehow slipped Ativan into Cole's food or drink, drugging him before he got into the car to drive.

When I arrive at the house, Mum is instantly concerned.

'What's this emergency you mentioned, Jennifer? What's happened?'

I can't go through it all with her now. 'Miller's gone missing, Mum. I'm going out to look for him.'

'Oh no! Did you have an argument or something?'

'No, but—'

'Miller's taken baby Rory,' Sylvie says helpfully. 'Sara's going to call the police if Mummy can't find him.'

'What?' Mum's face pales.

'I haven't got time to talk about it now, Mum. If I find Miller, I'll call you right away. Thanks for having Sylvie; see you soon.'

'Wait! Where are you going to look? Has Miller taken the baby without permission?' I hear her voice rising in panic. 'Do you want me to—'

'I'll call when I can. I have to go.' Mum's voice fades out as I run back to the car.

Think, think, think. Where would Miller go? He's on his bike and he's taken the papoose and Rory's changing bag. That doesn't make for a comfortable ride. Taking all that into consideration, I'm assuming he can't have travelled that great a distance.

My first stop is the school field where he used to play a lot of football. There are a few kids kicking a ball around. I wind the window down and shout over, asking if anyone has seen Miller but I get just blank faces in return and a couple of them cautiously shake their heads.

Next, I drive around the streets and past Central Avenue with its cafes and restaurants, just in case he's stopped to feed Rory on a bench there. But he is nowhere to be seen.

Next, I head out into the residential roads of West Bridgford. I'm not sure why because I'd imagine Miller would want to keep out of sight. But I have to try and cover all bases. He'd know that we were bound to come looking for him once we realised he'd taken the baby. I'm hoping he just took Rory on spec without considering the consequences and that, soon, he comes to his senses and brings the baby back home before this all gets out of hand.

'Where *are* you?' I say out loud. I pull over and call his phone again, but it goes to voicemail like all my other call attempts.

I sit, my stomach churning with the frustration of considering what to do next when I haven't really got a clue what I'm up against. I wonder where Sara is, where she's gone. I hope she's stuck to her word and not contacted the police yet.

I've got fifteen more minutes before the half-hour I asked for is up.

I rack my brains to think of any other place that might be worth checking. Anywhere that means something to Miller or is private enough for him to be fairly close to home but keep them out of general view.

CHAPTER 54

SARA

TWO YEARS EARLIER

The networking meeting was the most important one of the year, with a range of top business speakers attending.

With the VIP visitors queuing to be booked in, Sara started to panic. She didn't know half of the faces and people were getting irritated as she made mistakes.

A smart, efficient woman in her forties stepped forward and stood next to her, pointing out names on the guest list and directing people to the correct area while Sara moved to the next person.

When everyone had been processed, Sara finally breathed out. 'Thank you so, so much, you're a real lifesaver,' she told her helper.

'I'm Corinne Waterman.' The older woman offered her hand and Sara took it as she introduced herself in return. 'They should have never left you struggling on your own like that.'

'It's the agency. They send me out on these jobs and I never feel properly briefed. I'm going to be attending the meetings regularly now, so hopefully I'll make a better job of it next time.'

Corinne smiled. 'Well, I'm always around, so just shout up if you need any help.'

After that, the two women sought each other out at the long

and often tedious networking events. Sara found Corinne easy to talk to and, within a relatively short space of time, they became quite friendly, meeting up regularly for coffee.

Sara felt herself latching on to Corinne in that way she was prone to do, but this time, it felt like Corinne wanted friendship, too. Sara would pass on bits of gossip she picked up from the different companies she worked for and, on one occasion, earned Corinne's undying gratitude when she was able to share intimate details of a major tender that was taking place with one of Corinne's main clients in the running.

Corinne had taken Sara out for dinner at a Michelin-starred restaurant after that little coup and they'd kicked off with a bottle of champagne, most of which Sara drank herself, she'd realised afterwards.

She wasn't supposed to drink heavily on her medication, Sara knew that, but Corinne was her friend and she felt it wouldn't hurt, just this once.

Halfway through the meal, Corinne asked her about her family background and Sara, uncharacteristically, started to open up to this woman who she'd already come to trust. Fuelled by the drink she'd just consumed, the pent-up emotion began to pour out of her.

Corinne paid the bill after their main course and invited her back to her cosy flat, where she made coffee and Sara felt she could finally relax.

In just two hours, in the company of someone who wanted to listen, Sara had told Corinne everything, including her spell in the clinic when her father died, and the long-term medication she'd been told she must take to keep her mental health issues at bay.

'My dearest wish is to have my own child to cherish, to give him or her all the love and sense of belonging I never had myself,' Sara said sadly. 'But finding the right man, someone who'll cherish me and our child, is the biggest obstacle. All the best ones seem to be married and, although men are attracted to me, they never seem to stick around once they realise I have… issues that need to be medicated.'

After that, Sara and Corinne saw each other regularly through networking events but they'd also visit each other at their respective homes, watch a movie or just enjoy a catch-up and a chat.

One evening, as Sara was lamenting her longing to have a child, Corinne put down her coffee and looked at her intently.

'Look, I know this is highly irregular, but I know this guy… a really nice guy I work with who I happen to know is very unhappy at home. He's stuck in a loveless marriage and every time I see him I think of you, Sara. You two would make such an amazing pair and you'd also make the most beautiful baby.'

Sara laughed. 'Shame I didn't meet him before he got married.'

'So true.' Corinne picked up her mug again and stared into the dark liquid. 'To be honest, I think they'll split up before long. Someone is going to get an amazing guy when that happens. He's kind and understanding.' She looked up and met Sara's intense eyes. 'He's going to be at the next networking meeting. Maybe you could arrange to bump into him.'

Sara's eyes twinkled. She had no loyalty to anyone but herself. People had disappointed and let her down her whole life long. If this guy was unhappy in his marriage, then what was the harm in her getting to know him? She valued Corinne's opinion and it was clear her friend thought a lot of him.

And that's how it started. Until eventually, Corinne told her the real reason behind her interest.

'I want to break up his marriage,' she said. 'I want to make both of them suffer and then you can have him all to yourself.'

CHAPTER 55

NOTTINGHAMSHIRE POLICE

After they receive the call, Helena immediately contacts Jennifer Fincham.

'We've had a call from Sara Nordstrom alleging Miller has abducted her baby,' Helena says. 'Is this information correct?'

'He won't hurt him, DI Price,' Jennifer says quickly. 'It's some kind of protest he's making. He's so stressed, what with the death of his dad and – there's stuff happening I've been totally unaware of, which I need to speak to you about.'

'OK, but this is a serious matter and we'll need to get officers out looking for the missing baby,' Helena says firmly. 'Have you any idea where he might have taken the child?'

'Not far! He's on his bike and the baby is in a papoose. I've driven around the area but I've had no luck.'

Helena clicks her fingers in the air and Brewster looks up and then walks over to her desk. 'Please don't go anywhere, Jennifer. We're on our way to speak to you.'

'OK. I wanted to tell you that Miller had the sense to take Rory's milk and a changing bag, so he's clearly intending on caring properly for the baby.' Jennifer hesitates before adding, 'He is Miller's baby brother after all.'

*

Thirty minutes later, the detectives arrive at Jennifer's address.

'The CCTV footage of the park should be sent through to my phone very soon,' Brewster says as they walk up to the house. Jennifer opens the door and they go inside.

'We've been trying to contact Sara but she's not picking up,' Helena says. 'Have you any idea where she is?'

'No. She said she was going out to look for Miller and Rory herself,' Jennifer says. 'But there are lots of things I need to tell you about Sara.' She brings up the photographs on her phone. 'These are Ativan tablets I found in Sara's room together with a load of other medication. I've felt very tired and have slurred my words on a couple of occasions and I think she might have slipped a tablet in my drink.'

'Cole Fincham's bloodstream was full of this drug,' Helena remarks.

'Also, I've found out that Corinne Waterman, Cole's accountant, and Sara know each other,' Jennifer says. 'I don't know what that means yet but it feels very wrong.'

'They do? Neither of them have said so. And…' Helena frowns as the realisation hits her. 'That would mean there could be a clear conflict of interest when Cole signed legal agreements scrutinised by Corinne for the loans.'

'Corinne has led me to believe she's trying to find a loophole in the agreements,' Jennifer explains. 'She said she'd advised Cole not to go with the loans but he wouldn't listen. But now… I think there might be something sinister behind it all. Some kind of revenge plot.'

'Revenge for what?'

'I turned up unexpectedly at Corinne's offices to confront her about knowing Sara. Her business is called CB Associates. I now realise this is because her maiden name was Brace.'

'The same surname as Rhea, who Cole had an affair with,' Brewster murmurs.

'Exactly. She had a framed "sisters" photograph in her office showing her with Rhea when they were younger. I'm certain Cole didn't know about the connection; he would have said so when we got back together. But I still can't work out why Corinne kept her connection a secret.'

CHAPTER 56

JENNIFER

The two detectives told me they have officers out looking for Miller and baby Rory so I haven't got long. It's just occurred to me where he might be, and I have to check it out in case he's there.

It's just a small park close to the school where I'd often walk with Miller to take Sylvie on the swings and slide for fifteen minutes after the school run. If I can find Miller myself I can calm him down, find out exactly why he's got himself into this mess so I can help put him in a better light with the police.

Miller would usually sit on the bench, playing some game on his phone while I kept Sylvie entertained but when we walked, we'd all chat and laugh and it was a rare chance to get a little time together without devices butting in. I miss those times so much.

I park the car a little way down the road and walk to the concealed entrance behind a little cluster of trees. When I see movement, I hesitate, wait for my eyes to adjust. Then I see my boy, sitting on a bench, his head in his hands.

'Miller?'

He jumps up, pure panic distorting his features.

'Wait!' I call out as he dashes towards his bike. I almost throw up when I see he hasn't got the baby.

I run over and get to him just as he straddles the cycle. His face looks tear-stained and weary. 'I have to go, Mum. The police will take me away for what I've done… to prison.'

'Miller, where's the baby?' I grab his arm. 'Where's Rory?'

Panic rises in me and I grip harder.

He shakes me off and tries to push off to move the bike but I stand in front and hold the handlebars, my voice firm and deep. 'No! You cannot run away from this. You *have* to tell me where the baby is, right now.'

'He's… safe. He's OK, honest, Mum.'

'That's not enough! Where is he?' I shout now.

'Someone has him… he's safe.'

I feel faint with fear. 'You've *given* the baby to someone? How could you do that!' I grab his arms and shake hard. He loses his balance and falls sideways on to me, the bike toppling and knocking us both over.

Miller scrabbles to get to his feet, standing on my legs in the process and causing me to cry out in pain. He's about to take off when he looks down and realises I'm distressed. He extends a hand and I hoist myself up to standing.

'Mum, please… I have to go. The police will come and—'

'Who's got him?' I sit up. 'Who did you give Rory to?'

His face falls and he leans forward and whispers something.

'What? I can't hear you.'

He leans in closer and says something. A roar of disbelief blasts through me and I start to shiver. 'Oh no… what—'

'I have to go, Mum. It will be OK. I… I love you.'

Seconds later he's gone and I'm still sitting here, trying to compute what Miller has told me. None of it makes sense, but I get to my feet and run to the car.

And on the way, I call the police.

CHAPTER 57

I drive too fast and speed across town and over the river. I park outside the house and go to rush inside, except I can't get in because the door is locked.

I hammer on it. 'Mum! It's me. Open up.' There's no response so I run around the back where Mum often sits with the kids at the table playing some game or other. The room is empty.

I call Mum's phone and I hear it ringing. Redoubling my efforts, I bang on the door, the windows and I shout through the letterbox. When there's no response, I push open the letterbox and press my ear to it. I can hear voices upstairs.

Suddenly I hear thudding feet and the door opens. I fall inside and look up to see Damian standing there, his face tear-stained.

'Mum and Gran are shouting at each other upstairs,' he says breathlessly. 'Sylvie is hiding in my room.'

'What?' I spring to my feet and run upstairs. The shouting gets louder, crashes and bangs coming from what I know to be Ellen's bedroom. I turn off into Damian's room and he follows me in.

'Sylvie, you can come out now. Your mum is here,' Damian calls out.

The wardrobe opens and Sylvie emerges, frightened and rushing into my arms.

'It's OK.' I kiss the top of her head. 'Don't be scared, Sylvie.' I look at Damian over her. 'What's happening in there? Why are they fighting?'

Damian stares without speaking but Sylvie says, 'Aunt Ellen has Rory, Mummy. He's poorly and Grandma wants to call the ambulance to help him.'

'Wait here.' I rush over to the door. 'Watch her for me, Damian.'

I burst through the door into Ellen's bedroom and, for a second, both women freeze in shock. When they see it's me, they continue to scream at each other. I rush over to where Rory lies on the bed. He's not a blue colour like the other day and he's breathing OK, but he doesn't look quite right to me.

I step outside on to the landing and call an ambulance. I've just finished the call when Ellen springs at me from behind, snatching the phone. 'I said no ambulance!' I push her away as hard as I can and she hits the wall. She bounces off the hard surface and flies at me again, her face contorted like a wild banshee.

I push her again. 'Enough! Calm down, Ellen, think about the kids.' She stands there in shock for a moment, her eyes wide.

I rush back into the bedroom and Mum is sitting next to Rory, stroking his face. She looks exhausted. 'Mum, what's happened? What's wrong with the baby?'

'He was fine and then, as I held him, he went a sort of funny blue colour and I was certain he'd stopped breathing. I jiggled him, held him upright and he spluttered and seemed to recover. But he doesn't look right.'

Exactly what had happened at the house when Sara accused Miller of hurting Rory. I feel a rush of relief that I've been proved right... Miller didn't hurt his tiny brother.

'Why did Ellen tell Miller to take the baby? What the hell is wrong with her?'

'I don't know how we're going to sort this out, love.' Mum shakes her head, bewildered. 'Ellen apparently convinced Miller to take the baby because she says Sara is unstable and will hurt him. That's what we were arguing about… the fact she involved Miller in her crazy scheme.'

Ellen has barely set eyes on baby Rory *or* Sara. Why does she care so much? I glance at my watch. Five minutes since I rang for an ambulance. Rory is breathing steadily enough but he doesn't look well.

'Ellen was the one who told Miller to take the baby?'

'She said she's taking strong medication for a very serious mental health problem.' Mum starts to cry. 'Jennifer, I want you to know I had no clue what was happening behind our backs. I didn't know about Cole, or—'

'None of us knew about Sara and Cole at the time, Mum. I've since found out some information that blows all that out of the water. What's the medical issue that—'

'No, I mean, I didn't know what *Ellen* was doing… with Cole!'

'What do you mean?' My voice is low and quiet and the world seems to stop.

'Ellen was blackmailing him. She's admitted to me she threatened Cole. Said if he didn't pay her off, she'd tell you about him having a child with Sara.'

'She… she knew about their affair?'

All the hours I've spent talking to Ellen, trying to make her feel better about her future. Lending her money without Cole knowing… convincing her to come to the Halloween party. If Ellen knew Cole was having an affair, *surely* she'd have told me?

'I wouldn't call it paying me off.' I look up at Ellen, who stands, arms folded, in the doorway. 'It's true he was paying me an amount each month to keep my mouth shut, if that's what you're referring to.'

'You took money and let the affair carry on behind my back? Behind your niece and nephew's back? How… how could you?'

'I'm sorry.' She looks down. 'At the time, the money was all that mattered. I... I had serious debt problems, Jennifer. I tried to talk to you about it but—'

'I thought we were close. I thought—'

'You're in denial about everything!' she shrieks in frustration. 'You wouldn't have believed me even if I'd told you because you're trapped in your perfect little bubble where nothing ever goes wrong. You wouldn't even listen about that medication. You put the phone down on me. Something had to be done to blast the whole thing open.'

The jealousy and resentment is ugly when it finally spills from her lips. It has been years and years in the making. It has brewed and fermented itself all the times she's watched me, happy in my family unit, enjoying a successful life where we'd take holidays and live a pleasant existence.

'You knew Cole had a child with her, Ellen?'

She glances at Mum, who looks away. I can tell by the sickened look on her face Mum has not been party to the information.

Ellen walks further into the room. 'A friend I worked with in one of my temporary jobs saw him at the maternity clinic with Sara. She recognised him from a few family photographs I showed around at work a couple of years ago. She sent me a message asking if you two had split up.'

'Oh no...'

'If only you'd have snapped out of your denial. I mean, I just couldn't believe you'd missed all the signs again. I tried to talk to you about my worries but you blanked me constantly, just as you continue to do.'

I can't believe what I'm hearing.

But Ellen hasn't finished. 'Then you moved Sara into the house and you *still* didn't want to listen! Miller was really scared.

He felt very unsafe in that house and he opened up to me about it. He came here after school and broke his heart about the situation, told me some of the awful things she'd done.' So *that's* where Miller went instead of football training. 'Then I saw the pictures of the medication you sent, I got really scared for all of you. I knew I needed to do something radical before one of the kids got hurt. I had an idea and Miller came through.'

'I didn't tell you it was Sara's medication.'

'And why not? Because you were scared I'd cause a scene! You'd captured her name on one of the photographs but I could have guessed who it was prescribed for. The medicines included anti-psychotic drugs prescribed for psychotic depression and delusional thinking. She lives in a world of make-believe, Jennifer. First with her imaginary relationship with Cole and then after his death, she moved on to her delusions about becoming part of your family.'

She looks at the baby.

'Little Rory was in grave danger, as were your own kids. But Rory looks so much like Cole that she could snap without warning. If you couldn't see it, then it was down to me to do something about it. At first I wasn't sure how I could intervene and then you sent the photographs and I knew I had no choice. The whole situation needed to be brought to a head and that's why I enlisted Miller's help. That boy has more clue than you about the danger of Sara Nordstrom.'

CHAPTER 58

COLE

SIX MONTHS EARLIER

When Cole's receptionist told him he had a visitor, he felt like screaming. Six months ago he had creditors breathing down his neck for unpaid bills; now he had people hassling him for other stuff. Stuff that couldn't be solved by a quick bailout, like a brand new baby son his family knew nothing about.

He'd like nothing more than to instruct his receptionist to send the person away but when she said their name, he instinctively knew he would cause so many more problems for himself if he did so.

He walked across his office, down the short hallway and out into the foyer. His visitor stood waiting, her eyes pinned to the door he emerged from. He forced a smile on his lips.

'Lovely to see you, Ellen,' he said brightly. 'Please, come through.'

When she sat down across the desk, he knew. He knew that, somehow, she'd found out.

'I know what you're up to, Cole,' she said simply. 'I know everything about you and Miss Sara Nordstrom and, of course, your new baby son that my sister knows nothing at all about. If I go to Jennifer, your marriage will be over and you can kiss goodbye to your family because you've been here before, haven't you? I can't believe you've cheated on her again.'

'Let's say you have a point… why haven't you already gone to Jennifer?' Cole said coolly, thankful she couldn't sense his rising panic.

'Because I've come here to strike a deal with you.'

He laughed, hoping it would mask his shock.

'OK…' He dragged out the word and gave her a condescending smile. 'I'll indulge you. For now. So, what's the deal?'

'You'll pay me a lump sum and, after that, a monthly amount to keep my mouth shut. Simple, really.'

'I see.' He pasted an amused expression on his face. 'And this "monthly amount"…is that to continue indefinitely?'

'No,' Ellen says. Then quickly, 'I mean, I haven't decided on the finer details yet.'

'And if I refuse your terms, then what?'

She shrugged. 'I go to Jennifer.'

'What do you think Jennifer will say when I tell her you tried to blackmail me? That you were willing to say nothing about my supposed infidelity, so long as you got your grubby little hands on some cash?'

Ellen stared at him for a moment. He saw resentment spark in her eyes. 'See, that comment says everything about you, about Jennifer… even your kids. You all talk about money like it's nothing, Cole. But when you haven't got any, money is everything.'

'I've been on my uppers too, you know,' he responded gruffly.

'I'm not denying money has been tight at times, but to my knowledge, you haven't been unable to order in a pizza on a Saturday night, or have to choose between topping up the electric meter or sending your son to football practice.'

Cole knew she was exaggerating. Jennifer had never said she was struggling for money… not that bad, anyway. It was no use arguing with someone as clueless about business as Ellen was.

She had done precisely nothing with her life. Got herself pregnant by some loser who'd left her in the lurch and spent most of her time criticising and making snide remarks to Jennifer about what an easy life she'd got with Cole.

He wouldn't waste his breath trying to explain to her the crippling anxiety of being on the verge of bankruptcy. So much so you'd sign anything for an escape route. *That* was having money problems, not managing without pizza when your waistline could do with missing a meal anyway.

'First, tell me what you know,' he said, watching her sly face. 'Tell me exactly what you're keeping from Jennifer.'

'You're having an affair with a woman called Sara Nordstrom. She lives in a fancy apartment in Lady Bay and has just given birth to a bouncing baby boy. Your son.'

It occurred to him she had wasted herself, working in lowly hospital jobs, when she was clearly quite resourceful. The trouble she could cause for him didn't bear thinking about. But she'd got one detail wrong.

'I saw Sara a few times before I came to my senses. The woman is delusional. She's convinced herself I'm going to leave my family for her. She has me in a financial stranglehold so I have to string her along for now, but when I've made enough money to pay her off, that will end. I will confess to Jennifer and then she can do her worst. I believe my wife and I are strong enough to withstand an affair.'

'Another one, you mean?' Ellen jibed. 'If I go and see Jennifer this afternoon, it will be too late for your silver tongue. You'll be out on your ear before you can say, "Forgive me, darling… I've done it again." This time, there's a baby involved.'

Twenty minutes later, Ellen walked out of Cole's office with a done deal. A ten-thousand-pound down payment and then five hundred pounds a month to keep quiet.

Cole didn't know how he'd end up resolving this one, but he had faith that he would. Somehow, things would work out so the payments could stop.

He felt confident something would happen to get him out of the fix. Something always did.

CHAPTER 59

JENNIFER

The doorbell rings and Mum rushes to the bedroom window. 'It's the ambulance,' she says. She picks up Rory carefully and takes him down, leaving Ellen and me staring at each other.

'I'll be down in a minute, Mum,' I say.

Ellen looks contrite. 'For what it's worth, I'm sorry, Jennifer, I really am.'

'Sorry Cole died, you mean,' I reply bitterly. 'Taking your monthly cash bonus with him.'

'I'm sorry. I am. But that money wasn't to satisfy my greed. It made a massive difference to Damian and I,' she says, no trace of regret in her voice. 'For the first time in a long time we could afford decent food, treats and the odd outing together. It wasn't being spent on designer shoes and handbags.'

'If it wasn't greed, then why did you keep asking me for money, too? The day of Cole's death you asked me for a hundred quid to tide you over.'

'That was just a smokescreen! If I'd gone from asking for loans every couple of weeks to asking for nothing, you might've smelled a rat. You knew I wasn't working, so I had to keep up appearances. And it worked. You never suspected a thing.'

'*Loans*? A loan is paid back, Ellen. You never did.'

'I… I wanted to. I just never seemed to be in a position where I could. I did struggle with the guilt of what I was doing to you, Jennifer. I wanted to stay away from you, but when Cole came over, he said you'd be so disappointed if we didn't come to the party. So I—'

'Hang on. When was this?'

She hesitates. 'I... I can't remember. My mind's gone blank.'

A prickle starts at the back of my neck. 'Why did he come round?'

She's silent for a few seconds before sighing. 'I'll tell you because it will make you feel better. He came round here the day before the accident to tell me "the game is over", to use his exact words. He said he was going to tell you.'

I feel myself pale. 'He was going to tell me he was leaving me for Sara?'

Ellen shakes her head. 'He was going to tell you about what had happened with Sara. He was going to tell you everything, including his arrangement with me. He'd turned the tables on me.'

I sit down, stunned.

'He knew he should never have got involved with her. It was just a fling for him, something to take his mind off the business heading for failure. He saw her a few times, jumped at the chance to borrow the money. He naively viewed it as a business arrangement; he never anticipated Sara getting pregnant. She'd told him she was on the contraceptive pill.'

I pinch the top of my nose. 'I don't understand, Ellen. He carried on seeing her and yet I've found out from her landlord he wasn't actually living there. He showed me CCTV of her trying to hug Cole at the door and him turning away. But she said they were madly in love and—'

'Sara is mentally unstable, Jennifer. Seriously so. Surely you've seen that, living in the same house as her? Cole told me...' She looks out of the window before continuing. 'He told me she'd set out in the beginning to get herself pregnant by him, thinking he'd leave his family for her. She thought she'd sealed the deal by gaining financial power over him, too. He couldn't believe she was so organised, as if all this stuff had been planned.'

'I think she was part of some kind of revenge plot with Corinne Waterman, Cole's accountant. I can't go into it now but it turns out Corinne's sister was Rhea Brace, the woman Cole had an affair with.'

'The woman who took her own life?'

I nod.

'Well, Cole told me he wasn't having an affair with Sara. She was basically a distraction when he was low and she made the rest of it up in her head.'

'Miller saw them together in the car.'

'Because he had to string her along to stop her telling you. She threatened to ruin his life if he cut her out. He cared about his baby son, he worried for him, he said. He had a phone just so she could contact him and she'd send hundreds of texts and photographs even though he said he never replied to them. She'd tell herself stories of how they were going to be together soon. She was getting out of control and he knew he had to do something. He decided to tell you himself before she did.'

I think about the messages and photos Miller said were on the silver iPhone.

The way she'd constantly talked about how Cole wanted to leave us and move her in… the personal items in her bedroom that are carbon copies of my own. Maybe she'd bought those items herself.

Could it be that everything Cole had supposedly told her – his plans for them to live together, his commitment to her – had all been in her head?

Now I know about her connection to Corinne Waterman, it's clear she would have known all about us before she even met my husband. She could have observed me, bought the same clothes, even had a bracelet replicated like the one Cole had gifted me on our wedding anniversary. I've seen the CCTV, seen Cole turning on his heel and walking away from the house… Sara had a financial hold on him as well as being pregnant with his baby. Cole had looked as if living there was the last thing he'd wanted.

Now the police know about Corinne's involvement and the fact she was Rhea Brace's sister. That puts into question the integrity of the financial agreements Cole signed. I bite my lip and squeeze my eyes closed.

I can only pray none of them find out the final nugget of truth.

CHAPTER 60

SARA

Her head feels as though it's exploding. Where is her baby? Where are the police?

Rory is all she has in this world, and she has to do something. She has to find him and get away from all this stuff that is swirling round and round in her head.

She pushes the last bottle of tablets into the bag and stuffs it back into the wardrobe. She doesn't need all this medication the clinic had said she must take. They don't know what's best for her. She's OK now, feels better. She just has to find her baby boy and everything will be fine with her new family. Jennifer, Miller and Sylvie.

She knows exactly who she needs to see. The person who is to blame for a lot of this mess.

Sara gets into her car and drives to the office block in Wollaton. She takes the lift up to the fifth floor and walks into reception.

'I have an appointment with Colleen… Corinne!' she tells the receptionist. Her head is swimming. She feels like she could run a marathon or climb a mountain. 'I'll go directly through.'

'Sorry, madam, I'll have to check. Take a seat please.' The woman picks up the phone and says a few words as Sara paces around the small foyer. 'That's fine, you can go through.'

Sara walks into Corinne's office.

'Ahh, Sara! How are things at… are you OK? You look a bit spaced out.'

'I need to speak to you right now, Corinne. If you think I'm taking all the flak from this, you're sadly mistaken. As Cole Fincham's accountant, you're in even deeper than I am because all of this was your idea.'

'As I recall, as soon as you saw our good-looking prey, you were more than happy to go along with it.'

'You played me from the start,' Sara says, her eyes narrowing. 'Befriending me at those networking events, me spilling out my problems to you. You made me feel important, as if there was something in it for both of us. But you used me just the same as everyone else to get revenge for your sister's death. But Rhea took her own life, didn't she? It wasn't Cole's fault.'

'He used my sister and then he cast her aside.' Corinne spits out the words. 'That wife of his was implicit in her death too. They both knew she was young and vulnerable but they didn't care. Someone was there that day, the day she died at the flat, and I believe it was Cole Fincham. He might have even encouraged her to take an overdose so his life was made easier.'

'You said you never told him Rhea was your sister! You just carried on working for him despite what he'd done.'

'Revenge is a dish best served cold,' Corinne says simply. 'I only found out about his involvement when Rhea died and her friends told me at her funeral. If I'd confronted Cole, he'd have just cut me out of his life, got another accountant. I knew if I could bide my time, I could destroy Cole and his wife and really make him pay.'

'You knew he did all that and then you put me in danger, too. I… I honestly believed you were my friend.'

'I confided in you, told you everything about what happened to Rhea. I was honest, Sara. You were fully aware so the fact he did the same to you – dumped you the second he'd had his way – that's your own fault.'

'You told me he was unhappy with his family! You said he'd want to be with me.'

'You weren't supposed to fall in love with him and get pregnant, you fool! You got too involved. I just wanted to break his family up, have them lose their fancy house and give them both some real emotional pain. This madness… moving in with the family, trying to somehow fit in with their lives. I warned you not to do that.'

'I kept your secret. I never told anyone I even knew you because I thought you cared about me as much as I cared about and trusted you.'

'Time is up.' Corinne stands up and points at the door. 'Leave or I'll have no option but to call the police. I know you haven't been taking your medication; I can tell just by looking at you. They won't believe a word you say. They'll realise you're mad as a hatter and they'll take your baby into foster care. Never come here again.'

Sara moves closer, coming to Corinne's side of the desk. She lifts a paperweight off the desk. Corinne jumps back, holding up her hands.

'Sara, don't do anything silly. We can work this out. We can. Let's just sit down and relax. You can tell me all about what's been happening. OK?'

Sara does not move. 'It's not OK. You told me it would be simple, that I would keep my son and get Cole's house and now Cole is dead and Rory has already been taken away from me… I have nothing!'

'Calm down. I can help you get Rory back.'

Sara raises the paperweight above Corinne's head, then throws it at the display cabinet, shattering the glass front. The door flies open and the receptionist appears.

'Is everything alright – oh!' The woman backs up. 'The police are on their way, Corinne.'

'Now you're going to end up in prison, Sara,' Corinne baits her. 'You'll never see your boy again.'

Sara looks wildly around the room and then rushes forward to the French doors overlooking the street. She tugs at the handles and then spots the key that's in the lock. She turns it.

'No! Careful!' The receptionist runs across the room.

'Leave her!' Corinne yells as Sara yanks the doors open. The sky looks so grey and vast, like another world.

She jumps, launching herself over the Juliet balcony. Into a world that's better than this one for her and Rory.

CHAPTER 61

NOTTINGHAMSHIRE POLICE

TWO DAYS LATER

'So Corinne the accountant essentially targeted Sara Nordstrom as the perfect vehicle to exact revenge on Cole Fincham from the start?' Superintendent Della Grey asks as her two detectives take a seat in her office.

'Yes, ma'am,' Helena says. 'Cole Fincham had an affair with Corinne's younger sister, Rhea. He was unaware of the family link and Corinne only found out when it was too late and Rhea had died. Corinne was patient, waited years to get revenge on Cole. She found the ideal candidate in Sara when they met at a networking event. The two women became friends and a lonely Sara confided in Corinne about her mental health problems. Corinne could see that Cole wouldn't be able to resist Sara's charms and she became obsessed with breaking up Cole's family in revenge for her sister's death.'

'So Waterman was the brains behind the plan to ruin Cole and break up the family?' Grey says.

'That's right,' Brewster says. 'Waterman convinced Sara that Cole would be ideal husband material if she could only get him away from his wife and kids. Through her financial knowledge, Corinne also instigated the loans Sara afforded him and drew up the punishing agreements to secure ultimate control of him. Together, they made a formidable team.'

'Still, it seems radical that Sara would purposely get pregnant for the sake of forcing someone into a relationship.' Grey frowns.

'Sara suffered from delusional depression,' Helena explains. 'She had a lonely childhood and was desperate for a child and her own family. She genuinely fell for Fincham. The fact that she had a hold on him financially, too, was an added benefit. But Sara was unwell. We've since discovered she'd been in and out of clinics and suffered with delusions, which meant in addition to living out fantasies in her head as if they were real, she also experienced intense and crippling loneliness. She became obsessed with settling down with Cole Fincham to the point she truly believed it was imminent. The medical clinic confirmed they'd tried to contact her as she hadn't collected her latest prescription. She'd reduced and then stopped taking her anti-psychotic medication. She jumped to her death from the fifth-floor balcony of Waterman's office.'

'And Waterman has admitted that Fincham actually confronted her before his accident?' Grey says, consulting her notes.

Brewster nods. 'Yes. He'd already told Ellen Pendlebury, Jennifer's sister, that he'd spotted inconsistencies in the loan agreements. Additional pages that he was convinced Corinne Waterman had illegally inserted into the agreement after he'd already signed. Thanks to ANPR and mobile phone mast data, we knew he'd been in the Wollaton area immediately prior to the fatal accident. When presented with this evidence upon the death of Sara Nordstrom at her office, Waterman confessed she'd struck Fincham with a golf club in the midst of a disagreement.'

'Waterman said she panicked when she thought she might have killed Fincham. Then, he stood up, wobbled a bit but walked out of her office,' Helena adds. 'She most probably thought she'd gotten away with whacking him so hard, but she'd inflicted the primary injury that would kill him.'

'Around forty minutes later, as Rolly McAfee discovered, Fincham suffered the fatal second injury,' Brewster confirms. 'His brain quickly swelled and caused his untimely death.'

CHAPTER 62

JENNIFER

SIX YEARS EARLIER

Jennifer dropped seven-year-old Miller at school and then sat outside Cole and Rhea's little flat until Rhea came out and went about her business.

Her heart was broken. She knew the healing could not begin while she was in denial that Cole had left her and Miller, but still, she simply could not stop. Watching the two of them became an all-encompassing obsession. Seeing everything they did together was slowly killing her but it was also her oxygen.

Sometimes, when it all got too much, she'd go to Cole's office and, past caring what other people thought of her, she'd purposely cause a scene in the foyer. Beg him to come home, tell him how Miller cried himself to sleep at night. Promise him she'd be everything he wanted if he'd only come back.

But he remained resolved and, after a few times, he'd stopped coming downstairs to see her altogether and the building's security guard would escort her from the premises, her head hanging in shame and sadness.

After a while, Jennifer transferred the focus of her attention on to Rhea. Followed her everywhere on the high street, to her doctor and dentist appointments. She found out the hairdresser she used and made false bookings. She followed her into department stores and alerted the security staff she'd seen Rhea stealing goods, would watch with glee as she was hauled into the back rooms to have her bags searched.

But one day, Rhea had turned the tables. She'd suddenly arrived in the playground at the end of school when Jennifer had stood with her usual group of mums, all parents of kids in Miller's class and none of whom knew about Cole's affair or the fact he'd left home.

'Jennifer?'

She'd turned round to see who had said her name.

'You have to stop following me!' Rhea had yelled right in Jennifer's face, causing the other women to scatter back a little. The playground had fallen deathly silent as people further away had shuffled closer to see what the fuss was all about. 'She's following me everywhere, telling lies about me. My advice is to stay away from her!'

As she'd walked away, she'd grinned at Jennifer and whispered: 'Don't underestimate me, you mad cow.'

Jennifer had turned back to the group, shaking. 'My husband has left me to be with her,' she'd sobbed, visibly shaking. 'It's true, I have been following her… I don't know why I do it. I'm just making it worse for myself but… I hate her! I hate her so much!' The last bit slipped out, her voice high and thin. But those final few words had been so full of vitriol, she'd seen one or two of the women she knew less well recoil.

Jennifer felt relieved when others stepped closer to her and offered a hug or a consolatory stroke of the arm. She'd begun sobbing uncontrollably, rambling on about Cole's betrayal. She'd always been quite a private person but she just couldn't seem to stop that day. Sam, the mum she knew best, drove her home while one of the other women collected their children.

Jennifer had quickly collected herself and her outburst hadn't happened again. Still, a few mums started standing in a different part of the playground, so the group quickly shrank in size.

Jennifer regretted losing control in such a public space. Some people were genuinely sympathetic but to others, she'd just provided the gossip for the week. Rhea had simply walked away but Jennifer had to show up every day to pick up Miller. It wasn't a fair fight.

Jennifer had known she couldn't let Rhea get away with that. She just couldn't.

Only six and a half months later, Cole was home where he belonged. He'd tired of the tiny bedsit, of Rhea's penchant for partying, and he admitted he'd missed the easy comforts of home. He and Jennifer had talked for so many hours and it was obvious that Cole had learned a very valuable lesson about how much his family meant to him.

One day when Miller was at school and Cole was away on site all day, Jennifer called at Rhea's flat. She banged on the door and a dishevelled, bleary-eyed Rhea staggered to open it in a grubby nightgown. How the mighty fall!

Jennifer had lost two stone in weight when Rhea had stolen him from her. She'd bought a new wardrobe, had her hair freshly styled and coloured and she looked good.

'I've come to enjoy the moment of seeing you now my husband has come back to me,' Jennifer said. 'I wanted to tell you that we're happier now than we've ever been.'

Rhea tried to close the door on her but Jennifer pushed her way in. The place was tiny, just one big room. She tried to imagine Cole living here and failed. What had he seen in Rhea?

The coffee table in front of the sofa was littered with tablets and medication bottles.

'What do you want?' Rhea said, collapsing on the sofa. 'Just leave me alone. I've nothing to live for.'

And then Jennifer had understood. She'd caught Rhea in the exact pitiful moments of her taking an overdose.

'I loved him, you know,' Rhea had slurred, sickening Jennifer. 'I really, really loved him.'

Jennifer glanced at the piles of tablets and the bottles. 'Do you know what he told me? He said you disgusted him in the end. That he thought of me whenever he was with you.'

'No!' Rhea gasped. 'Don't... please don't say that...'

'One day, he said he just woke up and realised what he'd left behind. Now he's back home and he just wants to forget all about you.'

'I don't want to be here, in this life,' Rhea sobbed. 'If that's what Cole really thinks, I might as well not be here.'

'Don't let me stop you.' Jennifer dropped her voice. 'I just think you need to know that Cole never wants to see your face again.'

Rhea stared at the scattered pills on the coffee table. She looked at Jennifer, her face pale and wretched. 'I can't stand this pain any more.'

'I know all about *that pain*.' Jennifer shrugged. 'I had it for months and months, remember? You humiliated me, taking my husband away and even belittling me in the school playground. Don't expect any sympathy from me because you won't get any.'

As Rhea covered her face with her hands and began to quietly sob, Jennifer slipped away, closing the flat door and leaving the building without seeing another soul.

Cole came home white-faced a few days later. Someone in his office told him that a neighbour had found Rhea. She'd taken an overdose and called an ambulance but it had arrived too late.

'People will say it's my fault,' he'd whispered, clearly shaken. 'That she took her own life because of me. Why wouldn't she have reached out to someone, asked for help?'

Jennifer had laid a sympathetic hand on her husband's arm. 'I guess we'll never know,' she said.

EPILOGUE

JENNIFER

PRESENT DAY

Miller picks up his baby brother and swings him in the air above his head, Rory squealing in delighted terror. 'What time is everyone coming, Mum?' Miller calls.

'Everyone should be here in an hour,' I answer him. 'Are Joel and your other mates coming?'

'Yeah, and we're all going bowling after the party.'

Rory turns one today, a bright beautiful boy who looks more like his brother, Miller, every day. We found the DNA certificate amongst Sara's paperwork at the flat when I returned the CCTV equipment to Mr Friedmann. As I'd always known, Rory is Cole's son. But now I prefer to refer to him as Miller and Sylvie's brother. The paperwork at the flat also revealed receipts for Sara's matching bracelet, the so-called engagement ring and the expensive evening dress. Paid for with her own credit card, Cole hadn't gifted her with those things after all. It was another product of her delusional thinking.

I watch my eldest son now, his face bright and animated. He's like a different boy these days. He has a good friendship circle at school and he plays for the school football team again with Joel. When Sara died and it became apparent she literally had nobody, there was no way I could let Rory be taken into care.

Miller and Sylvie are his blood relations and I'm as close to a mother as he will get.

We went down the official channels and Rory's adoption came through just last week, coincidentally, the day he took his first steps.

Between us, Mum and I look after him, and Miller and Sylvie really pull their weight, too. I can't be around Ellen these days, after learning she knew all about Cole's affair, but Damian often comes over to see his baby cousin. Maybe one day I'll trust my sister again but it's not happening anytime soon.

On Sara's death, all her assets passed to Rory to be held in trust until he is twenty-one. When the legal agreements were declared null and void because of Corinne Waterman's corruption, the house reverted to our joint ownership. As Cole had died, it became part of his estate, which has now passed to me.

Corinne has been struck from the Institute of Chartered Accountants for her part in the loan scam. She has also been charged with the manslaughter of my husband and is awaiting her trial. The business has since gone into liquidation, so Fincham Developments is no more.

With Mum's support and encouragement, I'm back working in school part-time in my old position as a teaching assistant. I hope to take my qualifications further in a couple of years and train to be a teacher. It feels good to have a step on the career ladder again.

I can never put right my part in what happened to Rhea. I was half-crazy myself at that time; that's the only defence I have. But I hope my decision to keep Rory with us, his family, goes a small way to making up for the terrible thing I did… even though her death will always haunt me because I had the chance to stop it happening.

When Sara Nordstrom moved in with us, I'd felt so powerless. But eventually, I realised that I'm no longer a vulnerable teenager on the streets. Now, I am capable of steering my own life and choosing the best path for myself and my children, even in the face of adversity.

I look around the kitchen. We picked up platters of sandwiches from a local bakery and Mum baked a selection of her fantastic cakes – Victoria sponge, carrot cake, coffee and walnut loaf – that everyone loves. Sylvie and Miller have put up banners and balloons for Rory's birthday and we've used lots of Sylvie's glittery, homemade pictures to pretty up the walls. There is no fancy marquee, no caterers and no firing up of the outdoor kitchen.

Just a simple, small family gathering with all the people we care about.

What could be better than that?

A LETTER FROM K.L. SLATER

Thank you so much for reading *The Girlfriend* and I really hope you enjoyed the book. If you did and would like to keep up to date with all my latest releases, just sign up at the following link. Your email address will never be shared and you can unsubscribe at any time.

www.bookouture.com/kl-slater

My writing ideas come from all sorts of places and the initial idea for *The Girlfriend* came from my agent. Ideas often start as a collaboration between myself, my agent, Camilla, and my editor, Lydia, and I really enjoy brainstorming ideas as it's such a fantastic way for me to get excited about the next story. No matter how interesting or compelling the idea, that spark of excitement is essential in order for me to start building the characters and themes and to begin a book.

I have always been fascinated when reading true-life accounts of women who discover their partner has been living a separate life of which she has been entirely unaware. It's easy, I think, to wonder how it would be possible for one half of a couple to shield and conceal another existence, another life, and yet it happens and the stories keep on coming.

When my agent raised the concept of nesting, it seemed a good fit with this 'other life' idea I've had in my head for some time, and so I got to thinking – with the help of that wonderful magical phrase 'what if' – what might happen if our protagonist's husband dies and the other woman comes to the door and reveals not only that she's been living with him and bore his child, but she's bankrolled the family's whole life and owns everything, including their home? A nightmare scenario and rich pickings for a psychological thriller, I think you might agree!

How might it feel to be in our main character, Jennifer Fincham's shoes, then? To have such a conflict of emotions… the fury and shock clouding the grief of losing the man you loved, the fear of losing your home, rendering yourself and your children homeless… suddenly, there is lots for me to explore and untangle and WHAM!… I'm writing *The Girlfriend*.

This book is set in Nottinghamshire, the place I was born and have lived in all my life. Local readers should be aware I sometimes take the liberty of changing street names or geographical details to suit the story.

I do hope you enjoyed reading *The Girlfriend* and getting to know the characters. If so, I would be very grateful if you could take a few minutes to write a review. I'd love to hear what you think, and it makes such a difference helping new readers to discover one of my books for the first time.

I love hearing from my readers – you can get in touch on social media or through my website.

Thank you to all my wonderful readers… until next time,

Kim x

klslaterauthor.com

KimLSlaterAuthor

KLSlaterAuthor

klslaterauthor

ACKNOWLEDGEMENTS

Every day I get to write stories that excite me for a living, a wondrous career I waited many years to do full-time. Best of all, I'm lucky enough to be surrounded by a whole team of talented and supportive people.

Huge thanks to my editor at Bookouture, Lydia Vassar-Smith, for her expert insight, editorial support and valuable brainstorming of ideas.

Thanks to ALL the Bookouture team for everything they do – which is so much more than I can document here. But special thanks to Sarah Hardy for expertly managing my online cover reveals and publication days and to Editorial Manager Alexandra Holmes, who ensures the completed books are ready for the keen eyes of my wonderful readers!

Thanks, as always, to my wonderful literary agent, Camilla Bolton, who is always there with expert advice and unwavering support at the end of a text, an email, a phone call. Huge thanks to Camilla for helping develop the initial concept of *The Girlfriend*. Thanks must also go to the wonderful Jade Kavanagh, who works so hard on my behalf. Thanks too to the rest of the team at Darley Anderson Literary, TV and Film Agency, especially Mary Darby, Kristina Egan, Georgia Fuller and Rosanna Bellingham.

Thanks to copyeditor Donna Hillyer and proofreader Becca Allen, who have worked hard to make *The Girlfriend* as smooth a read as possible.

Thank you to my writing buddy, Angela Marsons, who is a brilliant support and inspiration to me in my writing career. Like all good friends, she's my go-to person for a moan, a laugh and our recent chats about dentistry…

Thanks to my friend April Fawcett, who reads and recommends my books, and to loyal reader Gail Hazley, to whom I made a slightly drunken promise to use her favourite setting for my next book… I delivered, Gail!

Massive thanks go to my family, especially to my husband and daughter, who are always so understanding and willing to put outings on hold and to rearrange to suit writing deadlines.

Special thanks to Henry Steadman, who has worked so hard to pull another amazing cover out of the bag.

Thank you to the bloggers and reviewers who do so much to support authors and thank you to everyone who has taken the time to post a positive review online or has taken part in my blog tour. It is always noticed and much appreciated.

Last but not least, thank you SO much to my wonderful readers. I love receiving all your wonderful comments and messages and I am truly grateful for the support from each and every one of you.

PUBLISHING TEAM

Turning a manuscript into a book requires the efforts of many people. The publishing team at Bookouture would like to acknowledge everyone who contributed to this publication.

Commercial
Lauren Morrissette
Hannah Richmond
Imogen Allport

Contracts
Peta Nightingale

Cover design
Henry Steadman

Data and analysis
Mark Alder
Mohamed Bussuri

Editorial
Lydia Vassar-Smith
Nadia Michael

Copyeditor
Donna Hillyer

Proofreader
Becca Allen

Marketing
Alex Crow
Melanie Price
Occy Carr
Cíara Rosney
Martyna Młynarska

Operations and distribution
Marina Valles
Joe Morris

Production
Hannah Snetsinger
Mandy Kullar

Publicity
Kim Nash
Noelle Holten
Jess Readett
Sarah Hardy

Sales
David Murphy
Jess Harvey

Typesetting
Ramesh Kumar

Dear Reader,

We'd love your attention for one more page to tell you about the crisis in children's reading, and what we can all do.

Studies have shown that reading for fun is the **single biggest predictor of a child's future life chances** – more than family circumstance, parents' educational background or income. It improves academic results, mental health, wealth, communication skills, ambition and happiness.

The number of children reading for fun is in rapid decline. Young people have a lot of competition for their time, and a worryingly high number do not have a single book at home.

Hachette works extensively with schools, libraries and literacy charities, but here are some ways we can all raise more readers:

- Reading to children for just 10 minutes a day makes a difference
- Don't give up if children aren't regular readers – there will be books for them!
- Visit bookshops and libraries to get recommendations
- Encourage them to listen to audiobooks
- Support school libraries
- Give books as gifts

There's a lot more information about how to encourage children to read on our websites: **www.RaisingReaders.co.uk** and **www.JoinRaisingReaders.com**.

Thank you for reading.